# DISAPPEARANCE
## *of a*
# SCRIBE

DANA STABENOW, born in Alaska and raised on a 75-foot fish tender, is the author of the award-winning, bestselling Kate Shugak series. The first book in the series, *A Cold Day for Murder*, received an Edgar Award from the Mystery Writers of America. Contact Dana via her website: www.stabenow.com

# DANA STABENOW

# DISAPPEARANCE *of a* SCRIBE

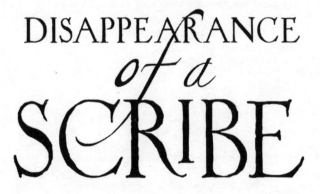

**HEAD ZEUS**

An Aries Book

First published in the UK in 2022 by Head of Zeus Ltd
An Aries book

9 7 5 3 1 2 4 6 8

A catalogue record for this book is available from
the British Library.

ISBN (HB): 9781800249776
ISBN (XTPB): 9781800249783
ISBN (E): 9781800249752

Typeset by Divaddict Publishing Solutions Ltd.

Printed and bound in Great Britain by
CPI Group (UK) Ltd, Croydon CR0 4YY

Head of Zeus Ltd
5–8 Hardwick Street
London EC1R 4RG

WWW.HEADOFZEUS.COM

For Carl Marrs, again,
this time for saying the word "pozzolan" in my hearing
and thereby inspiring the plot of this book.

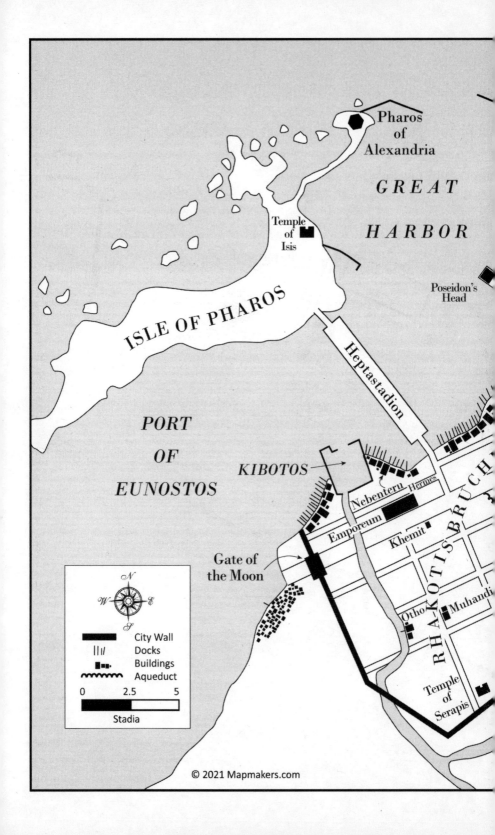

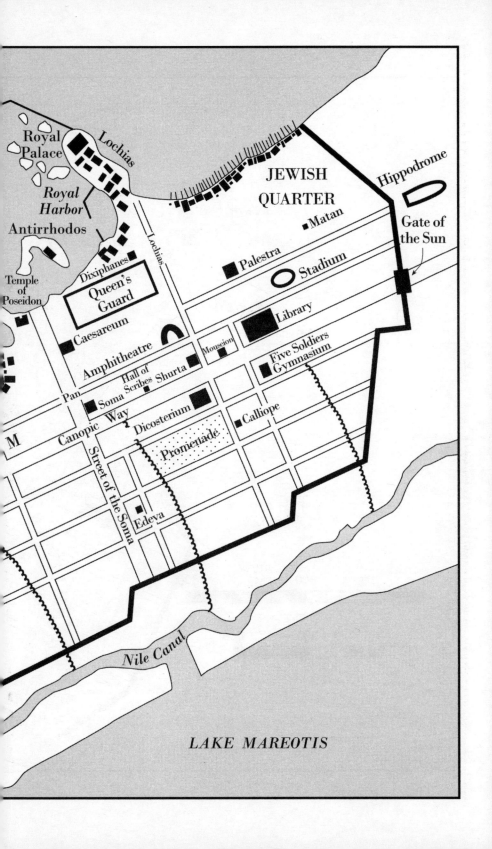

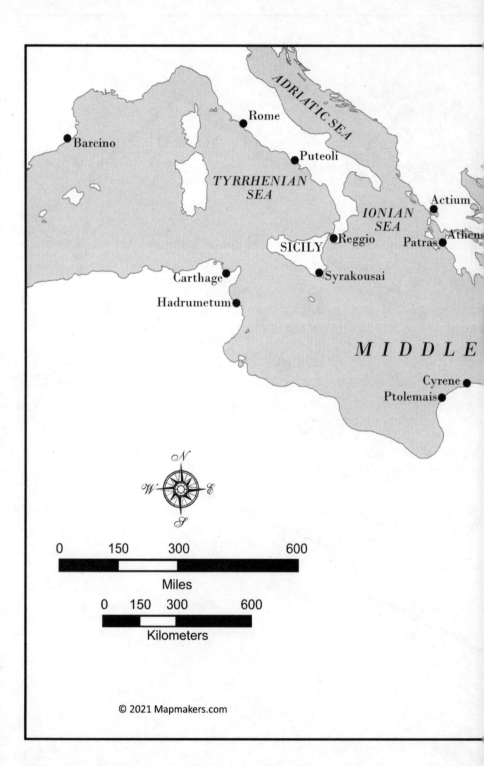

Barcino

Rome

Puteoli

ADRIATIC SEA

TYRRHENIAN
SEA

IONIAN
SEA

Actium

Athen

Patras

SICILY

Reggio

Carthage

Syrakousai

Hadrumetum

MIDDLE

Cyrene

Ptolemais

N

W                E

S

0        150        300                    600

Miles

0     150    300              600

Kilometers

© 2021 Mapmakers.com

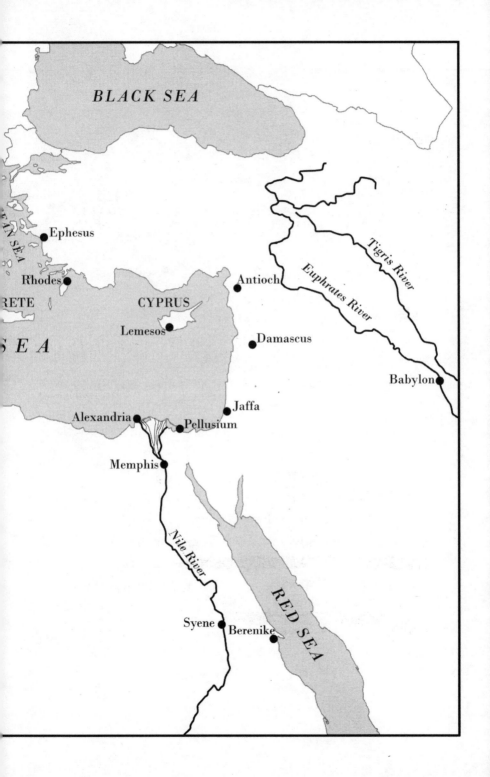

# CAST OF CHARACTERS

| | |
|---|---|
| Ahmose | Friend of Grafeas |
| Ampelius | Apprentice to Dixiphanes |
| Apollodorus | Partner in the Five Soldiers |
| Archeion | Owner of the Hall of Scribes, wife Eirene, son Grafeas |
| Aristander | Head of the Shurta, the Alexandrian police (wife Merti) |
| Arsinoë | Cleopatra's sister |
| Aurelius Cotta | Caesar's cousin and trusted aide, Roman legate to Egypt |
| Babak | A street messenger (in company with Roshanak, Agape, Narses, Bradan) |
| Caesarion | Son of Cleopatra VII and Julius Caesar ("Little Caesar") |
| Calliope | A hetaira |
| Calvus | Otho's guard |
| Castus | Partner in the Five Soldiers |

| | |
|---|---|
| Charmion | Cleopatra's personal servant and administrative aide |
| Cleopatra VII | Queen of Alexandria and Egypt |
| Crixus | Partner in the Five Soldiers |
| Dejen | A member of the Shurta |
| Dion | Apprentice to Dixiphanes |
| Dixiphanes | The Royal Architect |
| Drest | Otho's guard |
| Dubnorix | Partner in the Five Soldiers |
| Fulvio | Cotta's manservant |
| Galene | Food cart vendor |
| Goyo | Hibernian guard, ex-soldier, works for Khadiga (with Taki) |
| Grafeas | Missing scribe, son of Archeion and Eirene, betrothed of Raia |
| Hagne | Tetisheri's mother |
| Hunefer | Tetisheri's husband, deceased |
| Iras | Cleopatra's personal servant and head housekeeper |
| Isidorus | Partner in the Five Soldiers |
| Julius Caesar | General, Senator and Consul of Rome |
| Keren | Student of medicine, member of Tetisheri's household |
| Khadiga | Builder of Alexandria |
| Khufu | A member of the Queen's Guard |
| Kyros | Minor noble of Alexandria, student at the Five Soldiers |
| Laogonus | Owner and captain of *Thalassa* |

| | |
|---|---|
| Linos | Advisor to Ptolemy XIV |
| Matan | Lapidary, jeweler |
| Menes | A member of the Queen's Guard |
| Minius | Captain of the *Cameli* |
| Muhandis | A builder of Alexandria |
| Nebenteru | Tetisheri's uncle and partner in Nebenteru's Luxury Goods, owner/captain of the trade ship *Hapi* |
| Nebet | Hunefer's cook, now a member of Tetisheri's household |
| Nenwef | Friend of Hunefer, Ahmose, and Grafeas, son of Menes of Thinis |
| Nephilim | House guard for Matan |
| Nike | Hunefer's former slave, now a member of Tetisheri's household |
| Oengus | A seller of rare books in Rome |
| Otho | The Master of Builders in Alexandria |
| Phoebe | Cook for Uncle Neb's household |
| Polykarpus | Advisor to Ptolemy XIV, secretly advisor to Arsinoë |
| Ptolemy XII | Cleopatra's father (Auletes) |
| Ptolemy XIII | Cleopatra's brother, deceased (Theo) |
| Ptolemy XIV | Cleopatra's brother, husband, and co-ruler (Philo) |
| Ptolemy XV | Cleopatra's son by Julius Caesar (Caesarion) |
| Raia | Daughter of Muhandis |
| Rhode | Cabrio driver |

| | |
|---|---|
| Simon | Greek crew on the *Hapi* |
| Sosigenes | Current Librarian of the Great Library, advisor to Cleopatra |
| Taki | Saxon guard, employed by Khadiga (with Goyo) |
| Tamir | Servant to Khadiga |
| Tetisheri | Friend and confidante of Cleopatra, partner in Nebenteru's Luxury Goods, current Eye of Isis |
| Titus | Wealthy Roman plebeian |
| Vitruvius | Roman engineer and architect |
| Yasmin | Aide to Sosigenes |
| Zotikos | Cleopatra's personal physician |

Honestly, I think historians are all mad.

—JOSEPHINE TEY

# PRÓLOGOS

This couldn't be happening.

Therefore it wasn't.

He explained that to the men at work around him. He could see them laughing. It took a moment before he realized he couldn't hear them. He could see them talking to each other. Their lips were moving. He tried tapping his ears to alert them to the problem but for some reason he couldn't move his hands.

He searched his mind for his last memory. The dolma, of course. Had there been something in the dolma? In the grain, perhaps? Was it making him hallucinate? He had heard of the disease that sometimes attacked old grain. But no, he had bought that same snack from Galene every afternoon since his father had introduced them on the way to his first day at work. Her cart served only the finest food made from the freshest ingredients. She was a little more expensive than the other vendors in the area, true, but you got what you paid for in Alexandria as you did anywhere else.

The world around him rocked, and him with it. He puzzled over this for a moment. Was it an earthquake? He blinked around, and saw a bright light sweep across a glimmering sea.

Why, he was on a boat. How had that happened?

He was jolted out of his thoughts when they raised his feet and placed them in an amphora. It was a very large amphora, the size used to ship olive oil only with a much larger mouth. The lip on the mouth came all the way up to his knees. It was empty but for his feet. He stared down at them, perplexed. His legs were bound at ankles and knees. How very odd, not to mention unbefitting one of his rank and family connections. He tried to tell the men this, too, but they only laughed. Again. And he couldn't hear them. Again.

He shook his head, trying to clear his ears, and this time they did clear, at least partially, although it made his head hurt worse, which was when he realized his head did hurt. He blinked again and found that he was sitting on a thwart in the open hold of the boat. A large boat, he thought, looking up at the full-bellied sail over his head. The light he had seen swept over the sail and disappeared again. It must be the light of the Pharos. The heavy swell that made the hull rise and fall confirmed that they were on the open sea. It wasn't an earthquake after all, and the swell indicated that they were outside the lee of the island the lighthouse stood on.

He'd had no plan to make a sea voyage, had he? No,

certainly not. His work required good solid land beneath his feet. "Why?" he said.

The men laughed again. This time he heard them. It was not a pleasant sound. He knew none of them. One, who looked like a soldier in civilian clothes—you could always tell a veteran by their erect posture, a byproduct of marching in Roman legions for twenty years—this man slapped him on the shoulder and said, not without sympathy, "You noticed what you shouldn't have, boy, and worse, you talked about it. There is no forgiveness for that, and no pardon."

This made no sense to him, either.

They were mixing a concoction in a large bowl from some white powder they tipped from a canvas bag and cups of water from a leather bucket. A little powder, a little water, some vigorous stirring with a wooden stick, repeat. When they were done they poured it over his feet, filling the amphora halfway up his calves. He stared down at it, bewildered, wriggling his toes. It felt very grainy. Standing over him, the men argued if it was enough.

"*Arketa*," the soldier said with finality. "That stuff is worth our weight in silver. The boss won't be happy if we waste it." He nodded at the pot. "And rinse that out before it hardens."

He understood finally, and his mouth opened wide in a soundless scream.

He was still screaming when he went over the side, the weight of the amphora and its contents dragging him down. The water closed over his head. He tried to take a breath and choked as the water rushed in and the air bubbled out of his nose and mouth and lungs. He tried to cough, tried to twist his hands free of their bindings, tried to pull his feet free of the amphora.

It was just before dawn. The last thing he saw was the golden light of Ra rising up over the eastern horizon as he descended into the ever-darkening depths of the Middle Sea.

# 1

The scroll was written in Greek. The hand was neat, the label tied to the scroll easily read.

*The sixteenth máthima of the twenty-seventh Eye of Isis*

*By her own hand for the record*

*Twelfth Bay, Seventh Shelf*

*The Room of the Eye*

*Great Library, Alexandria*

Máthima was a Greek word with several meanings. It could represent general knowledge, or knowledge of the sciences in particular. It could be a statement of beliefs, or it could be the guiding principles of a particular faith. It could mean something that is taught, a lesson.

She raised her head. The room in which she sat had high ceilings pierced by four skylights. On a clear day, the table top was illuminated with all the light one could wish for. The shutter that closed over the skylights was opened and closed by a series of ropes and pulleys ending in a thin cord secured to a cleat mounted next to the door.

Additional light was provided at need by a dozen oil lamps hanging from brackets carefully spaced around the room and as carefully shielded. Fire was the nightmare that had haunted every Librarian from Demetrius of Phalerum on. The current Librarian, Sosigenes, already a professional paranoiac by virtue of his position, had been further traumatized during the recent siege when Caesar had ordered the burning of the ships in the harbor and that fire had jumped to shore. It had not reached the Library itself but it had burned down a warehouse containing books belonging to the Library and that was enough for Sosigenes to ban any open flame in any room under his supervision from the Library to the Serapeum. It was forbidden for any library patron to light, extinguish or remove a lantern without an employee of the Library standing by, and if anyone was caught doing so they could be banned from the premises for a year. Sosigenes had only had to make good on that threat once to inspire full compliance. Scholars, astronomers, architects, engineers, doctors, philosophers, authors, playwrights, composers, professional people of every persuasion came from all over the known world to study and research at the

Library. It was not a privilege anyone was willing to put in jeopardy, especially when full board and room came with it, courtesy of the royal family. Scholars were always hungry.

The sole exception—to this rule or any other—in the sprawling edifice and its satellites, so far as she knew, was the room in which she now sat. Her gaze dropped to the shelves that covered all four walls from floor to ceiling. They were carefully labeled, reign by reign and Eye by Eye. The oldest documents occupied the space to the right of the door and were yellow with age. Tetisheri had touched one when she entered the room for the first time an hour before, fully expecting it to crumble beneath her fingertip. It didn't, and she didn't understand why until she discovered the tiny cisterns in the four corners of the room. Together they formed barely a trickle of water but it was enough to support a trace of moisture in the air, which kept the documents from completely drying out and falling to bits. Someone had given a great deal of thought to the design of this room.

A square wooden table sat at the center of the room, at which she was now seated on a square wooden stool. On the table was a volume between wooden covers bound with waxed twine, very thick. The binding allowed the volume to be disassembled for the addition of more documents, trimmed pages made from papyrus or parchment and in a few cases vellum. The symbol of the Eye of Ra had been traced onto the facing cover and then burned in over the tracing, forming a charcoal outline whose pupil seemed to follow her wherever she moved around the room.

She reached inside her tunic to find the badge of office bestowed on her the previous month by Cleopatra Thea Philopator, Lady of the Two Lands, beginning to be called by some Cleopatra the Builder, already called by others Cleopatra the Whore. It, too, was a representation of the Eye of Ra but this one was a work of art, made of nacre and turquoise circles inlaid on a base of lapis lazuli. It was unique among the insignia of the royal court, and as distinctive and as identifiable as the gold cobra the queen wore on her brow.

Even though, Tetisheri thought, few people ever saw the Eye, or ever wanted to. She certainly hadn't.

She held the pendant up to the light. The Eye of Isis in this form was no mere symbol of the goddess whose avatar sat on the throne. It was an actual, physical manifestation of the eye and ear and mouth of the ruler of Alexandria and Egypt. The power it represented was second only to the power of the throne itself. It compelled instant obedience to any order. Among other legends accruing around the office it represented, it was said that the first view struck a terror so intense as to make the viewer fall down in a faint.

Terror was not what it had inspired in Tetisheri. Far from it. Tetisheri, a partner with her uncle in a prosperous trading firm and fully occupied with concerns of her own, had not sought the office, had not expected it, had not wanted it, and had tried to refuse it. But her friend had asked her to assume its title and responsibilities, and her friend was the Queen of Upper and Lower Egypt and would not be denied.

The book on the table was an index in which all the máthimas of all the Eyes of Isis were catalogued by ruler, date, name of the Eye, and location on the shelves. The pages therein were bound with the most recent additions first. The Ledger of the Eye, a list of every case history of every inquiry made by every Eye of Isis from Kataskopos, Eye to Ptolemy I, to Khemit, last Eye of Auletes, Ptolemy XII, Cleopatra's father, and first Eye of Cleopatra VII.

The most recent máthima and therefore the first one to which the Ledger opened concerned a missing person, a young man, Grafeas, son of Archeion. The relevant scroll lay open before her, one end continually trying to roll up again. She slipped the chain of the Eye over her head and used it to weigh down that end. The other end immediately began to curl. There was a pair of scroll rods on a shelf but she didn't want the tedium of threading the ends of the scroll through the slots, during which effort something always tore, which she would certainly hear about, at volume, from Sosigenes. She used her small leather purse to weigh down the other end, and began again to read.

Archeion was the patriarch of a family of scribes who traced their ancestry back to Herodotus. Their legend was that the Father of History had spent enough time in Egypt to take an Egyptian wife and father an heir on her. Archeion's family claimed to be a direct descendent of that offspring.

Well, and she'd heard less likely stories. It wouldn't have

been the first or even the thousandth time a foreign-born man had adventured into Egypt to become the progenitor of a family. It was a custom that endured through today, as witness the three-month-old baby boy presently at Cleopatra's breast.

Which reminded her, Tetisheri's birth gift, a teething ring carved with interlocking wooden animals, polished to a beautiful shine that did justice to the original myrtle, had still to be delivered. If Little Caesar was as precocious as his doting mother boasted, it was a gift that could not be given too soon.

The scroll she was looking at was her precursor's last case but one. Khemit had had no opportunity to document her final investigation, which had ended in her murder and precipitated Tetisheri's stepping into her shoes as Khemit's avenger and successor.

It was why she was here in this room, to write the first máthima of the twenty-eighth Eye of Isis. She had written it, as witness her ink-stained fingertips and the neatly tied scroll of papyrus deposited in lonely state on the shelf below the precisely stacked shelf of Khemit's máthimas. "In the Reign of Cleopatra VII Thea Philopator, by the hand of Tetisheri, twenty-eighth Eye of Isis," the shelf's label read. The scroll had its own label, "In the Matter of the Missing Bullion." The missing bullion was a fortune in newly minted drachmas that Tetisheri had recovered after the murders of an Eye, a Roman monetale, and an Egyptian nobleman, an attempt on her own life, a mad dash across the Middle Sea which had included an encounter with pirates, and another fraught chapter written in the continuing unhappy relationship between Cleopatra VII Thea Philopator and her brother, Ptolemy XIV Philopator. Altogether more excitement than was absolutely necessary and Tetisheri was not anxious to repeat it. Which might be one of the reasons she was in the Library, reading through a lot of dusty old records.

She sighed. There was no love lost between Cleopatra and Ptolemy, the latter known familiarly as Philo. They were married, true, but only by command of Julius Caesar in an attempt to return Egyptian life to some semblance of normalcy following the Alexandrian War, not to mention staving off accusations back in Rome that Caesar was turning the richest country on the Middle Sea into his own personal fiefdom. Cleopatra and Ptolemy were co-rulers in name only and a good thing, too, as her brother allowed himself to be ruled by a duo of corrupt and venal counselors who had been scheming to kill Cleopatra from the moment the wedding ceremony was concluded. It seemed to Tetisheri that half of the queen's attention was subsumed by putting out fires lit by the kinglet's counselors.

Kinglet. Her lips curved upward in a reluctant smile. It was Apollodorus' title for him and it fit so well that Tetisheri was in danger of inadvertently using it out loud in company, which would never do.

She looked back at Khemit's last report. She had had a notion that she could not do better than read through past investigations documented by the previous Eyes, at least through Philon, he who had been first Eye to Auletes, also known as Ptolemy XII Neos Dionysos Philopator Philadelphos, also known as Cleopatra's father. Auletes had died only four years before and many of the people involved in his Eye's investigations would still be alive today. There could be some residual resentment which might inform her investigations going forward.

Khemit's last full report wasn't long. Grafeas, eighteen years old and his parents' only child, had gone missing one afternoon on the way home from work. Work was in his father's business, the Hall of Scribes on the Canopic Way between the Soma and the headquarters of the Shurta. Halfway between law enforcement and the courts, Tetisheri thought, a good location for scribes who rented themselves out by the hour. Scribes did a rousing business with plaintiffs and defendants in turn, working both sides of the aisle and then hiring themselves out to the courts to take the minutes of the cases. Each party would want a record of their own, written with their own interests in mind, especially if the verdict went the wrong way and they planned an appeal to the queen. A lucrative and enduring profession, scribe.

Grafeas had been working on half a dozen different cases before the courts. There was a breach of promise; a claim of personal injury against a shop owner by a chronic plaintiff whose name was known to everyone from Rhakotis to the Royal Palace; two property disputes, one involving ownership and the other damages; a case of construction fraud remarkable only because it involved the Royal

Architect; and a complaint against the City of Alexandria by a neighborhood near the Gate of the Sun in the matter of inadequate policing. Khemit had contacted the plaintiffs, defendants, and prosecutors in each case. All claimed they had no fault to find with young Grafeas' professional efforts on their behalf. She had also contacted the various judges, none of whom had found anything to complain of in young Grafeas' conduct in their courtrooms.

So, on the surface nothing of interest in his professional life, and Khemit had moved on to his personal life. The young scribe had been betrothed to Raia, daughter of Muhandis, a builder of some repute in Alexandria. Khemit had interviewed both and reported the father sad at the loss of such a promising young man to the boy's family, to his own family, and to his community. The daughter, her father said, was too devastated to speak to anyone and Khemit had left herself a note to return to the house to pursue the interview another time. If she had done so, she had not added an account of the visit to her report.

Grafeas had lived with his parents, their home in a neighborhood near the Soma, an easy walk to work. Khemit reported that the house was not larger than their needs but very comfortably appointed. Archeion had last seen his son leaving the Hall of Scribes at Eleventh Hour, an hour early because he said he had to run an errand for one of his clients. Archeion did not know what errand or which client. After that Grafeas was meeting friends for a class at the Five Soldiers Gymnasium. A food vendor on the Canopic Way between the Shurta and the Library reported that Grafeas, a customer well known to her, had bought a dolma minutes later, and that was the last that anyone had seen of the young man.

Khemit had found the two friends he had been going to meet after work at the Five Soldiers, Nenwef and Ahmose. The three of them met at the gymnasium twice a week without fail and they were at a loss to explain why he had not appeared this time. Asked if he had reported any problems at work or in his personal life, they nudged one another and sniggered (Tetisheri reading between the lines) and intimated that Grafeas was resigned to his upcoming nuptials. The marriage had been arranged by her parents and his, and he was prepared to do his duty by his family. She might be part-Egyptian but her father was very rich, and further he was in construction, which augured well for future business. There was always someone suing a builder.

The aridity of Khemit's voice wafted up from the page like a wind off the desert.

In short, Tetisheri thought as she sat back, there seemed to be no discernible reason for Grafeas' disappearance. He had a good reputation at work. He was beloved of his parents, and of his betrothed as well, evidently. Khemit reported his friends as being young men of good family and reputation.

Three days later, as the law provided for, Archeion and Eirene reported him missing to the Shurta. A month later, at the bottom of the scroll, Khemit had written "Unresolved," followed by the date and her name and title.

The one thing Tetisheri didn't understand was how this mysterious disappearance had come to Khemit's attention, and why Khemit had felt the need to investigate it. Grafeas' family, while respectable and certainly storied if indeed it included Herodotus as part of their ancestral line, wasn't a noble one. There was no mention in Khemit's account of either Archeion or Eirene forming part of any Ptolemy's court, such as it was, given how mobile and transitory that court had been in those days of internecine warfare. People went missing every day, voluntarily and involuntarily. Surely ordinary missing persons came within the purview of the Shurta and not the Eye of Isis?

A question best left for another day. She replaced the Eye around her neck and secured the purse to her girdle. The scroll was rolled up and returned to its proper place on the proper shelf. She stood for a moment, letting her eyes run over the shelves again. So many Eyes, so many inquiries, so many royal concerns, represented here by so many máthimas that went back more than three hundred years to the time of the first Ptolemy, the man who first dreamed of the Great Library. The man who handed down to each of his descendants that passion for collecting all the knowledge in the known world beneath one roof.

This roof.

She looked up and saw the shadows beginning to grow long against the ceiling. She straightened the Ledger of the Eye so that it sat in the exact center of the square table, and slid the square stool beneath it just so. She walked to the door and released the cord that controlled the shutters from the cleat. The shutters closed, plunging the room into gloom.

She listened at the door. All was quiet without. The door opened on silent, well-oiled hinges. She stepped into the hall and closed it behind her. The key turned soundlessly in the lock.

The hinges of the door were on the inside and the door itself was set flush with the wall and had been painted the same white. It was free from sign or adornment. Users of the Library who penetrated this far would pass it unseeing. Unless, of course, they looked up and saw the tiny Eye painted on the wall above the door almost where it met the ceiling. Someone else might mistake it for a smudge of dirt, or a cobweb.

But people seldom looked up.

A man said something, too distant for her to hear the words, and was answered by several others in chorus. She turned and walked swiftly through the many connecting halls leading to classrooms and carrels and rooms named for donors of the collections of books within, made voluntarily or otherwise, coming at last to the office tucked just inside the front door.

Sosigenes was at his desk. An untidy tumble of dark hair made him seem at first glance younger than his years, but a closer inspection revealed the lines across his forehead and bracketing his mouth. The stooped shoulders of the scholar complemented the thin, drooping nose that gave him an uncanny resemblance to an ibis, that long-billed, long-legged bird that stalked the streets of Alexandria and left its calling card on every clothesline and park bench in the city. "Did you light the lamps?" he said.

"I did not, Sosigenes. The skylights were more than sufficient. How is Yasmin?"

He looked around, as if Yasmin might magically accrete out of the walls. "Oh. Fine. She's overseeing the copyists. Homer. Both books."

"A new translation?"

He shook his head. "A replacement. The last edition was stolen."

She was startled. "From here? From our shelves?"

His faint smile was an acknowledgement of the possessive pronoun. "It's an ongoing problem for any library, Tetisheri, but here especially, just because of the sheer volume of our inventory and because we open our doors to everyone in the world. Books have walked out the door tucked under chlamyses and togas every day since Ptolemy I. But lately…"

"What?"

He rubbed his eyes. "It's almost as if the thefts are organized."

"How so?"

He dropped his hands and leaned back in his chair. "They are targeted, for one thing."

"Targeted?"

"Yes, the oldest volumes regardless of their authors.

Illustrated editions especially. Particular favorites include Astyanassa's *Of Erotic Postures* and Elephantis' *The Nine Forms*."

She stared at him.

He pointed a finger at her. "Don't you dare, Tetisheri! Don't you dare laugh!"

Her shoulders were shaking. "But, Sosigenes—"

"They are also stealing maps," he said grimly, "and the older the better. Eratosthenes and Anaximander are most popular."

All impulse to laughter died in her. "Does the queen know?"

"Some. Not about the most recent."

"When was the most recent?"

"Last week. A very old copy of Hecataeus' *World Survey*."

"How was it discovered?"

"Yasmin went to lock up the map room, which we have taken to doing every evening of late. She noticed some disarrangement of the shelf dedicated to his works. She sent for me and we compared the maps on the shelf to the room's index. We have other copies of it, but that was our oldest version, and irreplaceable."

"If the room is locked at night, then someone who visited it during the day must have stolen it."

"Yes, and the only way to have stopped him or her would have been to keep the room locked to everyone all the time. Impossible. We're a library, Tetisheri. We are *the* Library." He scrubbed his hands through his hair. When he dropped them again his curls stood out like the snakes on the bust of Medusa in the lobby. "The sum of all human knowledge resides within these four walls. I am not meant to close the doors to the world when it comes seeking that knowledge."

"No," Tetisheri said, almost absently. She was thinking. "Find a student you and Yasmin trust. Have them sit in that room from the moment you unlock the door to the moment you lock it again. Have them take the names of everyone who visits." A ghost of a smile. "And of the visitors to the room that houses the collection of erotic literature, too. All the rooms subject to predation. It won't help find your missing manuscripts, but at least potential future thieves will be put on notice that someone is watching."

He brightened. "It might discourage them, you think?"

She thought rather that the thieves would find some other, more ingenious way to do their work, but she said, "It can't hurt. I'll stop by in a few days to look at your lists."

He looked lighter of spirit just by virtue of having shared his burden. "Willingly."

"Sosigenes, some of the máthimas of the Eye are very old. Have you given any thought to having them copied before they crumble into dust?"

"The only two people who are allowed inside that room are in my office now, and given current events I don't think we need to offer potential thieves more opportunities. Are you volunteering your services?"

"Very funny. Rotate the task between the younger scholars, letting each one copy only, say, five. You could bring the scrolls to them in a room where the door was locked from the outside, and when they were finished, take the scrolls away again. All they need to know is that they are copying old documents as an exercise to improve their penmanship. Start with the oldest documents first and work forward. The task needn't be accomplished in a day."

He tapped his lips with a finger as ink-stained as her own. "I will think on it, Tetisheri."

With that she had to be content.

"Do you have the key?" he said.

She held it up. "If you're not here, how will I get into the room?"

"I am always here."

But he wasn't, and they both knew it. She looked around his office. It was a small space for the Librarian of the Great Library of Alexandria, and it was crowded with shelves stuffed with all manner of scrolls and volumes and documents and artifacts. Was that a lump of gold? Between the figure of a voluptuous woman carved from an elephant's tusk and a tiny wooden model of a sundial? "I could send a workman to inset a small cabinet into the wall behind one of your shelves. It will open and close at a touch. No key necessary."

Sosigenes frowned. "He must never speak of it."

"He is a man trusted by the queen herself."

He thought it over, frowning, and then gave grudging assent. "Very well."

"Thank you, Sosigenes." She cocked her head. "Is it true you helped Caesar with his new calendar?"

He gave an abstracted nod, already reaching for a stylus. "I did. Why?"

"What month is this now, again?"

"September. Or no. October."

"And the day?"

He tutted impatiently. "The eleventh. Haven't you seen the annual calendar the Library put out? I made sure many copies were made and distributed across the city and all the way up the river to Syene. Here." He searched his desk and produced a sheet of papyrus. It was lined horizontally and vertically, forming six grids on both sides. "See? First month, January, what was once called Pharmouthi, and so on."

She'd seen it before. There was one posted in the kitchen at home, another over-sized one on the wall of the warehouse, and a third and fourth in both hers and Uncle Neb's offices. "Thank you, Sosigenes," she said gravely. "Is it true you and Caesar added two months to this year?"

"We had to," he said testily. "The calendar was out of alignment by a full quarter of a season. Of what use is a calendar if you can't look at it and know when the Nile floods?"

"And there are seven days in the new week, instead of ten? And different months have differing amounts of days?"

His eyes narrowed and after a moment his face broadened into a smile. "Have done teasing your old teacher, Tetisheri, and get thee gone about the queen's business!" The smile faded and he said anxiously, "You're sure you didn't light any of the lamps?"

She laughed and departed, laying a bet with herself as she went that within five minutes he would be scurrying off to the room she had just vacated to see for himself.

# 2

Apollodorus was waiting for her at the bottom of the marble steps that ran the length of the building. He was facing the Way, a broad boulevard stretching the breadth of the city from the Gate of the Sun in the east to the Gate of the Moon in the west. A full plethrum in width, there were two central lanes for chariots and for people on horseback and tradesmen delivering goods in donkey carts. They were divided by a median planted with trees and shrubs and featuring fountains and benches, and bordered on either side by lanes for pedestrians. Here traveled the lifeblood of the city, slaves and servants laden with bags and packages, mothers scolding children into line, scholars declaiming to students, street vendors filling the air with their cries, trying to sell out before they had to pack up for the evening. At one time or another during every day, all of Alexandria was on parade along the Canopic Way. It was the best free show in the known world.

But Tetisheri's eyes were on the nearer prospect, a figure she could recognize at any distance in any weather. She had never wondered why until this year.

He was tall but not so tall as to set himself too much apart from his fellow man. He was trim in figure but the muscle was there for anyone with the eye to detect it. His hair was fair and thick and clipped close as a soldier's, as he had once been. His knee-length tunic was well made, of good material but dyed an unostentatious brown and girt with a plain leather belt with a plain bronze buckle. One hand rested on the hilt of the gladius that hung from his belt in a boiled leather sheath. His lower arms were bound with wide leather guards worked with the double-headed eagle of Thrace. The guards were oiled and supple but showed signs of scarring, which one could imagine had been incurred in battle.

The man, too, bore the scars of those same battles, old and white, one across an eyebrow, another down a cheekbone, another, deeper, one across a calf. It was an eloquent history of service under arms, although his face was otherwise curiously unlined. She realized she had never asked him how old he was, and that he had never volunteered the information.

He turned and she felt again that faint shock at meeting those clear green eyes, the color straight out of the olivine mines of Punt. Their gaze was so direct and so entirely without judgement that she felt she could tell him any black secret from her past and he would not condemn her.

In fact, she had, and he hadn't.

He smiled at her, and such was the effect that it took a moment for her to remember that she had feet and that they worked. She paused one step above him so that she could look straight into his eyes and met his smile with her own. She saw the effect in his expression and thrilled to it. "Tell me you're not here because I've been summoned anywhere."

"I'm not here to summon you anywhere but to your dinner."

"I am relieved to hear it."

He laughed, a deep, attractive sound that resonated in her very bones, and attracted attention from women and not a few men passing by. They descended to the street and turned right.

"Do you mind if we make a quick stop at the Five Soldiers?" he said.

"Never."

"You really are the perfect woman."

She laughed, causing a man walking the other way to take a second look. She hoped she wasn't glowing.

They crossed the Way at the first intersection, dodging a carriage carrying a group of sunburnt Romans the worse for wine back from the afternoon races at the Hippodrome. One of them hung over the side, calling out invitations to every woman he saw, young or old, pretty or not, to join them at their lodging to help them spend their winnings. Matrons glared and girls giggled and non-Roman men of every race and creed manifested a common cause in despising the lords and masters of the known world.

"At least no one's throwing anything," Tetisheri said.

"At least." He looked down at her. "You look unaccustomedly sober. What troubles you?"

She told him of the thefts at the Library, and when he stopped laughing she said with asperity, "Yes, hilarious. I admit I laughed, too. But it is books of all kinds that are being stolen, Apollodorus, valuable ones, rare copies, irreplaceable and therefore priceless. Maps, too, copies that date back even to the days when some of the greatest scholars and artists lived and wrote. Sosigenes has scribes copying out Homer's works because the shelf copies have disappeared right off the shelves."

He shook his head gravely. "Terrible. Definitely, what the world needs is more copies of *The Iliad* and *The Odyssey*." He caught her hand before it smacked his shoulder and tucked it into his elbow. "All right, all right. You're going to do something about all this, I expect."

"I suggested that a student be stationed at the doors of various collections to take the names of everyone who enters."

"That will slow the thefts in the short term but determined and informed thieves will no doubt find a way around such actions." He frowned. "Looking at it from the other end of the transaction may be more successful."

"You mean—"

He nodded. "Who receives the stolen goods? And why?"

"'Why?' Isn't it obvious?"

"You mean to sell them for profit?" She nodded. "Well, yes, of course, that is the motive that would first spring to mind, but there could be others. Someone could want a particular edition of a favorite author to keep for their very own." He grinned. "Or as an instruction manual ready to hand in pleasing one's mistress. So to speak."

"Apollodorus!"

He blinked at her innocently. "What?"

Still arguing, they turned left off the Way. The gymnasium was a single story building made of stone set back from the street with a double wooden door at the center. A frieze of open cutouts in a repeating Greek key design lined the walls beneath the eaves of a roof of terracotta tiles. Two highly polished bronze statues stood on marble plinths on either side of the door. One was the figure of a man in the act of throwing a javelin, the other of a man bent double about to hurl a discus.

A second frieze had been added below the first. This one was painted, an abstract design in reds and blues and greens and golds. It was very bright. "Dub went out of town again, didn't he."

"Unfortunately. This time it was an alleged artist who couldn't pay his bill. We can't watch Isidorus all the time. Alas." He opened the door and held it for her.

Inside was a large room with a floor covered in mats. All four walls were lined with weapons and shields from every army in the known world, representing some that no longer existed. Outside at the back, Tetisheri knew, was another space as large again, this one covered in sand, reserved for group practice. Crixus and Castus were attempting to impart the intricacies of close work with spears to a class of young lordlings.

One she knew. Nenwef, friend to Hunefer, her late, unlamented husband. He saw her at the same moment she saw him. They exchanged a long, hostile look before he deliberately turned his back on her, wiping the blood from the scratch on his arm. The young man next to him nudged him and made a remark which made the group laugh heartily. Nenwef laughed, too, although the set of his shoulders told her he hadn't appreciated the joke as much as the rest of them had.

Dubnorix lounged languidly against the opposite wall, watching without enthusiasm as two middle-aged men with matching paunches stepped cautiously through riposte drill, gladii held gingerly in their hands. The blades came together with a dissonant clang. One combatant dropped his sword and shook his hand, swearing. Drops of blood splattered his tunic. Dub rolled his eyes, pushed off from the wall, and sauntered forward to give instruction.

"Dear me," Apollodorus said in a low voice meant only for her ears. "I suppose it would help if Titus could see farther than a hand's width in front of his face."

"Titus?"

"The one who dropped his sword. A Roman, actually. A plebeian. I understand his father prospered in trade. Titus came to spend it all in Alexandria, as one does when one inherits wealth and isn't allowed to use it to buy his way into the ranks of Roman patricians. Kyros is helping him buy his way into the ranks of Alexandrian patricians instead. Kyros being a scion of the Knife."

"Ah." The Nomarch of the Knife was as legendary for the number of children he had fathered as he was for his inability to provide for them all. His children were either married off or apprenticed as soon as they came of age, while he kept having more by new wives and concubines. Kyros appeared to be one of the eldest. "So these are some of your new evening classes?"

He nodded. "They've been so popular we've gone to three sessions a week. We're overcharging to keep the classes small but we've still got waiting lists for all of them. At this rate we're going to have to hire more instructors."

One of the reasons the Five Soldiers was the most success-ful gymnasium in the city was the man standing next to her. Everyone wanted to boast of knowing him, of recounting the day in class when the renowned Apollodorus, retired legionary, friend and advisor to the Lady of the Two Lands herself, the man who had personally smuggled her into the private interview with Julius Caesar that had forever changed the future of Alexandria and Egypt—well. A man could dine out for a year recounting the day Apollodorus had personally demonstrated the proper grip on a gladius in thrust. But all she said was, "I didn't know upper-class Alexandrians were so bloodthirsty."

"I don't think they are, as a rule. Mostly they hire out their mayhem. But I think the late war traumatized everyone."

She was inclined to agree. The Alexandrine War had lasted four long, bloody years as Auletes' children fought over the Two Crowns. The Roman cohorts marching in and out to support one claimant or another had not provided a sense of security. It was no wonder Alexandrians were lining up at the Five Soldiers Gymnasium to learn how to protect themselves. Certainly it was obvious that many of them could use the instruction.

Isidorus charged through the door in the back wall, spotted them at once, and broke into a trot. The light from the oil lamps that hung round the room shone off his scalp, which he had begun to shave when he started going bald. "Sheri, by Sobek's balls! It's good to see you, beautiful girl!" He picked her up as if she were a featherweight, which she knew very well she was not, and whirled her around and set her down again to beam up at her. "What brings you into this sweatshop full of pretenders, every one of whom you could take blindfolded? That is, if you've been practicing?" He frowned at her, and all that was needed was a curled beard and curlier horns to complete the resemblance to Faunus.

She was flushed and laughing. "I have, Is. I would not dare otherwise to show my face here."

He beamed at her. "That is good to hear, beautiful girl." He cast a disparaging look at Apollodorus. "It shows you have some sense." He flicked her temple. "Remember, your most important weapon…"

"... is the one between my ears." She'd heard the admonition often enough that she could recite it in unison with him. "I remember, Is."

He gave a satisfied nod. "Good."

Apollodorus winked at him and looked over his head at Dubnorix. He nodded at the back door and headed in that direction. Dub bestowed upon Tetisheri his most devastating smile, the one proven to make all the ladies go weak at the knees, excused himself and followed. His pupils, looking relieved, downed swords and headed for the refreshments.

"Are the classes for girls filling up, Is?"

"Of course. During the day only, so far, although Crixus says he is wooing some promising matrons by way of that dressmaker of his."

Crixus had been laying romantic siege to a dressmaker in the Royal Quarter for months. "Any joy to be had there?"

Is waggled his eyebrows. "Let us just say there is a spring in his step this month that wasn't there last month, beautiful girl. And how is your friend, our august queen?"

"Between rebuilding Alexandria and Egypt after the last war and being a new mother, she has her hands full."

"And what does she hear from Caesar, that mightily victorious general and the father of her child?" Is held strict if nontraditional views on the responsibilities of parenthood, and in his view Caesar fell woefully short in this regard. It might have had something to do with the fact that Caesar had not bothered to wait upon Caesarion's birth before leaving to put out some provincial fire. There were always fires in the provinces. There was not always a new child to welcome into the world, as Is had pointed out tartly on more than one occasion, Julius Caesar had cause to know.

Tetisheri returned a slight shrug, but thought it wise to turn the subject. Fortunately, Khemit's account of her last investigation sprang readily to mind. "Is, do you remember a young man named Grafeas? He met friends here twice a week. This would have been about two years ago, when the war was still going on."

"I don't—"

"He was a scribe, of the Hall of Scribes, owned by Archeion. He was Archeion's son."

Is's brow cleared and he snapped his fingers. "The young man who disappeared! Of course I remember. There was a woman nosing around, asking after him—"

"Khemit?"

His eyes narrowed, and he took a long, deliberate look at the fine chain that was all that could be seen of her badge of office. "Yes," he said after a significant pause. "Khemit."

So Is knows, she thought. And if Is knew, then Dub and Crixus and Castus knew as well. So much for the traditional secrecy shrouding the identity of any Eye of Isis. Aristander knew, too, but then the head of the Shurta always did. "What did she want to know?" she said, drawing his eyes back to hers, hoping that her expression was uninformative. It was something that required practice, of which she hadn't yet had a great deal.

Is's eyebrows drew together. "He was in my class—unarmed combat—and I gave her the names of his two friends who took the class with him."

"What were their names?" They were in Khemit's notes but even as new to the post as she was, Tetisheri knew to check everything twice, if not three times, if not every time the opportunity presented itself.

"They're both here tonight. Ahmose is one of them. He's still a student. Some real talent there. I'm trying to nudge him toward the Queen's Guard." He nodded at a young man in the long weapons class, notable for a musculature that was Achillean in aspiration. "The other is some scion of a noble house, and someone much more interested in his reflection than in blade discipline." He pointed with his chin at the young man who looked like a ten-year-old boy standing next to Ahmose. "Nefer? Nitwit?"

With foreboding she said, "Nenwef, son of Menes of Thinis?"

Is snapped his fingers. "That's it!"

At that moment Nenwef said something to Ahmose and sauntered over to the refreshment table set against the wall beside the door. He poured a large cup of water and drank it down in one long swallow. He looked over his shoulder at her and flexed a muscle. She kept her face expressionless.

Is cocked his head. "You know him?"

"Unfortunately."

"Want to talk to him?" Is half raised his hand to beckon Nenwef over.

"No," she said. "I really don't. He was a friend of Hunefer's."

Isidorus looked at her in silence for a moment. "Want me to throw him out?"

Some of the ice that had formed around her heart when she had seen Nenwef melted. "No, certainly not. His money's good." She smiled. "Or at least his wife's is."

He knew her well enough to recognize the effort that had gone into the smile. "The offer stands." She said nothing more, and he shrugged. "Why all the questions about Grafeas?"

Nenwef stiffened. Interesting, she thought, and didn't bother to lower her voice. "He's still missing. His parents remain citizens in good standing of Alexandria, and they are owed answers. Did Khemit say why she wanted to know?"

He shook his head, and she read the message in his eyes easily. *She didn't have to.*

Nenwef dallied over another glass of water before walking back to his class, ostensibly ignoring them both. He smacked Ahmose on the back and said something. Ahmose seemed to protest. Nenwef shook his head, and without taking leave of his instructors entered the door leading to the changing rooms.

Is shared the latest in local gossip while Tetisheri listened with half an ear, watching as Nenwef emerged again, now dressed in elaborate attire that was some clothier's bright idea as to what the rich wore for street clothes. Nenwef always had dressed above his station and his purse. He waved at his friends and walked out the front door. He wasn't moving slowly.

"Is the long weapons class over?" she said.

"No."

The door in the back wall opened and Apollodorus came in alone. He walked across to them with an unhurried gait, and smiled down at her. "Ready?"

She smiled at Is and followed Nenwef out the door. He was a diminishing figure at the corner of the Way.

The crowds had dwindled and Tetisheri saw Nenwef hail a cabrio. "Hurry," she said.

"Why?"

"I want to see where Nenwef goes."

"Nenwef?"

They emerged onto the Way as Nenwef's cabrio driver slapped the back of his horse with the reins.

Tetisheri looked up and down the street for transportation. A cabrio turned into the Way from Lochias. Apollodorus shouted and waved and he pulled up in front of them. "Where to?"

Tetisheri pointed. "Follow them. Don't get too close."

"Oh now, lady, but I've been at work since dawn and I want my dinner—"

Apollodorus climbed in beside her. "Follow them, and keep your distance."

The driver gulped and clucked at his horse.

In a low voice Apollodorus said, "Why are we following Nenwef? I would have thought—"

"I mentioned a name to Is and Nenwef overheard me. He left in a hurry."

"Why do we care?"

"It was the name of a missing man from one of Khemit's cases. He was never found. In her report of the investigation she listed two of his friends. One of them was named Nenwef. Isidorus told me Nenwef was friends with this Grafeas. I want to know why hearing me speak his name would move Nenwef to quit his lesson early and leave in such a rush."

Apollodorus grunted and settled back into the cabrio's seat. It was a plank of unvarnished wood fitted snugly into the half circle shape of the back of the cabrio. The driver stood in front of them, holding the reins. A pair of shurta on patrol nodded at Apollodorus as they passed. A food vendor was hauling his cart towards home. A group of students oblivious to everything but a heated argument over the character of Euripides' Medea (heartless mother or abused wife?) nearly trampled a rose garden planted in the median. An ibis that had been prospecting for bugs raised an indignant squawk and flapped off to try his luck on the shores of Lake Mareotis, narrowly missing one of the offending students with a healthy squirt of rich yellow excrement.

Tetisheri craned her neck to look ahead. Their driver was maintaining a discreet distance between Nenwef's cabrio and their own. She relaxed back onto the seat. "By the way, how did you know I was at the Library?"

"I stopped at the house on my way back from the port.

Nike informed me that dinner would be served promptly at Fourteenth Hour and that it was Nebet's lamb in apricot sauce tonight and that if we wanted any of it we'd best not be late."

"Was Uncle Neb home?"

"I didn't see him. Is he away again?"

She nodded. "He's on his way back from Puteoli."

"What's in Puteoli?"

"Construction materials." A brief silence, while she wondered how to put her question in the most delicate terms. There was much he couldn't tell her of his service to their queen. In the end she decided on the straightforward approach. "You've been away yourself."

"Have I?" He glanced down at her.

"I haven't seen you for a ten-day at least, and you said you were coming back from the port." In spite of herself she heard the note of accusation in her voice.

He heard it, too, and his grin flashed again. "You've been keeping count, Sheri."

She turned her head so he wouldn't see her blush.

It was late afternoon, that time of day when everyone was on their way home. They traveled the length of the city before their driver slowed. "He's turning, sir."

"Left or right?"

"Left."

She looked at Apollodorus. "Into Rhakotis."

He grimaced. "Which street?"

"Canal Street, sir."

The street that followed the Nile Canal, which connected the harbor to the Nile. "Follow him as far as you can."

Canal Street was half the width of the Canopic Way and crowded with shops selling everything to do with the construction trade. Here a small shop with a kiln taking up most of the room made and sold nothing but clay roof tiles. There a stall displayed racks full of hammers great and small. Progress was slower although many of the owners were preparing to close up shop. All of the shops had apartments over them, where most of the owners lived. Construction after the war was so fierce that the tools and materials of the trade were fetching premium prices, which made them targets of opportunity for every band of thieves in the whole of Alexandria and Egypt.

As they traveled deeper into Rhakotis, the houses on Canal Street became larger and spaced farther apart, with property going down to the edge of the canal, which they were now able to see. Gradually some of these homes became flanked with construction yards with walls around them and double doors made of solid wood with heavy bronze hinges and locks. All of the doors boasted at least two guards, heavily armed.

Their driver pulled up. "He's stopped, I think. Yes, he's paying off his driver and getting out."

"We're close enough to home," Tetisheri said to Apollodorus. "We can walk from here."

He nodded and got out. She pulled out her purse and dropped enough coins into their driver's hand to make him whistle cheerfully as he maneuvered his equipage around to return the way they had come.

Tetisheri and Apollodorus found a shadowed corner across the street. Nenwef was haggling with the driver of his cabrio, a stout man whose face was turning a deep, dark red.

The cabrio had stopped before an impressive collection of buildings set beside an equally impressive length of the Nile Canal. The central structure was a house built in the classical Greek style. Both sides were covered with scaffolding all the way up to the roof. The front of the house, however, was free of construction debris and open to the admiring gaze of passers-by. There was much to admire. A carved pediment illustrated what appeared to be the entire life story of Alexander the Great, painted in colors that would have made Isidorus weep with envy. In one scene Aristotle lectured the young Alexander. In another Alexander dribbled out a handful of grain to mark the borders of the city, and battles, battles everywhere, from Halicarnassus to Hydaspes. Ptolemy I Soter appeared often, looking enough like Alexander to be his twin, although the sculptor had taken care to differentiate the two men by giving Alexander a helmet with wings and Ptolemy one with a hooded cobra, a broad hint at his future as the first Ptolomaic king of Alexandria and Egypt. The cornice framing the frieze, it went without saying, was elaborately keyed.

This masterpiece rested on not one but two rows of

columns, the first Corinthian, the second Doric, one set back from the other on a deep porch. The columns were heavily illustrated with the histories of the various Ptolemy kings and queens, and again painted in bright, saturated colors, predominantly red and blue. A small drive curved around a garden oval, in the center of which a tall, elegant fountain stood. It was not yet in operation. Across the drive a broad marble staircase led up to the columned portico.

On the right was an enormous space twice the size of the house, surrounded by a brick wall that had been stuccoed and painted a soft cream, one could only suppose the better not to shame the grandeur of the main building. The massive doors were spread wide and looked into a yard filled with industry, carpenters, joiners, woodworkers, masons, painters and more hard at work at their individual crafts. On the left more buildings similarly stuccoed and painted stood. Warehouses, Tetisheri thought, as the estate evidently came equipped with its own dock, too, as manifested by the masts of several vessels visible beyond the roofs of the various buildings.

Apollodorus whistled beneath his breath. "That's not a house, that's a mansion."

"That's not a mansion, that's a palace."

A woman descended the marble steps of the house, a sheaf of papyrus in hand, the skirt of her shapeless linen tunic kilted up to show strong calves in thick leather sandals. She wore a wide belt with pockets suspended from it. Nenwef saw her and ended his argument with the cabrio driver by turning his back on him and hastening away. The driver hurled curses after him, mounted his cabrio, and slapped the reins against his horse's back hard enough that it snorted and lunged forward, barely missing a workman coming down the street with a box of tools on his shoulder, who added his own comments.

The woman paused on the bottom step. In her late thirties or early forties, she had thick black hair caught back in a knot that was more to do with being kept out of her way than with style. Her figure was thickset but not fat, her skin browned by the sun, and even at this distance Tetisheri could see that her jaw was heavy and her chin pronounced. She did not look pleased to see Nenwef.

"Greek, do you think?"

Apollodorus nodded, watching. They couldn't hear the conversation but Nenwef looked excited, while she looked more and more forbidding. He spoke quickly, gesturing. She asked a question and he shook his head violently, shrinking from her. She grabbed his arm and asked again, and again he shook his head. She shoved him away from her, and came down the last step. He caught at the fabric of her tunic and she slapped his hand away contemptuously. It must have hurt because he cupped his hand reflexively and said something to her receding back. She paused to give him one look over her shoulder. He took a step back, still cradling his hand. She snorted, reached into the purse suspended from her belt, and tossed a handful of coins in his direction. They skittered all over the flagstones of the driveway. Nenwef scrabbled after them on one hand and his knees while she disappeared through the doors of the yard.

He got to his feet, carefully tucked away the coins, and looked around, evidently for his cabrio. He said something that looked like a curse and walked down the street the way he had come, cradling his arm.

Apollodorus pressed Tetisheri back into the shadow and she had just enough time to see the smile on his face before he kissed her. Startled at this public display of affection, she raised her hands to his shoulders as if to push him away before she realized the kiss was to put his back to Nenwef and conceal her from Nenwef's sight. It would have been difficult to explain away her presence, and he would never forgive her having witnessed his humiliation.

She relaxed and let her hands slide up and around Apollodorus' neck and found herself pressed into the corner where the shadows lay. His hand knotted in her hair to pull her head back and his knee pressed her legs apart, settling himself in between them, firmly, so there could be no doubt of his arousal. A hot flush of desire swept over her and she made a sound deep in the back of her throat. She raised up on her toes as his hand slid over the curve of hip.

Someone rang a bell loud enough to be heard over the thud of Tetisheri's heart and they pulled apart and looked around. Tetisheri had to blink several times for her vision to clear enough to see the scene through the doors across the street, where everyone inside was downing tools and packing up for home. The woman with the belt stood just inside the door behind a scribe, who counted out a day's pay into eager hands and marked each sum next to a name. The workers poured out into the street, walking in twos and threes, most of them making in the direction of the Way.

"Come on," Tetisheri said. She reached for Apollodorus' hand without looking. It slid into hers and she tugged him into the stream of workers.

Some of the men stopped for a drink at cafes and tavernas but enough of them continued toward home that she and Apollodorus could mingle without occasioning comment. By a miracle no one recognized Apollodorus. Tetisheri smiled at a young carpenter and that was enough to start a conversation. "We couldn't help but notice the house you were working on."

Someone snorted. "It's hard to miss."

His friend elbowed him in the side.

"Who is it being built for?"

The snorter spat. "The Master of Builders himself. I guess he's decided he needs a house that lives up to his new title."

"What are you complaining about?" his friend said. "His coin is as good as anyone else's."

"And the foreman? Who is she?"

"The lady Khadiga," he said readily. "She's not the foreman, she's Otho's contractor."

The man walking next to him sniggered. "That's not all she is."

"Quiet," the first man said, looking involuntarily over his shoulder. "I shudder to think what she'd do to you if she heard you say something like that. That is not a forgiving woman." He looked forward again. "But she pays well."

"Somebody does," his friend said.

After which they seemed disinclined to pursue the topic any further, and turned the discussion firmly to speculating who would win the next gladiatorial contest in the Hippodrome.

# 3

They parted from their new friends when they reached the Way, crossing it to walk through the Emporeum. Here, Tetisheri was obliged to stop and say hello to every shopkeeper and business rival who called out her name, which was most of them. She and Apollodorus helped old Kurush put up his shutters, put their shoulders to Elon and Beulah's cart to start them on their way home, and admired Izem and Tifawt's new baby. Before anyone else could claim their attention they crossed Hermes Street and were navigating the warren of homes and warehouses that filled in the area between Hermes Street and the docks.

The tang of salt air grew stronger and the last gulls were heard squawking their way home to their roosts. In short order they came to the walled house that sat next to the massive warehouse with the sign, "Nebenteru's Luxury Goods." As they approached, the door to the house was flung back and Nike, the slender maid from Nubia who had lived life as a slave in Hunefer's house until freed by Tetisheri, and now, within the space of months, ruled Nebenteru's household with a rod of iron, stood outlined in the door. She was letting her hair grow out and it was wrapped in a length of red cloth, the same cloth her dress was made of. She looked like a living flame.

While she didn't scold them for their tardiness they both felt chastised anyway, and followed her meekly into the back of the house to a room that opened onto a walled garden. It held a long table and a sideboard. "Will Keren be joining us?"

"She sent word to say she would be late at the infirmary this evening."

Tetisheri poured water from the pitcher into a bowl set on a sideboard. She started to wash her hands, caught Nike's condemnatory eye, and stepped back to wave Apollodorus forward, as was his right as guest of the house. His lips quirked but he washed his hands and accepted the towel proffered by Nike with a nod of thanks that was nearly a bow. When Tetisheri's hands were deemed sufficiently clean they proceeded to the table, where there were only two places set. Tetisheri looked at Nike. "Aren't you joining us?"

Nike tossed her head, and the wild curls peeping out of the red cloth bounced in emphasis. "Who will eat with Phoebe and Nebet if I do?" And off she went to the kitchen.

"I sense a conspiracy," Apollodorus said, sounding amused.

"As do I."

"One that smells delicious, however, and I'm hungry."

"As am I."

The table was laden with bowls of the aforesaid lamb in apricot sauce served on a bed of grain, cucumber in yogurt and herbs, and fennel sliced thinly with onion garnished with mint and dressed with honey. There were fresh-baked barley rolls on the side and apples and cheese for dessert, and a lovely wine from Chios, crisp and fragrant and not so potent that it would catch fire from being set too close to the candle flame.

Nike had seen fit to place the one lone lamp behind a vase full of red roses from Phoebe's garden. The scent perfumed the air with enough sweet intensity to rival the lamb, which took some doing, and the light from the flame filtered gently through the blooms.

Definitely a conspiracy, Tetisheri thought, pushing away her cleaned plate and reaching for the water pitcher instead of the wine to refill her glass.

Apollodorus took a refill of the water without comment and leaned back in his chair. "Nebet can cook."

"Indeed she can."

"Phoebe all right with a second cook cluttering up her kitchen?"

"Phoebe likes to learn, and Nebet is only semi-retired."

"Is she one of yours?"

"Phoebe?" She smiled a little. "She was my first."

"Tell me."

It was one of the things she loved most about him, that he wanted to know how she spent her days, and what he had missed in her life. More of a contrast to her former husband there could not be. "We were in Rome, with Auletes and the queen, begging Pompey for money."

"Before my time."

"Just barely, but yes, and how lucky you were. It was dueling banquets during our entire stay, one night at an Optimas', the next at a supporter of the Populares."

Apollodorus raised his eyebrows. "You dined with the Populares? Pompey must have been pleased."

"Auletes was always alive to the possibility of regime change in Rome, and he was adept at keeping a foot in any camp that looked like it might make a try for power. At any rate, this particular banquet lasted all day, everything edible growing, walking, swimming, or flying was represented, everything came to the table either on ice or on fire, and everything I could manage to eat of it was absolutely delicious. Until dessert." She fortified herself with a swallow of water. "Dessert was a parade of cakes baked and iced in the shapes of birds. Herons, swans, hawks, doves, cranes. And, as it happened, their maker had conceived the excellent notion of mixing live birds in with the fake, in cages formed of almond paste and icing embedded with pistachios. Works of art, really. Until two of the live doves managed to eat themselves out of their dovecote and began to fly around the room looking for a way out."

Apollodorus looked as if he were trying hard not to laugh. "And who could blame them."

"Indeed. They immediately began demonstrating their

displeasure on all available surfaces. You know how everyone makes fun of Caesar's combover? I doubt that anyone there that evening ever will again, because as it turns out a shiny scalp makes an excellent target."

Apollodorus lay back in his chair and a laugh boomed out. Laughter was a good look on him, brightening his eyes and deepening the creases at the corners of his mouth, and she paused for a moment to enjoy the view. "Yes, it was very funny. At first. Less funny when Scipio, wiping the dove excrement from the side of his face, roared out for the person in the kitchen responsible for the cakes to be brought before him at once." She turned her goblet around between her fingers. "It was Phoebe. To this day I don't know if she was responsible for the cakes or if whoever was in charge of the household staff decided she was an acceptable scapegoat. She wouldn't tell me." She nodded at the apples. "But I have noticed that she seldom serves anything but fresh fruit, nuts, and cheese for dessert, and anything more complicated will only be a simple custard or a fruit tart. Never anything elaborate."

All trace of laughter gone, Apollodorus said, "What did he do?"

"He beat her, personally, right there in front of us, until she was bleeding from above her knees to her shoulders and her arms down to her elbows. And then he commanded she be strung up by her wrists at his front gate with a sign hung round her neck reading, 'Disobedient slave.'"

When she stopped he said, "And?"

45

"I expect he meant her to hang there until she died. Let it be a lesson to you and all that, although I don't know what that lesson would have been, precisely."

"Don't incorporate livestock into the sweet course?"

"Very likely."

"What did you do?"

She took comfort in the certainty of his tone, that he knew she would have done something. "I waited until Twentieth Hour and went back and cut her down. She could barely walk but I managed to get her home and hidden in my room. The next day I smuggled her down to the *Hapi* in Ostia."

"Ah, Neb was there, was he?"

She nodded. "His was one of the ships Auletes had commandeered for the voyage. He grumbled the entire time over how much trade he was losing."

"I can almost hear him. Did you tell Cleopatra?"

"By the Eye of Ra, no. She and her father had enough trouble on their hands as it was."

"But she knew."

Tetisheri sighed. "She always knows everything. It's alarming."

"And so you brought Phoebe home with you."

She nodded. "I told her the same thing I tell them all, that she could stay or go, but if she wanted to stay and cook for us that it would be as a freedwoman and she would be paid a fair wage."

"Neb went along with this?"

"There was some initial upset, but then Phoebe started cooking on the voyage home. He's been doubling her salary every year or so ever since, out of fear she'll leave us."

"Sabazios knows I've never had a bad meal at this table. I'm sorry I missed that party, though." He stretched out a hand and took her own in it. Her heart skipped a beat in the way the foolish thing always did. "Life can be like this, too, Tetisheri. A good dinner, a quiet evening, the enjoyment of each other's company."

"We serve the queen," she said in a low voice. "It is not exactly a calling conducive to a quiet life."

"What were you doing at the Library?"

She was surprised by the change of subject. "There are records left by the ones who came before me." Even here, safe at home, the habit of secrecy was ingrained. She'd spent entirely too many of her formative years with Cleopatra. "I thought it might help if I read through some of the more recent cases." Her lips tightened. "Since I have no experience in investigating anything, it might be the only way I can gain some."

"And that was how you learned of this Grafeas, and that Nenwef was his friend."

"Yes."

"Why did we follow him?"

"I think he told that woman, Khadiga, that I had been asking Is about Grafeas."

"And that means—"

"I don't know. Yet." She toyed with her glass and looked

up with a rueful smile. "Khemit wrote 'Unresolved' at the bottom of her report. It bothers me."

"You said this young man disappeared, what, two years ago?"

"Yes."

He shook his head. "How many investigations did Khemit do altogether?"

Again she was surprised by his question. "She numbered her last one the sixteenth máthima."

"So sixteen investigations total, I assume not including the one concerning the theft of the new issue?"

"She did not survive to write an account of it, as you well know."

An appreciative twinkle appeared in his eye, and she wondered crankily why it was that any show of annoyance in her amused him.

"Sixteen investigations in, what, four years?"

"Yes."

"Which comes to an average of four inquiries per year. Not an inordinate amount of work."

"And what about you? You, too, are in her service. You're gone half the time on her orders."

He stood up, pulling her to her feet. He raised her hands to his lips and kissed them both in turn, and then drew her to him to kiss her mouth. Just like that, she was back in that shadowed corner, his touch turning her body into molten gold, all running into a puddle at her own feet.

He pulled back and her eyes opened slowly. A thrill of

excitement ran up her spine at the expression in his. "I resent it," she said, her voice trembling a little.

He traced the line of her throat with his mouth, biting here, licking there. "Resent what?"

"Resent how much more experience you have with this than I do."

His head raised, all trace of amusement wiped clean from his face, but all he said was, "The better to please you, *agape mou*."

"Sophist," she said.

"We were taught so by the best." He kissed her again, and took a step back, holding her off by her shoulders when she would have followed. "I should go."

"You could stay," she whispered.

"I would not shame Nebenteru's house so."

"Then where?"

He slid his hands around her neck, nudging her face up, and kissed her again, his lips warm, his teeth and tongue teasing hers. "It's not where, Tetisheri, it's when."

He kissed her hand again, and then turned it to kiss her palm.

Her hand closed over the warmth he had left behind as she watched him fade into the night.

# 4

H is last remark had interfered with her dreams and was interfering again with her work the following morning. What did he mean, when, not where? She felt he was being unnecessarily cryptic. It annoyed her. Men were supposed to be simple and easy to manage. Every married woman she knew said so. Cleopatra had certainly played Caesar as well as her father had ever played the flute.

Yes, Tetisheri had endured an abusive marriage but here she was, a full partner in one of the most respected and successful trading concerns on the Middle Sea, a liberator of oppressed women wherever she found one, a valued friend of the queen, a servant to her country. She had traveled extensively. She spoke many languages. She was known to people in power the length of the Nile and she numbered among her business correspondents kings in, among other places, Judea, Tunis, and Cappadocia, traders from Corinth to Corduba, and people from every walk of society in between. By no measurement could she be construed as a victim. She feared that Apollodorus did. Or else he would have stayed last night. She had invited him to stay, in so many words. And he had walked away. She wanted to be angry with him. She wanted to be furious.

And yet she was uneasily aware that he might not be entirely in the wrong. With Cleopatra in hiding and Uncle Neb on a year-long voyage to Punt she had had no allies to protect her from a political marriage forced on her by her mother. Hagne herself had married for money, holding up her nose at her husband's people, who, in her family's opinion, had come from far too far up the river, who had welcomed his death, and who had lost no time in wiping the stain of his blood from her daughter by marrying Tetisheri to an impoverished noble who needed money to buy his way into the royal court.

It had been a nightmare of a marriage, but it had not broken Tetisheri. She could still laugh. She could still cry. She could still love.

She scowled down at the latest communication from the Nomarch of the Ibis, who was emoting all over his message about a late shipment of garum. Since he had some of the troops Caesar had left behind quartered in his nome she could understand his agitation over the shortage of something the average Roman considered essential to every meal, but really. She took up her stylus to write a short, pithy reply when there was a soft knock at the door. "What?"

She realized how bad-tempered her response sounded and turned to apologize. Nike stood in the doorway, back as straight (and as rigid) as an obelisk. Her expression gave Tetisheri to understand that she, Nike, would overlook her, Tetisheri's, ill-mannered ill-humor this one time. "Aurelius Cotta has called and begs a moment of your time."

Tetisheri said a very bad word. Nike put her nose even higher in the air. "I put him in the parlor. I will bring cakes and a cooling drink."

"No cakes, no drinks. The last thing we want is to make Caesar's legate comfortable in our house."

Scandalized, Nike vacated the area with an outraged flounce.

Tetisheri, ruffled and determined not to show it, took time to neaten her desk and lock away her correspondence, including the aborted letter to the Nomarch of the Ibis. It was probably for the best. It would have been unfair of her to treat his concern as frivolous. She had learned from people who housed workers of any kind that food was invariably the single most important thing to everyone in employment. Soldiers and travelers from Rome required garum to spice everything but their wine. Miners from Gaul made a stew with herbs, marrowbone, and root vegetables, and wouldn't go to work without the promise of a full bowl at the end of every day. Laborers and gladiators from Magna Germania refused to raise a shovel or a sword without a large mug of small beer to start and end their work.

Uncle Neb told a hilarious story about a group of laborers putting up yet another temple in the Port of Mumba, because evidently there were never enough shrines and temples in

Mumba. The laborers had come from all over the East, bringing their various special talents in painting and carving and masonry with them. Their common staple was rice, which delighted the rulers of Mumba, who foresaw an easy, cordial relationship for the duration of construction. Not so easy or so cordial, as it turned out, because each group ate a different kind of rice and each cooked their rice in a different way. There weren't quite riots but until the city fathers had adjusted the menu accordingly, work had not gone forward with the celerity it otherwise might. It had been, Uncle Neb said, a shocking demonstration of power on the part of the workers, although it would have cost you your life had you said it out loud within the walls of Mumba.

She was obliged to give herself a mental shake. She was stalling, hoping Cotta would grow tired of waiting for her and leave. He would instead be prepared to wait until the doors to the Underworld opened for both of them, and she knew that, too. She rose to her feet and looked at Bast, the slim, ebony cat with eyes as blue as Tetisheri's own, who condescended to share Tetisheri's home with the rest of them. "Well? Shall we find out what this Roman wants? Again?"

Bast, curled into a ball on the corner of the desk that received the most sun, yawned and stretched and moved sinuously to her feet. She gave Tetisheri her usual slow blink, the one that always found Tetisheri wanting, and leapt from the table to land soundlessly in front of the door. She looked over her shoulder and gave voice.

"We're not in a hurry, remember," Tetisheri told her.

"Cotta needn't think he has only to snap his fingers to see how high we'll jump."

Bast gave her an admonitory look and strolled from the room.

Tetisheri smiled. Bast would expect any audience to wait upon her presence until she chose to honor them with it.

In her turn, Tetisheri fussed with her stola, a loose-fitting, floor-length white tunic, and picked up her palla, a length of deep blue, finely woven linen, and took the time necessary to arrange it in a correctly draped fold around her shoulders. The obsidian amulet of the goddess Bast hung from a silk cord round her neck, and she checked to see that it was properly centered. She smoothed back her hair and stepped outside of her office, pulling the door closed behind her, to find Keren waiting for her in the hallway.

She was a slim girl with dark eyes, olive skin, a snub nose, and shiny black curls in a thick cloud around her face and shoulders. "Off to see the legate?"

Tetisheri sighed.

"Here's some good news to temper this visitation by one of the self-proclaimed gods bestriding the Middle Sea." Keren produced a scroll. "Uncle Neb is back, or so Simon says, who brought the message."

Tetisheri's face lit up. "Oh, good!" She reached for the scroll and broke the seal, reading it quickly. "He's offloading the cargo at the Royal Harbor. He says they'll bring the *Hapi* around to our dock when he's done and to hold dinner for him."

"I'll tell Phoebe."

Tetisheri raised an eyebrow. "Simon, hmmm?"

Keren might have blushed. She did toss her head. "I'm off to the Library. Yasmin found an old text in the archives that she says contains drawings of the human body in layers all the way down to the bone."

"What fun for you."

Keren stuck out her tongue. "I'll be home for dinner."

"Did you invite Simon?"

Tetisheri received no answer, just a back clad in gaily striped linen receding rapidly toward the front door. She smiled to herself and followed at a leisurely pace, pausing in the doorway of the parlor.

Gaius Aurelius Cotta, legate of Rome to the Court of Egypt and Alexandria, cousin to Gaius Julius Caesar himself, was very much at his leisure, sprawled comfortably in the room's most substantial chair. He bore a superficial likeness to his cousin, with more hair. The real resemblance came from the fact that both were soldiers. Both men were at fighting weight, both never left home without a gladius strapped to one hip and a long knife to the other, and both studied a style of civilian dress that facilitated an ease of movement and the ability to hide any blood spilled during the day.

Of course, Cotta was made instantly identifiable by the scar on the left side of his forehead, inflicted by the downstroke of a sword held by an Arveni chieftain, a blow it was said had been meant for Caesar and that had been deliberately taken instead by Cotta. No attempt had been made to hide it, as Cotta had his hair clipped as close to his skull as Apollodorus did his. His tunic was knee length and belted beneath a toga draped over one shoulder and one arm in the approved Roman style. His sandals were serviceable. He wore a small signet ring on his right forefinger. Tetisheri couldn't see the device on it from the door.

Bast was in residence in a chair opposite, delicately occupied with a thorough washing of her left front paw.

"Ah, lady," Cotta said in Latin, rising to his feet and gazing with warm appreciation on her face. "Thank you for taking the time to meet with me as I descend upon you without warning." His gaze traveled her from head to toe and back again, the glint of admiration in his eyes plain. "I see that I find you in your usual excellent health."

She inclined her head. "Aurelius Cotta."

He took no notice of the frost on her greeting, but then he was adept at not noticing things he did not want to see. "Please, join me for a moment in this most pleasant room. Allow me to pour you some of this excellent fruit punch your servant brought to me here."

She perched next to Bast, the straightness of her spine rivaling Nike's own, and accepted a glass made of a thin, translucent alabaster that showed off the rich red of the juice to advantage.

"A cake? No? Ah well, you ladies are always looking after your figures. We soldiers require fuel and I must say these little cakes are a most delicious means of taking it on. You must prevail upon your cook to share the recipe with mine."

Tetisheri sipped her juice and thought dark thoughts about Nike, and darker thoughts about Cotta, who dared to act as host in a home not his own.

He chatted, mostly to himself with occasional monosyllabic noises from Tetisheri, about the news lately from Pontus, of Caesar's five-day victory at the Battle of Zela, and the escape of Pharnaces II following the battle and his subsequent murder at the hands of his son-in-law, Asander. "And so back to Rome, I believe, with, alas, no visit to Egypt to break his journey."

He bestowed a sympathetic smile on Tetisheri, who met it with one of her own. "My queen will be prostrate with grief."

His eyes glinted with appreciation of her sarcasm. Not entirely devoid of a sense of humor, Cotta. It would be much easier to thoroughly dislike him if he were. "But will carry on with her duty to Egypt and Alexandria nonetheless."

"As any responsible monarch would do."

"Certainly those chosen by Caesar," he said smoothly.

"And by Isis Herself," Tetisheri said, just as smoothly.

He had the audacity to laugh out loud and, still laughing, offered to refill her glass. She shook her head and he refilled his own and sat back to regard her with a steady gaze that, while it wasn't quite unblinking, was certainly alive to every change of expression on her face. "I hope the trade is going well?"

Bast decided that her paw was sufficiently clean. She placed her feet in a perfect square, curled her tail around them in a no-less perfect arc, and regarded Gaius Aurelius Cotta with a stare of her own. Hers was, in fact, unblinking. Cotta, wisely, pretended not to see it.

"I believe we are able to provide food and shelter for ourselves and our dependents for the foreseeable future, as well as accrue a respectable profit."

Unperturbed by her tone, Cotta said, "I saw the *Hapi* dock at the Royal Harbor this morning and went down to give Nebenteru my regards. He tells me he can't keep up with the orders for construction materials he receives from builders."

Tetisheri felt that they had at last arrived at the reason for Cotta's visit. In one way she welcomed it as it meant the time of his departure was that much nearer. In another, she was uncertain as to what, exactly, his true purpose was and she was wary of imparting any information that would help him in achieving it. A merchant's life was by definition a competitive one. She also had a lively appreciation, first, of her responsibilities to the throne as the Eye, and, second, of Cleopatra's opinion of anyone who abrogated said responsibilities either accidentally or deliberately.

Mostly she just wanted Cotta out of her house. "Does he," she said in response to his last remark.

"It isn't surprising. Much damage was done to the city during the late war, all of which your queen seems intent on repairing. The reconstruction of the Heptastadion is now complete, did you hear? In seven days, no less. Quite the undertaking, and very popular with the citizens of

Alexandria." Cotta smiled. "Your queen has earned a new title, did you know? Cleopatra the Builder."

No, she thought, how could I possibly know what nicknames my own people are calling my own queen? "A compliment, I should think."

"Indeed. I understand that repairs to the Pharos are also well underway. After that, I believe the next major project is to restore the warehouses that were burned?"

When your general ordered the ships in the harbor to be set on fire, Tetisheri thought. "There will be no replacing the books that were stored inside," she said out loud.

He looked sympathetic again. "Unfortunately, I fear that you are right. I know Caesar regrets that no less than we do. Still, there are always new books to buy, as your uncle well knows." He produced a twinkle. "He gave me to understand that a smaller part of his cargo this trip included books purchased in Rome from one Oengus, a bookseller known to him there."

Oengus was a dealer in fine manuscripts and had been responsible for finding a complete and unusually clean copy of the Theban plays in remarkably good condition. Sosigenes had nearly fainted when he saw them and Cleopatra had even been moved to reimburse Nebenteru's Luxury Goods for the full purchase price. The plays now rested in a place of honor in the Library and were much studied by those masters who considered themselves sons of Melpomene.

Always supposing the plays were still in the Library. It

occurred to her that it might be useful to know who the Alexandrian Oengus was, before Cotta recalled her to the topic under discussion. "But the larger part of his shipment was, of course, pozzolan from Puteoli."

She tilted her head in polite inquiry. He was happy to enlighten her ignorance. "A volcanic ash, which mixed with lime and water serves as a mortar. When it sets, the walls it forms are quite literally immovable. It is much prized in seaside construction, as it stands up remarkably well to salt water."

"Fascinating."

"Indeed, and rare, since the only known deposits are in Puteoli and Santorin."

Ah. And now they came to the heart of the matter. "Rare indeed." And since both were places under Roman authority, the profits—and taxes—accruing to the mining of pozzolan benefited exclusively Roman concerns. It was not a monopoly they would care to see challenged.

"I understand your queen has some interest in finding pozzolan deposits in her own country."

And there it was. She returned his bland smile with one of her own. "Does she?"

"Well, and why wouldn't she? There is so much to be done, so many streets and buildings and public facilities to be repaired, so many new buildings and temples to be constructed. It's understandable she would be keen to find such a resource nearer to home." He made an expansive gesture. "Granite, of course, Egypt has in plenty, as witness the many deposits in Syene." No mention made of the ancient, awe-inspiring structures made of said granite that lined the Nile, as nothing could possibly compare to the modern roads and aqueducts of Rome. "But Egyptian cement is of an inferior quality. Or so those deposits found thus far have proven to be."

She raised her eyebrows, and he laughed again. She was, of course, delighted to be able to afford him so much amusement.

"Very well, I see you will not be drawn on the subject, lady." He drained his cup and stood up. Bast leapt to the floor and took up her place between them as if by right, staring up at Cotta. He looked down at her with amusement. "You have a fierce defender here, lady." He raised his eyes to the pendant she wore. "Twofold, it would seem."

"Bast blesses me with her favor."

"I'm sure it comforts you to think so." He shook his head. "Romans are god-ridden enough, Jupiter knows, but you Egyptians have us beat."

Stung, she was betrayed into indiscretion. "In that as in so many things."

He laughed again, looking and sounding enchanted to be insulted. It must happen so seldom as to be a novelty to him.

She saw him to the door, as one does when playing host in Alexandria, however reluctantly, and waited as he paused on the doorstep. The midday sun poured inside in a golden shaft, outlining his face and figure. He personified the future of the Middle Sea and very probably the entire world. Egypt was the past, Rome the future, if nothing other than by sheer force of arms, and Tetisheri was honest enough to admit it. It did nothing to ease her resentment.

He saw it and was disposed to be kind. He readjusted his toga, that emblem of the conquerors of the known world. "Should you fall into conversation with your queen, lady, I would appreciate your dropping the hint. For her ears only, of course."

She did not insult either of them by pretending to misunderstand him, nor by pretending she would not report news of his visit to her queen. He gave her one long, last, lingering look, head to toes and back again, but he did not repeat the mistake he had made at their second meeting of touching so much as her hand. He could be taught, it seemed. Yet another thing to hold against him. He waved at the servant standing at the head of the horse harnessed to his chariot. "Come, Fulvio, we are away."

Fulvio, fair and square and in appearance every bit the soldier his master was, stepped lightly into the chariot and waited only for his master to step up beside him before slapping the reins against the horse's back. She and Bast stood in the doorway to watch them drive off.

She looked down at Bast. "Patronizing ass."

Bast's blue eyes laughed up her.

# 5

S he returned the tray of punch and cakes to the kitchen, there to give Nike a hard stare. Not noticeably cowed, Nike offered her an empty plate and she joined Nike, Phoebe, and Nebet for a midday meal of salad with goat cheese and olives and herbed rolls hot from the oven. Tetisheri listened to the latest gossip with one ear while she debated inwardly between writing to Cleopatra of Cotta's latest visitation and delivering her report in person.

"The Nomarch of the Oryx has found a bride for his son at last."

"No!"

In person was always the best option, and she could deliver the baby gift at the same time. Done.

"Indeed, I heard it from Tuya in the marketplace this morning, and she had the word straight from her father, who is visiting from Syene."

Tetisheri's ears pricked up at that. News from Syene

was always of interest to Cleopatra. Which was not to say she didn't already know of it. Her intelligence service was second to none over the length and breadth of the Middle Sea. Tetisheri harbored some suspicion that Apollodorus might have something to do with that.

"Remind me, why was the son so undesirable to the other nobles again?"

"The Oryx's section of the Nile is infested with crocodiles. It is difficult to find farmers to work the soil, since Sobek seems to regard it as his personal hunting ground and unleashes his creatures on anyone who gets too near the water."

A general shudder and a flashing of signs to ward off the evil eye. "Why doesn't he pay to have it cleared? Isis knows that since the war ended there are enough ex-soldiers standing around scratching their asses who would be only too willing to hire out their spears."

"You're not listening. He has no money."

"So he found a rich bride for his son?"

"So Tuya says."

"Not a noble one, would be my guess. Some rich merchant's daughter with social aspirations."

"An Egyptian?"

"Most likely."

A round of tsks. "Another poor girl sold for her parents' social aspirations."

Phoebe sniffed. "Like we don't already have enough of those."

Nebet looked at Tetisheri and elbowed Phoebe hard in the side.

"Well," Tetisheri said, "at least the queen may once again see some revenue from the Oryx." Never let them see you cry.

"Herminia sings next month at the Odeum," Nebet said, rather obviously changing the subject. "No, truly, I heard it direct from the Rostra yesterday afternoon."

"Herminia! What is she singing?"

"*Lysistrata.*"

Gales of laughter this time. "Oh, of a certainty, we cannot miss that. What a fortunate thing that Nebenteru has returned! I'll ask him to ask Ninos for tickets."

"Good idea! He refuses Neb nothing since that business last year. We will declare a household holiday and go in a body on first night." Phoebe nudged Tetisheri. "Eh, Tetisheri?"

"What? Herminia? *Lysistrata*? Oh yes, I think we must go. Of course Uncle Neb will get tickets. Even if they were sold out, after that business with that actor Ninos would put in an extra ring of seats if Neb asked him to."

"What business?" Nike was too new to the house to have heard the tale of the actor, the soldier, and the live goat. If Phoebe retold the story with advantages, who could blame her? Neb certainly did every time he told it.

The gossip ran out and everyone returned to their duties. Tetisheri wandered back to her office and stood for a moment staring out of the window.

She should return to her correspondence, not least of which was a perhaps more temperate response to the Nomarch of the Ibis than was her first draft. But she had been sitting long enough for one day, and Cotta's visit had made her restless.

Or so she told herself. She wanted to see Apollodorus again, with a kind of hungry ferocity she had not known before, and that had kept her awake most of the night. But she had no idea where he was in the city today and she was of no mind to scour all the ways and lanes and alleys looking for him. He knew where she lived.

She wanted to be here to welcome Uncle Neb home but she didn't know how long it would take to offload the *Hapi* and then bring her back out of the Royal Harbor, around the Isle of Pharos and into the Port of Eunostos and thence to their dock, less than half a plethrum from where she stood. He had said he would be home in time for dinner. She would see him then.

She wondered if Keren would invite Simon, and smiled to herself.

Bast had resumed her station, although she'd followed the sun to a spot to the right of the last one. She raised her head and regarded Tetisheri with a cool, blue stare.

"Yes, yes, I know. A written message is always at risk of going astray." Tetisheri sighed and reached for her cloak, a heavier weight of linen than her stola, woven in darker shades of blue. She retrieved the Eye from the hidden cabinet constructed by the same man who would build the one in

Sosigenes' office and slipped it over her head. She never left the house without it. In public it was now who she was, whether the public knew it or not. Halfway out the door of her room she turned back and found the gift for Little Caesar and tucked it away in the leather purse fastened to her girdle.

She stopped in the hallway. "Nike? I'm going to the Palace. I'll be back in time for dinner."

"You'd better be!" Phoebe said, shouting from the kitchen. "I'm making salt-baked mullet with pomegranate sauce and roast chicken with olive stuffing and I don't want them sitting around drying out waiting for you to get home!"

"You never make me two courses when I'm home alone," she said in a lowered voice, and raised it again to say, "Bolt the door behind me!"

They hadn't been quite so security conscious until recently, when she had been kidnapped by Ptolemy XIV, Cleopatra's brother, husband and co-ruler, and very nearly killed. Between them Apollodorus and Cleopatra had greatly reduced the risk of something like her abduction ever happening again. But still. She pulled the door closed and waited until she heard the bolt thrown across behind it. A thud of a fist on the door was answered by one of her own and she was off.

The walk through the Emporeum was the usual friendly gauntlet of greetings and waves and smiles but at this time of day all the vendors were surrounded by customers and they had little attention to spare for her. She slipped through the dark warren of connecting streets to emerge onto the wide majesty of the Canopic Way and into the presence of Ra in all his golden, glaring glory. It only made her think even better of Alexander the Great, that he had chosen this site for the world's greatest city precisely where the heat of the inland desert met the cooling onshore breezes of the Middle Sea.

She was about to cross the street when a cabrio pulled in front of her, obstructing her way. She looked around with what she felt was pardonable irritation. "Excuse me, sir, but I believe pedestrians have the right of way here."

"Indeed they do, but a conveyance picking up passengers is allowed a brief stop, I believe. It is Tetisheri of House Nebenteru, is it not? May I offer you a ride? We appear to be going in the same direction."

All her senses went on the alert and she took a careful step back, only to tread on someone's toes. She looked around to see a solidly built man in a nondescript tunic with a businesslike gladius strapped to his belt. His hair was cut close to his scalp and his square face set in unsmiling lines. He had the foursquare solidity of the Roman veteran and nothing less than the authority of a tesserarius. He met her eyes with an impersonal gaze. He was definitely on the job and he wouldn't work cheap.

She looked back at the cabrio which held the man who must be his employer. He was smiling at her, showing a set of well-kept teeth. It was not an expression that engendered any feeling of warmth or humor or, for that matter, safety.

Thick through the torso with massive thighs, he looked more like an Iberian bull than a man. He would do well in the arena. His hands were large-knuckled and covered with old scars, but now they were softened by lotion and his nails were neatly pared, as if he'd once had to work for a living and had since moved up to a position in life where he did not. He was dressed plainly in a well-tailored tunic of a dark green weave that included threads of darker green silk that sparkled discreetly in the sun, and his sandals were made of fine leather in the very latest style.

"And you are?" she said.

His smile didn't change but his eyes did. A man used to people knowing who he was, then. As to that she had a pretty fair idea but she refused to cater to his ego by saying so. He gave a slight bow from his seated position. "Otho the Builder, lady."

She threw him a sop. "Ah. Otho, the Master of Builders, is I believe your full title."

Predictably, he preened a little. "Some call me so indeed, lady. You've already met Calvus, my manservant." He waved. "We are, as you so rightly pointed out, obstructing traffic. Again I ask, may I offer you transportation? As I said, we seem to be going in the same direction."

She felt a distinct pressure at her back, as if she were being herded. She looked over her shoulder and smiled, imitating his master as best she could. "One moment, please." She slipped away without seeming to notice Calvus' hand outstretched as if to stop her, or the frown on his master's face that stopped the gesture in mid-reach. She walked to the corner and surveyed the collection of boys clustered there. She found one who looked clean and reasonably well fed, choosing as she always did on the theory that the most reliable messengers were always the ones who made the best living and showed it in their appearance. "Your name?"

"Babak, lady."

She held up a drachma, one of the new ones with Cleopatra as Isis and Caesarion as Horus suckling at her breast. "There is another of these waiting for you at the home of Nebenteru the Trader. You will find it next to his place of business, Nebenteru's Luxury Goods, a warehouse that sits just off the docks to the east of Kibotos on the Port of Eunostos. Are you familiar with the area?"

"I am, lady. On the other side of the Emporeum, across Hermes Street. It isn't far."

She appreciated his crisp manner. "Knock at the door and tell whoever answers that Tetisheri is in the company of Otho, the Master of Builders, and to expect me home by dinner. Repeat that back to me, please."

He repeated it word for word. "Good." She gave him the drachma. "Quick as you can, if you please."

The coin disappeared. He saluted and was off at a trot, threading his way through the busy crowd with no undue fuss or bother.

She walked back to the cabrio, where Calvus stood waiting to hand her up. She took the seat opposite Otho, who looked annoyed but was trying to hide it. She had wasted five minutes of his time that he had allotted elsewhere. She didn't apologize.

Calvus mounted the step next to the driver and they were off.

"You are cautious, lady. I practice caution myself, so I appreciate it in others."

Tetisheri made a production of adjusting the folds of her cloak before looking up. On the ledge at the back of the cabrio stood the driver and Calvus, both affecting the expression of the professionally deaf. "We have not met, I believe."

"We have not before today, no," he said, "but long have I heard good things of Nebenteru's, that trading partnership most favored of the queen. Why, it has attained renown in ports all over the world. You and your excellent uncle make your home next to your warehouse, on the docks east of Kibotos, I believe."

"You are too kind." She permitted herself a slight smile. She who had traveled far and met folk from many lands could not place his nation of origin. At first look she would have said he was Roman, but his coloring was too fair and his height and build were more on the order of an Alemanni. He was definitely an immigrant because while they were speaking in Greek, the *lingua conventus* of Alexandria, his vowels were too flat for him to be a native speaker. "I would have thought that the fame of Otho, Master of Builders, would have far eclipsed our own."

He shrugged. "It may be that I have helped in some small way to facilitate the queen's determination to see the city whole again."

She inclined her head a fraction in acknowledgement of his modest accomplishments.

In fact, there was nothing modest about them. Otho had been elected Master of Builders by the builders' guild the day after Ptolemy XIII had killed himself while trying to swim the Nile in a full suit of armor and it had become manifestly evident that Cleopatra would be queen. Otho's elevation was a decision accepted by all and, as Tetisheri understood it, welcomed by most. He had been instrumental in the remodel of the Temple of Isis in Hermonthis and he had overseen the rebuilding of the Heptastadion in, as Cotta had rightly observed, only seven days. He was currently supervising the reconstruction of the Pharos, and if rumor served had his hand in a dozen other building projects around the city and outside of it, public and private. He was by anyone's account one of today's up-and-coming men.

She could have said all of this out loud, of course. It would be the politic thing to do, and Bast herself knew there was no better way for a woman to ingratiate herself with a man than to find ways to praise him. She waited, hoping she maintained an outward appearance of indifference while every sense was on the alert. People had disappeared in the city before this by being too certain of their own safety.

Fortunately, Otho was disposed to be chatty. "I hear that your uncle is recently returned from Rome?"

"He is."

"With a stop in Puteoli for the main part of his cargo. Pozzolan, as I understand it to be."

"As you say yourself, the queen is desirous of making Alexandria whole again."

"And grateful we builders are for it!" he said warmly. "It is indeed a blessing to have a ruler with such an excellent understanding of the imperatives of the construction trades."

"It must be," she said in a congratulatory tone.

A flash of irritation crossed his face and was quickly repressed. "We are fortunate to live in Alexandria, we who build, where all who are interested in the art and the science of such come to study."

"Genius, like water, always finds it own level," she said blandly.

They were proceeding very slowly indeed down the Way, pausing at every intersection to allow people to cross, giving precedence to anyone on or driving a horse or donkey who wanted to turn onto a side street. One could, if one were of a skeptical frame of mind, almost accuse Otho of attempting to prolong this conversation in order to milk it for everything he could get.

"As I understand it, you are Neb's full partner?"

She was irked by this uninvited use of Uncle Neb's diminutive but she took care not to show it. "I am."

"And you travel with him?"

"On occasion."

"An exciting life."

"Moderately."

He eyed her speculatively. "It is said you stand high in the queen's favor."

The weight of the Eye was heavy against her breast. "Is it?"

He forced a laugh. "Come, come," he said, "all know Tetisheri for the queen's schoolmate and confidante."

"Do they?"

He took a deep breath and let it out slowly, and the flush that had risen up into his face retreated. That kind of self-control was impressive and it made her all the more wary. And then he surprised her with a rueful laugh. "Lady, I believe we may have gotten off on the wrong foot."

"'We?'"

"Very well, I," he said. Unlike Cotta, his eyes weren't made for twinkling but he gave it his best effort. "Cry mercy, and let us begin again. I'm hosting a small reception at my home in Rhakotis on Seventh Day this week—or no, Sunday, as we must all now call it according to this dratted new calendar of Caesar's." His smile was more natural this time. "Nothing formal, just good food and good conversation between good friends and those about to become so. Would you and your uncle care to attend?" And then before she could answer he said, "And any others of your household who might care to join us are welcome, too. Your friend the doctor, perhaps? Keren, I think her name is."

She felt a chill run down her spine and from his expression

she could see that she had not hidden it as well as she might have liked. "I will inform my house of your kind invitation."

"The festivities begin at mid-afternoon, and I hope neither the company nor the refreshments will disappoint. You know my location?"

Indeed she was newly come to that information, but she shook her head.

"No? In Rhakotis, the new house next to the big fenced yard on the Nile Canal. Like you and your uncle, I live where I work. It makes for occasionally dusty days but the benefit of being able to keep my eye on the yard is invaluable. Perhaps you'd be interested in a tour during your visit."

"Very much so." Tetisheri became aware that they had left the Way and were drawing up at the northern end of Lochias. Calvus was instantly there to hand her down.

"A delightful conversation, lady," Otho said. "Thank you so much for relieving me of the boredom of my own company. I look forward to seeing you again on Sunday, and to meet the famous Nebenteru the Trader in person." A smile and a wave and they were off.

She watched them go. It was more than a little unnerving that she had been dropped within a five-minute walk of the modest entrance to the palace that she used when visiting the queen.

Especially as she hadn't said where she was going.

# 6

She turned and nearly ran into a young man approaching at a dead run. She didn't know him but he wore a kilt belted with the Feather of Maat.

"You are the lady Tetisheri?" he said, gasping her name out between gulping breaths.

"I am Tetisheri."

"Aristander sends you his compliments and begs you to accompany me. He says there is something you must see. At once."

She glanced up at the palace. "I'm sorry, but—what is your name?"

"Dejen, lady, my apologies."

"Dejen, I have business at the palace. Could this matter not wait until afterward?"

"No, lady, it cannot." The young man was emphatic. "Aristander said to find you and return you to him without delay."

"How did you find me so quickly?"

"I went first to your home. Please, lady, we must go. I have transport waiting at the corner."

Transport was a light chariot behind a pair of swift bays, all three of which were built for speed. The horses already wore a light sheen of sweat. The young man tossed a coin to the boy holding the reins and vaulted inside. He turned, extending a hand to pull Tetisheri up behind him. There was no seat and he barely waited for her to take hold of the crossbar before slapping the reins against the necks of the horses. They moved instantly into a trot, the shurta calling "Ho! Ho, there! Shurta! Make way!" in a carrying, surprisingly commanding voice in one so young. A magic word, shurta, scattering people to the four corners of every intersection.

When they reached the Canopic Way he cornered the chariot neatly and precisely into the center eastbound lane and smacked the horses with the reins. "Shurta! On business of the Shurta! Make way, you!" Everyone pulled over to allow them to pass and no one even yelled obscenities after them. There was a near miss with a fruit cart, as the old man hauling it was apparently deaf, constant checks from carts and wagons hauling construction materials, and the wheel on Tetisheri's side nearly clipped a middle-aged matron wearing a fearsome headdress woven of dyed raffia into a likeness of the many-breasted image of Isis. She squawked and her maid screamed and the matron's elderly gallant shook an impotent fist after them as they sped away, the flesh beneath his upper arm swaying back and forth like the belly of an overfed cat.

They were traveling west and after what seemed a very short space of time passed beneath the Gate of the Moon and out of the city proper. The road narrowed although it did not decrease in traffic and they were forced to slow their pace. A short time later they turned right and a few moments after that Dejen pulled the equipage to a smooth halt.

"Excuse me, lady—" He slipped past her to the ground and turned to hand her out. "We must go the rest of the way on foot, if you please."

Or if she didn't. Her cloak had been disarranged by the wind and she took a moment to restore it to some semblance of dignity before she followed him.

Even just outside the gate the city became much more recently built and much less orderly. The streets were narrower and more crooked, the houses were much less grand and of every size and shape and style. They were built of every material from driftwood to what looked like stone blocks looted from the Great Pyramids, although Tetisheri did wonder how the builders got them the fifty leagues from there to here. The Nile Canal, perhaps, and only during the recent conflict would the royal eye have been distracted enough to allow that to happen without severe repercussions. Cleopatra reserved all construction materials new and old to crown projects. But however it grew it was a mad jumble of construction jostling for a sea view, with the buildings nearest to water built barely above the tide line. One storm, one earthquake, and the beach would be wiped clean again.

They dodged flapping clotheslines and children's toys and abandoned carts and quarreling couples and shouting vendors and debouched at last on an endless curve of golden sand leading gently down to meet the glittering blue of the Middle Sea. At the edge of the water a small crowd of men were gathered around an object covered by a tattered cloak.

"Sir, the lady Tetisheri," her guide said, and effaced himself.

Aristander, who was kneeling, stood up. "Tetisheri."

"Aristander, well met. What—"

He twitched back the cloak and the words died on her lips.

It was a body, or rather what remained of one. The white skull grinned up at the sky. The stomach was excavated from front to back, leaving only the spine to attach the top half to the bottom. A few well-chewed ligaments remained to connect the whole.

But it was the bottom half that stayed Tetisheri's eyes. She knew she was staring, she knew her mouth was half open, but she simply couldn't help herself.

"By the claw and fang of Bast," someone said, and she realized it was her.

From just below the knees down, the legs were encased in cement.

"Rhakotis sandals," Tetisheri said.

Aristander nodded.

"I thought they were a myth."

"So did I." At this moment Aristander looked far older than his years, which numbered few more than her own. "And how I wish I still did."

She closed her eyes and swallowed, but against her lids all she could see was an ever-increasing swirl of images, a body sinking into the depths, arms grasping frantically, futilely at the water, reaching for any purchase, anything to slow the descent, leaving a stream of air bubbles behind—

She opened her eyes and saw he had a sympathetic expression on his face. She raised her chin, daring him to offer any sympathy.

Aristander was a slim man of medium height, with nondescript features that were useful in a profession where anonymity was an asset. Bright brown eyes looked keenly upon the world around him and never forgot a detail. That was to say, never forgot a detail his queen wished him to remember. One learned early on in the service of the queen the inconvenience of remembering things she wished forgotten.

He and Tetisheri and the queen were of an age and had been tutored together as children in the Royal Palace by all the eminent scholars in the Library from Sosigenes on down.

When Auletes, Cleopatra's father, had deemed it necessary for the queen as a matter of self-preservation to study the art of self-defense, he had included Tetisheri and Aristander to study that art with her as a matter of equipping her supporters with the skills to defend her at need. Thus it was that the two people most nearly concerned with law and order in her realm would be two of her closest friends from childhood.

For the first time, Tetisheri wondered who had selected her as the next Eye. She remembered Auletes as a man who made many bad choices and very few good ones, but that the most important one of all, his heir, had been his best choice by far. She looked at Aristander now and wondered if Auletes had singled him out as the head of the Shurta as well. Like her, he was much younger than the people who usually held such posts. Khemit had been in her forties.

But these mental wanderings were nothing more than avoidance of the matter at hand. "Who found it?"

He glanced at the body, covered again by the cloak. His men stood in a grim-faced ring around it, backs to the shrouded form so they didn't have to look at it. Their line had the additional benefit of hiding it from the view of the gawkers clustering between the houses. "There's a reef offshore. Two men were spearfishing." He nodded at two men Tetisheri hadn't noticed until now, young, thin, and brown, dressed only in damp shentis. Net bags and spears had been discarded nearby. They sat on the sand with their arms around their legs and their heads resting on their knees. Even their backs looked unhappy. Two of Aristander's men stood nearby looking as if they thought they should do something but weren't quite sure what. As Tetisheri watched, a third shurta returned with a large mug in each hand and a dripping leather pail over his shoulder. He offered them to the fishermen, who fell on them with cries of gratitude and drained them dry in one long, continuous swallow, and reached for refills.

Tetisheri could have used one of those mugs herself, whatever was in it.

"It was quite the shock, I imagine," Aristander said, his voice dry. "There they were, stalking the elusive bream, when suddenly this upright human skeleton loomed up out of the murky depths. One of them panicked and nearly drowned and had to be towed to shore by the other. They sent for the Shurta, and here we are."

"How did you get it out of the water?"

He nodded at a small boat idling offshore. "We whistled up the *Meri-Maat*. The fishermen agreed to dive for it—"

"I hope for a decent price."

"A very decent one, and, I might add, happily paid. When they found the—" he made a vague gesture "— we realized we couldn't get it into the boat, not without tearing the skeleton apart. So we had them fasten the ropes off to the, er, weight, and they guided the, uh, him while we pulled the weight to the shallows and brought him in from there."

"It's a man, do you think?"

He shrugged. "Just a guess. Tall for a woman. I had Dejen lie down next to it for a comparison."

An involuntary shudder rippled over her. "Any identifying marks?"

He opened the purse at his belt and held out a pendant on a tarnished silver chain. She held out her hand. "Ptah?" The figure was made of malachite and, while it wasn't an exemplary piece of the sculptor's art, the ostrich plumes, the sun disk, and especially the horns of the headdress were obvious even in outline.

"If the head had not remained attached to the spine we never would have found it," Aristander said. "And it isn't particularly conclusive anyway. Could have been a love gift, or something owned by a parent, or something he picked up from a street vendor because he liked the stone."

Tetisheri touched the figure of Bast at her throat. "Or he could be a follower."

"A priest?"

"Possibly."

"Or a carpenter, or an architect, or any one of a number of crafts that follow Ptah. The amulet itself, I've seen a thousand like it and so have you, carved from malachite or lapis or topaz or turquoise, any gemstone you care to name. It doesn't exactly narrow down his identity."

"No. Although the manner of the murder would suggest that he had been involved in the construction trade."

"It certainly makes a statement."

She handed the pendant back, and took a deep breath. "How long has he been in the water?"

"Well, as you can see, the body has been stripped nearly clean, which indicates it's been down there a while. A few weeks, at least. I'm hoping Zokitos can give us something more exact."

"I'd like Keren to take a look as well, if you don't mind."

A slight smile lightened his countenance. "And if I do?"

She made herself smile slightly back.

His eyes dropped to the chain around her neck. "That's what I thought."

"What about the, uh, the weight on his feet?"

He cleared his throat and looked back at the body. "You see the shape."

"It looks like an amphora made of solid stone."

"Yes. Well. It appears someone put his feet into an amphora or some similar vessel and filled it up with liquid concrete."

Her hand closed over the figure of Bast. "And then?"

"It would have to have been allowed to set for some amount of time, otherwise the cement might have dissolved in the water and he could have floated to the surface. Most corpses do within a few days." He shook his head. "I know nothing about cement. We'll have to find someone who does."

She thought of Cotta sitting in her parlor that very morning, inducting her into the mysteries of pozzolan. "What happened to the amphora?"

"My guess would be that it broke when it hit the sea

bottom. The shards could have been swept away by the current. Or—" he shrugged "—clay vessels dissolve if left in water long enough."

Her mouth was dry. With difficulty she said, "Would he have been alive when he went into the water?"

"We have no way of knowing. But no reason for him not to be."

She followed her thoughts out loud. "No one would go to this much trouble if they weren't trying to make an example."

He took a deep breath and expelled it slowly. "That is my belief as well."

"Although clearly they were trying to ensure that the body was never recovered."

"But just in case it was..."

"Yes."

They were silent for a moment. "Aristander, why am I here?" She turned to face him. "Surely bodies are found in suspicious circumstances at least once every day in Alexandria. What urgency necessitates the presence of—" She paused and emended her words to say, "necessitates my presence?"

He smiled again and answered her in a low voice. "You are correct, Tetisheri. If I called you to the scene of every crime perpetrated every day in Alexandria and environs the Eye of Isis would scarce have time to bite or sup. Our queen would definitely have something to say about the proper use of your office, and it would not be to my credit."

"Then why?"

He sighed. "Because, Tetisheri, this is the second such victim I have seen."

All she could do was stare at him.

He glanced away for a moment, as if her horror was too much to face. "Yes," he said as if she had asked, "I am afraid so."

He signaled to his men and they picked up the body, two men on the lump of cement, and carried it at a quick march through the crowd. He walked over to say something to the fishermen. They got to their feet and he gave them each something from the purse fastened to his belt and dismissed them. They looked relieved to quit the beach.

He walked back to stand at Tetisheri's side, having given her long enough to gather her composure and stiffen her knees. When she spoke she was proud her voice was steady. "Have you come to any notion of how to begin this investigation?"

"I'll show you the other body." At her look he grimaced. "We couldn't identify it, either, so it's still in the morgue."

For the second time her imagination followed that someone, still alive perhaps, plunging down, down, down through the water to the ocean floor, gasping out their last moments, hoping against hope there would be succor, a last-minute rescue, a miraculous intervention of one's own god even while their lungs filled with water and—

Her vision began to gray again and then she felt Aristander's hand in hers, the hand of friendship and fellowship, of a shared childhood then and shared duties now. "None of that," he said, and her vision cleared enough to see his stern expression. "Tetisheri, niece and partner of one of the most successful traders from Rome to Syene, friend to the queen, Eye of Isis—" he winked "—chosen of Apollodorus, whom all know to be that most discriminating of lovers—"

She could feel the blush rising into her cheeks and tried to yank her hand free, but he held her fast. "This woman, this Tetisheri, she does not faint." He looked over her shoulder. "And certainly she does not faint before people prepared to spread the news of it from the Gate of the Moon to the Gate of the Sun in less time than it takes to tell the tale."

She followed his glance involuntarily, and, indeed, the gawkers were still assembled, watching avidly. She stiffened her spine. Aristander gave a nod of approval and released her hand.

Her gaze fastened on a pier beginning to be built out into the water west of where they were standing. "What is that?"

He glanced over his shoulder. "Another attempt by greedy shippers to circumvent the port landing tax, I would imagine."

Now that she knew to listen for it she could hear quite clearly the cacophony of hammers and saws and curses. As they watched, one man, wielding a long pole to stir a large vat from a precarious perch on a shaky ladder, lost his footing and toppled in. There were shouts and a swarm of workers around the vat and the man was fished out covered in some white paste. He was tossed without ceremony into the sea, and everyone watched until he surfaced, snorting and blowing like a whale. A gale of laughter and catcalls followed him as he swam to shore, where he stood in water knee deep and cleaned himself off. "Since it's not inside the city walls, they think the queen won't notice?"

"Evidently."

She took a deep breath and exhaled slowly, straightening her shoulders and raising her chin. "Then one can only look forward with great anticipation to their discovering their error."

His smile was approving. "That's better. And to answer your question in full, odd occurrences and unexplainable circumstances come well within the purview of your office." His expression was bleak. "As such things only too often turn out to be political in nature, and therefore attract the attention of the Lady of the Two Lands."

Tetisheri exhaled on a long, defeated sigh. "Shall I brief the queen then?"

"Dejen is waiting to take you to the palace."

# 7

The queen was in her private parlor, and Iras, who had conducted Tetisheri into her presence, was immediately dismissed with a smile of thanks. Caesarion was suckling greedily at her breast, and as Tetisheri watched she jumped a little. "Ouch!" She gave her son and heir a severe look. "How dare you maul your sovereign about so, sir?"

"He can't possibly be teething yet," Tetisheri said.

"Then he has very sharp gums."

"This should help." Tetisheri produced her gift for the baby.

"Unwrap it for me, would you? Thank you. Oh, Sheri, the very thing! He can gnaw on that instead of on me. Oh, and it's delightful, what perfectly carved little animals. Although I doubt he'll be any respecter of the artist's work." She smiled up at Tetisheri.

When Cleopatra smiled, the singers said, the world stood

still. Tetisheri had known Cleopatra for far too long and been through much too much with her for her world to do any such thing, but it was still an extraordinary smile that made one feel as if the queen had given one a gift meant for themselves alone. Tetisheri had seen Cleopatra use that smile to devastating effect on recalcitrant Egyptians, Jews standing unyieldingly upon their dignity, grumbling Greeks, and arrogant Romans, singly or in groups and on occasion in armies. It might not in and of itself deliver her the contents of the city in question but it would certainly open wide the gates.

Her looks were almost nondescript by comparison. Olive skin, large, dark, thickly lashed eyes, a long, strong nose, a mouth wide and full-lipped. Her figure was good, her waist almost restored to its previous circumference, but again, not a figure that wasn't commonly seen on the streets of Alexandria any day of the year.

No, it was the woman within who was so extraordinary. She would have stood out in any crowd with or without her crown.

"Here." Cleopatra dumped the baby in Tetisheri's lap and pulled her dress into place. Caesarion, startled at this sudden change of scene, stared up at Tetisheri out of eyes that were just beginning to change from blue to brown. Cleopatra tossed her a towel and Tetisheri put it over her shoulder and put the baby against it, patting his back. He immediately burped in her ear, a long, replete sound. He fell asleep immediately, the burp changing to a delightful little snore. "Why is is it that when babies fall asleep they immediately gain twice their body's weight and temperature?"

"Enjoy it," Cleopatra said dryly, "sleep happens seldom enough with this child."

The room they were in was simply furnished with low couches and tables easy to hand. A broad window hung with undyed linen in an open weave looked out over the Royal Harbor. Across the Harbor entrance the Pharos stood tall, swarmed over by the workers busy restoring it to its former glory, after it had been so grievously wounded in the war. Nonetheless, it was still sending its light ten leagues out to sea, guiding merchant ships and fishing boats and Roman triremes safely into port again.

Charmion slipped inside with a tray and left with the baby. The queen poured steaming tea into simple pottery mugs. "I thought something warm on such a chilly afternoon would be welcome."

Tetisheri accepted the cup with a nod of thanks, and was grateful when the heat warmed her hands.

"A bit of cheese? No? Well, good, because I'm so hungry I could eat this entire tray clean." The queen loaded a plate. "Eating for two. Or it's what I tell myself."

Tetisheri smiled with an effort.

For a while the two friends sat in peaceful silence. A breeze tangled with the curtains and the shouts of sailors from passing ships could be heard. Thumps of hammers and the exasperated bellow of construction supervisors came only faintly across the water. It was almost a mille passus away, but then sound traveled over water.

Tetisheri drained her mug and realized she was completely and utterly relaxed for the first time since stepping into her own parlor that morning. She looked across the table at the queen. "You are a witch, Pati."

Cleopatra laughed and refilled their mugs. "I will take that as a compliment. Drink some more of this excellent tea and tell me all about it."

So Tetisheri spun her queen the tale, and Cleopatra held her peace until the very end, with Aristander's revelation that there had been two murders, not one. "Rhakotis sandals," she said. "I am chagrined to admit I have never heard of such a thing before now. Explain."

Tetisheri set down her mug with a hand she was pleased to see was steady. "I had thought it was a myth. More, a joke. You know what the builders are. Or perhaps it is more accurate to say what they like to appear to be. They make public examples of anyone they consider to have stepped out of line, so much so that that person usually has to change professions, because they will never work in construction again."

The corner of Cleopatra's mouth quirked in not quite a smile. "Examples, perhaps. But not homicidal ones."

"No. I had thought that was all it was, a reputation. If you were, say, caught with your hand in the strong box, or perhaps you overbid a project without telling your employer and lined your own pockets with the difference in the profits, or, horrors, done so and not shared those profits with your foreman. The guilds make it known that they would not bother calling for the Shurta, that they would handle it on their own. Most of the time all it involved was injuries only sometimes serious enough to call for a doctor. But there was also this persistent rumor that one of the ways they discouraged bad behavior was to fit the offender with a pair of Rhakotis sandals. The victim's feet were placed in an amphora. The amphora was filled with a liquid slurry of cement and allowed to harden."

"What kind of cement?" Cleopatra saw Tetisheri's expression and sat up. "Not pozzolan?"

Tetisheri stared at her. "Pati, the amount and arcana of knowledge you have accumulated between your ears never fails to astonish. Are we quite sure your head is of a normal size?"

"It is my duty as the mother of Egypt to know all her secrets," Cleopatra said demurely, if the Lady of the Two Lands could ever be said to be demure.

"I don't know what kind of cement it was, I'm afraid. It was green with some undersea plant. Aristander did not know, either. I will find someone who knows more about it for an expert opinion."

"If it was pozzolan, it was an inexcusable waste of a valuable commodity in short supply. For that alone, I will be inclined to be very severe indeed when the murderer is found." This was the queen speaking now, not Tetisheri's friend. "Tell me the rest."

"When it had hardened sufficiently the victim was dropped into the sea."

"Alive?"

"Very probably. I don't see anyone perpetrating this heinous a crime having the mercy to end the victim's suffering too soon. Aristander agrees."

Cleopatra contemplated this in silence for a moment. "Sandals because the cement encases the feet. Rhakotis because that is where in Alexandria most of the guilds who work in the construction trade are located."

"And where all the builders have their yards and most of them live," Tetisheri said, thinking of Otho. "Yes."

"Nasty."

"Very." Tetisheri rose to her feet and walked to the window, staring out at the Pharos, surrounded by scaffolding and swarmed over by men in shentis, torsos covered in sweat. Cleopatra joined her and they stood side by side, staring across the harbor entrance at the towering pile of hand-cut rock that at present resembled nothing so much as a massive ant hill. "How did you get up to the top to wave goodbye to Caesar, anyway? I was watching you from the deck of the *Thalassa*."

"I rode up on the hoist." She nodded at the wooden flat of supplies currently halfway up the octagonal section of the tower. "Dixiphanes arranged it."

No sooner were the words out of her mouth than the flat swung wide and hit the side of the inner tower with a crash that echoed over the water. The man riding with the supplies lost his grip on one of the suspending ropes and fell, screaming. He bounced off the edge of the square tower on which the octagonal tower rested and disappeared behind the wall of the fort that surrounded the base. His despairing scream ended abruptly.

Tetisheri imagined she could hear the thud of flesh and bone meeting stone. Shaken, she looked at Cleopatra, who was already moving swiftly to the door. "Iras? Iras! There has been an accident on the Pharos. Send someone to see how the man does. If he's dead, find out if he has family and what provision will be made for them."

"Majesty." A scurry of footsteps, cut off when Cleopatra closed the door. She rejoined Tetisheri at the window. In very short order they saw a small boat launched from one of the palace docks below and three oarsmen a side pulled rapidly toward the Pharos. They couldn't see what was happening behind the wall but another man climbed onto the flat and it continued its jerky journey skyward.

Cleopatra put her hand over Tetisheri's, and Tetisheri looked down to see that her fists were clenched so tightly her nails were digging into her palms. She unknotted her fists and saw that her palms were bleeding in three places.

Cleopatra fetched a wet rag and ointment. The bleeding soon stopped, but the red welts remained visible.

They looked out at the Pharos. The platform of the hoist had been unloaded and was now being lowered to be loaded again. Work continued. The work always continued.

"Not a job for the faint of heart," Cleopatra said. "Construction."

"No."

Charmion opened the door. "My queen, you must dress for the audience."

Cleopatra grimaced. "Antipater has sent another delegation."

Tetisheri pulled herself together, speaking in a determinedly light tone. "Is the ethnarch complaining about Herod again?"

"Antipater's sole form of communication is 'Send me money or I can't defend you from the dread king of Galilee.'"

"He can't defend himself from his own family now, never mind Herod."

"Tcha!" Cleopatra made a face. "A completely untrustworthy, utterly corrupt creature, but they do say he is gaining the ear of Caesar."

"I didn't know you'd met Herod."

"In Rome. He did his best to inveigle me into meeting him alone. I was ten at the time, if you recall."

Both women shuddered. It was generally understood that there were so many rumors about Herod only because so many of them were true. "Shall you send Antipater's minions packing, then?"

"Very likely."

"Good." She glanced at Charmion, who huffed out an impatient sigh and stepped outside the room, closing the door behind her with exaggerated care. "Pati, I was at the Library yesterday. Sosigenes told me about the thefts."

Cleopatra's expression hardened. "Yes?"

"Another map was stolen last week. Hecataeus' *World Survey*."

"May Isis herself seek out these thieves and rip the beating hearts out of their breasts." It was more of a prayer than a curse.

"Sosigenes seems to think these thefts might be organized. They're targeting the most valuable items." Tetisheri eyed her friend with some caution. "I didn't have the heart to say this to Sosigenes, and I barely have the courage to say it to you, but..."

"What?"

"When was the last time an inventory was made of the Library's contents? Scrolls, bound books, government documents, and maps? The collection entire?"

Cleopatra stared at her hard for a long, uncomfortable moment. "I will speak with Sosigenes," she said finally.

Tetisheri nodded. She really didn't want to say any more.

"Was there something else you wanted to tell me?"

Tetisheri blinked at her.

"A visitation you received this morning?"

This morning felt like a year ago and it took Tetisheri a moment to search her memory. "Oh. Oh." A long sigh. "Cotta. Yes, our esteemed legate deigned to grace my parlor, to bring us the news that Uncle Neb was back." She shook her head. "My apologies, my queen. I cannot think how it slipped my mind."

"Yes, well." Cleopatra squeezed Tetisheri's shoulder and smiled. "You have recently been through a fairly traumatic experience. I'll forgive it, just this once."

"My abject regrets and gratitude, O most high."

"Tcha!" the queen said again, this time giving Tetisheri's shoulder a light smack. "What did he really want?"

"Oddly, I believe Uncle Neb's cargo was what brought him hotfoot to speak with me."

"The pozzolan?"

"Yes. Cotta knows you have scouts up and down the Nile looking for pozzolan deposits. He's worried that you'll find one and that Rome will lose its monopoly."

"Why talk to you about it?"

"He knows I'll mention it to you."

Cleopatra grinned a very unqueenlike grin. "And I'm to be frightened off my search for the elusive pozzolan?"

"Well, and you are known by all to be a timid creature."

Cleopatra gave an exaggerated shiver. "All hail the Senate and People of Rome!" She shook her head. "If we do find a deposit, they'll expect me to tithe some overlarge portion of it, I'm sure."

Tetisheri was sure they would, too. "Cotta was very complimentary about the Heptastadion being repaired in just seven days."

"As well he should have been," Cleopatra said. "It was an extraordinary piece of work on everyone's part."

Not least the woman standing before Tetisheri now. "One thing more, my queen."

"Truly?" Cleopatra said. "You have had a busy day."

"You have no idea," Tetisheri said with feeling, and gave a quick accounting of the meeting with Otho. She mistrusted coincidence. Two men had been murdered by someone who understood how cement worked. Cement was an essential element of the building trade, as so eloquently expounded by Cotta that very morning and then emphasized by Otho immediately afterward.

"Not a chance meeting, I fancy," the queen said thoughtfully.

"Highly unlikely."

"Could anyone have overheard your conversation with Cotta?"

"Only Bast. And the people of my house are loyal. I have my own thoughts as to how Otho might have heard of my interest in Grafeas."

"Oh?"

The queen looked only politely inquiring but Tetisheri was not taken in. "Which I am not ready to share," she said firmly.

Cleopatra's eyebrows went up. "I see. Very well. I bow to the wisdom of the Eye." The tie that bound back the heavy fall of black hair was coming loose. She pulled it free and shook her head. "So Otho is hosting an event in his new house, and you're invited," she said thoughtfully.

"That's what the man said."

Cleopatra's eyes narrowed in thought. "I have heard tales of this new house of Otho's."

"I've seen it. Believe all of them."

Cleopatra raised an eyebrow. "Really. How very interesting."

Tetisheri squared her shoulders. "Majesty, is it your wish that the Eye of Isis investigate these two murders?"

"It is, my Eye." The queen spoke with equal gravity and formality. Echoing Tetisheri's own thoughts, she added, "I don't like coincidences, Sheri. That so valuable a resource so necessary to the restoration of Alexandria and Egypt to its former glory has been employed as an instrument of death sends me a message I cannot read. I don't like it."

The door opened. "My queen!"

"Peace, Charmion, I come. Keep me informed of your investigation, Tetisheri. And give my love to Uncle Neb."

As Tetisheri left the palace she passed the incoming delegation from Judea, a cluster of black-clad men with their earlocks rigorously curled and pomaded and their black robes starched to rigidity. To a man they wore the hungry look of the supplicant in any court.

Tetisheri escaped into the dimming light of the day and lost herself in the much safer embrace of the crowds on the Way.

Uncle Neb snatched her up into a comprehensive embrace. "Tetisheri! Flower of the Middle Sea!" She made a muffled protest from where she was squashed into his shoulder and he dropped her back to her feet. "Where have you been? I wanted yours to be the first face I saw when I came home." A rumble from beneath his tunic belied that statement. She grinned up at him and his head fell back and he let loose with a deep, rolling belly laugh that filled the house entire. "All right, all right," he said, chuckling, "and I want my dinner. You know Phoebe will let the roast burn before she serves it to a half-empty table." He raised a brow. "By the way, what was all that business with the message saying you were with Otho, Master of Builders?"

She smiled up at him. "Surety that I would return in time for dinner, Uncle, and as it happened, entirely unnecessary."

"Oh. Ah. Well. I tipped the rascal twice what he said you had promised and he went away rejoicing."

"Good." She stood back to survey him with appreciation.

Her father's younger brother was a big, burly man with black hair and dark eyes the same shape and as thickly lashed as her own but a deep brown in color. His skin was dark from both his heritage and his profession, which required long days on the water. He had of course changed from his ship clothes and she stood back to admire him in all his red-and-gold silk grandeur. "This is new, surely?" she said, fingering the fringed sash he wore doubled around his waist. Uncle Neb could give any court dandy a run for their sartorial money.

"Remember the spun silk I brought back from Punt? Tarset set her weavers to work on them at once and I claimed the first length."

Her eyes softened. Khemit had been a weaver, a successful one, and in her will she had left her business to her employees, chief among them her assistant, Tarset. Of course Uncle Neb had thrown business their way, and nothing would please him more than to parade his new finery the length and breadth of Alexandria and be asked where in the names of all eight of the Ogdoad of Hermopolis had he found such miraculous fabric.

Tetisheri walked around him, clicking her tongue in admiration. She reached up to give the pearl that was woven into the point of his black beard a gentle tug. "I don't know that I'm worthy to be seen in your company, Uncle."

He burst out laughing again. "Then what do I tell Apollodorus, who has been oh-so-patiently waiting your arrival?"

Her heart, that unreliable object, skipped a beat. "Apollodorus is here?"

"Come," he said, the pearl trembling with mirth as he threw an arm around her waist and swept her toward the dinner table. "Let us eat and I will tell you all the gossip in Rome."

"Is Caesar back yet?"

"I believe he is on his way, trailing clouds of Pontian glory behind him."

"And carrying chests full of Pontian treasure with him as he comes."

"It was undoubtedly one of the objects of the exercise." Nebenteru took the chair at the head of the table and beamed at the faces sitting around it. Apollodorus, already seated, smiled at Tetisheri, and the next thing she knew she was next to him, her hand held in his warm clasp beneath the table.

Keren was there, with Simon beside her. Keren wouldn't meet Tetisheri's eyes. Simon couldn't meet Nebenteru's eyes. The roast chicken was delicious but Tetisheri couldn't face the mullet, not with the events of the afternoon still vivid in her memory. Bast, also a guest although not at the table, made up for her lack of interest.

As one course succeeded another Nebenteru regaled them with the goings-on in Rome, fact and rumor. "Caesar, as he made sure we all know, came, saw, and conquered in Pontus. Some are saying he might be stopping off in Greece on the way home to clean up the last little nest of Pompey's band of Optimates."

"Cato?" Tetisheri said.

Nebenteru nodded. "The Younger, along with Metellus Scipio, Pompey's sons, and whoever else remains. There can't be many, and by this time they must know they're beaten."

"They're idealists," Apollodorus said. "Idealists never say

die until they do." He had cause to know that better than anyone, although at this table only Tetisheri knew it.

Nebenteru shook his head. "Sad but true. Let's hope they don't come here."

Everyone laughed, and after a moment Uncle Neb did, too. "Yes, now that I think of it, our queen would love to make a groom gift of the lot of them, tied up with a bow and delivered to Caesar with her best love. They must have that much common sense between them, that they would not willfully place themselves in so much danger."

"Again," Tetisheri said with a glance at Apollodorus, "idealists. They could see the writing on the wall when Caesar marched his troops on Rome. The end of this matter was a foregone conclusion from that day forward." She shook her head. "Pompey. Of all the idiocies perpetrated by Philo, that had to have been the silliest. If Pompey were alive today, he and Caesar could at least make a pretext of sharing power. Even if it would only have been the most obvious fiction, the warring factions might have been able to work together going forward. Certainly fewer people would be dead and our queen would not have been put to all the trouble and expense of rebuilding Alexandria, in some places from the ground up."

"You sound just like her," Uncle Neb said, laughing again.

"The best thing Theo ever did for Alexandria and Egypt was to imagine he could float in full armor." Apollodorus raised his glass in memory of Ptolemy XIII, and the rest of them followed suit in heartfelt agreement. Theo, the first of Cleopatra's brothers named Ptolemy, had not been universally loved.

Uncle Neb refilled his glass and passed the flagon to Tetisheri. "One especially pernicious rumor that I heard more than once, and mind you I was only in Rome for three days, is that there is a conspiracy building among certain of the senators to assassinate Caesar. Which will mean another internecine war in these interminable Roman wars that beset us all."

Keren rolled her eyes. "There is always a conspiracy by disaffected Romans to assassinate someone."

Simon, a slender Greek, was a quiet man even when he wasn't sitting at dinner with Keren's loud and opinionated family, but now he said, "I heard that rumor, too, onshore at Ostia. Everyone was talking about it."

"Not much of a conspiracy, then," Apollodorus said.

"And so less likely to be true," Uncle Neb said, cheering up. He disapproved of war in general. No matter how righteous the cause it was always bad for the moving of goods between seller and buyer. "One cannot effectively conspire if said conspiracy is exposed before the event."

"Doesn't mean it isn't true," Tetisheri said. "Caesar has too many enemies, and is too nakedly ambitious. If any of those old Republicans could wish him dead they'd do it in an instant."

"What did Cotta want?" Keren said.

Uncle Neb looked from her to Tetisheri. "Aurelius Cotta was here? The man is determined to be ubiquitous. He was down at the docks when we made port this morning, watching us unload."

Tetisheri glanced at Apollodorus, who looked unsurprised at the news. "Yes, he visited here shortly afterward. He's worried about the Roman monopoly on pozzolan."

"Has a deposit finally been found on this side of the Middle Sea, then?"

"Cotta doesn't know. That's what worries him."

"And the queen isn't saying?"

"Not to him, at any rate."

Uncle Neb smote the table with his fist, making all the dishes jump. "May Shu ever fill the queen's sails with a following wind! Good for her. Sometimes it feels as if the Romans won't be happy until they've sucked the entire country dry of resource from Alexandria to the Sixth Cataract."

Cheese, fruit, and savory biscuits served with a chilled sweet wine served as the last course, and soon afterward the party broke up. Keren escorted Simon to the door. Uncle Neb was about to adjourn to the kitchen to pay his compliments to Phoebe and Nebet when Tetisheri said, "Wait a moment, Uncle."

He paused, looking down at her. "Yes?"

"Is there a bookseller in Alexandria known especially for acquiring and selling rare editions?"

He raised an eyebrow. "We don't generally buy books in Alexandria to sell somewhere else, Tetisheri." He faked a shudder. "If the queen ever got to hear of it…"

She laughed. "No fear of that, Uncle. But is there one?"

He fondled the pearl dangling from his beard. "Alexandria is a city of scholars. There is always a brisk business in the buying and selling of books here. Students, now, are always looking for cheap editions of texts referenced by their teachers..." She shook her head. "But you mean new editions."

"Or old ones." She hesitated for a moment. "Rare ones. So old, so rare that a buyer might not inquire too deeply into its past history for the joy of acquiring it for their personal collection."

Both eyebrows went up. "I see." He waited, but when she said no more he nodded. "I will think on it, Tetisheri."

"Thank you, Uncle."

Apollodorus and Tetisheri were left alone at the table.

He was looking at her, a smile in his eyes. She could feel the color rising into her cheeks. "Again, I sense a conspiracy."

She couldn't help but laugh a little. "Again, your intuition is faultless. How did you know to come?"

"Neb sent a message around to the gymnasium as soon as he docked." He raised her hand to his lips. "It's nice to have so many of our friends and family cheering us on."

"Procuring, more like," she said, and this time he laughed.

He sobered. "I'm sorry you had such an uncomfortable afternoon."

She huffed out an exasperated sigh. "You're as bad as Pati for knowing everything that happens before anyone else."

"I saw Aristander briefly on my way here."

"The queen has called on the Eye of Isis to investigate."

"Have you any thoughts?"

She stared past him, her eyes narrowed in thought. "Tomorrow morning I will visit the Shurta, where Aristander has the bodies of both victims. I will ask Keren to join me."

"A good thought. Keren's medical expertise may help discover some clue as to the identity of the poor souls, at least."

"Perhaps."

"And then?"

"And then I thought I might call on Dixiphanes of Knidos."

"The Royal Architect?" Apollodorus made a face.

"Oh, I know he's a pompous, misogynistic, and xeno-phobic old windbag, but there is no one who knows more about building and construction in Alexandria than he does." She paused. "Except perhaps Otho."

"The Master of Builders?"

"Yes." She told him of that day's encounter. "The queen isn't wrong to dislike the coincidences. It is odd that on the very same day that Uncle Neb returns with a cargo of pozzolan, that Aurelius Cotta betrays his concern over the Roman monopoly of same, and that Otho, the Master of Builders, deigns to offer a mere trader a drive in his cabrio and an invitation to a celebration at his home, and on that same day cement has been used to murder not one but two people."

"It sounds as if one of the murders took place some time ago."

"Yes, but nevertheless."

"Nevertheless," he said, and surprised her with a quick kiss.

"What was that for?"

"You're a natural at this, Tetisheri." He got to his feet, pulling her up with him. "Let's go sit in the parlor."

"Why?"

"Because I want to kiss you again, and I don't want to do it here where everyone in the kitchen is crowded into the doorway so they can watch."

She looked over his shoulder and saw four heads disappear quickly from view, followed by the sound of muffled laughter.

He smiled down at her. "It might hamper my technique."

"Oh," she said, her heart beating a little faster. "Well, we wouldn't want that."

# 8

Alexandria's Shurta were housed in a large rectangular building set back from the Canopic Way. It was notable for its undistinguished frontage in a city whose architecture was adorned to an extent said to blind at high noon if stared at directly. The Shurta's building, by contrast, supported a single row of Doric columns with a narrow porch behind, and a single pair of unadorned double doors set into a wall that was otherwise a plain fitted stone facade painted white, like the columns, the cornice, the pediment, and the entablature. There was no frieze, either painted or relief. This severe lack of ornamentation was in stark contrast to the Great Library and the Soma to either side and to the Dicosterium across the Way, every available surface of which was bedizened and embellished and gilded and tinted to such a fervent extent that it would have satisfied an ego the size of Rameses II's.

Self-effacement was its own statement, Tetisheri thought, mounting the steps.

Obliquely echoing Tetisheri's thoughts, Keren said, "In a civilization that is four thousand years old, with a massive bureaucracy that results in at least one public beheading a month from a conviction for graft or embezzlement, how is it that you never hear of a shurta taking a bribe? You'd think the opportunities to buy oneself out of fines and arrests would be irresistible."

"In this reign? The queen put Aristander in charge."

"And in other reigns? Before Aristander?"

Tetisheri paused halfway up the steps and looked back at the morning's hustle and bustle along the Canopic Way. "You heard the story about the Roman visitor who killed a cat?"

"The mob tore him and his brother apart."

"And then?"

Keren shrugged. "It is never wise to offend Bast. All know her to take a swift and sure vengeance." She looked at Tetisheri expectantly.

Tetisheri touched the amulet at her breast. "The Shurta's chief at that time, Auletes' man, arrested the first ten citizens he could lay hands on whether they'd been involved in the riot or not, had them killed, and sent the bodies of the two dead Romans back to their families in Rome accompanied by the heads of the, ah, guilty."

"And then?"

"And then the mob relieved Auletes of his throne and put Berenice in his place. Sosigenes claims to this day it was the beginning of the Alexandrian War."

Keren thought it over, frowning. "I still don't see why—"

Tetisheri continued up the stairs. "Among the ten men, there was not a single Greek."

"What?"

Tetisheri nodded. "All Egyptians, every one. There is more than one reason her Egyptian subjects accept Cleopatra's rule so willingly. It isn't only because she gets all dressed up as Isis on earth." To the guards at the door she said, "Tetisheri and Keren, to see Aristander. He's expecting us."

Dejen winked at her. "Of course, lady. Follow me, please."

The narrow room ran the width of the back of the building. A long table stood over a deep, central gutter through which a stream of water had been induced to flow, in through an opening in the west wall and out again through a similar opening in the east wall. Rectangular vents lined the three exterior walls beneath the roof line, through which the smoke of incense burning in every corner continually drifted, carrying other, less aromatic, scents with it. A double door stood open onto a loading dock. The shrouded remains of someone were being loaded from the dock onto the back of a cart, from where it would be taken to the embalmers and the priests. Aristander was overseeing the operation from the door until he saw them enter. "Tetisheri," he said. "And Keren, how nice to see you!"

"It is good to see you again, too, Aristander. How is Merti?"

"She is well, and so is the child. We shall never be able to thank you enough."

Keren smiled. "I'm glad I was able to help."

Tetisheri nodded at the cart. "Anyone we know?"

"An old woman who wandered away from her home in Cypress Park three days ago. She was found in an alley in the Jewish Quarter, dead of exposure. It took us until now to find her family." At Tetisheri's look he shook his head. "The family are genuinely distraught, as it seems she was much loved, but she had been failing over the past year. It wasn't the first time she'd wandered off. But for their anguish over the way she died I would say they are relieved that she has passed on to the next life." He kissed the amulet of Maat that hung from his neck. "And here—" he gestured at the table "—we have our two mystery guests."

The table was wide enough for both skeletons and their footwear to be laid out side by side.

"Isis above," Keren said. Tetisheri looked at her, ready to comfort a fellow sufferer, but she saw that Keren was not so much shocked as she was intrigued. "They were both found underwater?"

"Yes," Aristander said. "As you can see, all we can do is guess as to when they went in."

Keren walked the length of the body on one side and then circled the table to walk the length of the second. The skeletons were both remarkably well preserved and intact and mostly attached at the joints. The weights that encompassed their feet were similar in size and shape—of an amphora, as Aristander had noted—although one was more discolored than the other, as if it had been in the water longer. The bones gleamed whitely against the stained wood of the table.

In a way this was worse than it had been the day before, the horror doubled. These had been living, breathing people, their lives truncated in calculated acts of sadistic violence that would have extracted the maximum amount of pain and terror before Anubis was allowed to welcome them home. Tetisheri took a deep and she hoped unobtrusive breath in through her mouth and exhaled through her nose. "What can you tell us, Keren?"

Keren raised her head. "They were both men. That is obvious from the length and weight of the long bones." She indicated the legs and arms. "The shoulders are wide, and if they were women their torsos would be longer. And their skulls—" She bent over the table.

"Yes?'

"The brow ridge, above the eyes, is larger than a woman's would be, and the brow slopes, where the brow of a woman is more vertical."

"Can you tell how old?"

She was examining one of the arms on the older skeleton. "From the generally good condition of the skeletons, I would guess that both were young, in their early twenties, perhaps. Oh."

"What?"

"This man had broken his right arm not long before he died. It was a simple fracture and it healed well. You must look closely to see the crack." She looked up at Aristander. "Is this the older one or the one from yesterday?"

"The older one."

She nodded. "There is more degradation of the bone in this one, so that fits." She looked up for permission and, receiving it, touched the leg above where it disappeared into the cement. "As you can see, the bones of this one are loose where they meet the cement. Not enough to slip free, but still." She reached across the table and touched the leg of the other skeleton. "This one, there is much less movement."

"Meaning?"

Keren stood up. "There are creatures in the sea much smaller than our eyes can see, and like all life they feed. In which case, I would have expected the feet to slip free of the weight. But it hasn't."

"Have you attempted to removed the... the weights?" Tetisheri said.

No one knew what to call them.

"We were afraid of destroying what is inside," Aristander said. "That there might be evidence that could be harmed."

"Would you try now? If they were still wearing footwear when their feet were placed into the cement, and there is anything left of it, it might provide a clue as to who they are. Or were."

Aristander looked at her and his eyes softened. "I'll send for tools and someone who knows how to use them."

"I'd like to stay to observe," Keren said.

"Of course."

"It would also be useful to know what kind of cement was used," Tetisheri said.

Keren and Aristander looked at her. "There are different kinds of cement?"

"There are." She met Aristander's eyes. "I will find someone today who can tell the difference and send him here. Please wait until then to remove the... it. Them."

Aristander inclined his head.

"There was an amulet with the victim found yesterday," she said. "Was there any identification found with the first victim?"

"They both wore amulets. Yesterday, as you saw, our victim lived under the scepter of Ptah. The skeleton from two years ago was found with an amulet of Seshat. The skull separated from the spine when it was taken from the water, as you can see." He pointed. Keren made an interested noise. Tetisheri repressed a gag. "It was merely good fortune that the chain tangled itself in his ribs or I expect it would have been lost to us."

"May I have custody of both, please?"

He looked at her. "You know you don't have to ask, Tetisheri."

The Eye of Isis could demand and not be gainsaid. It was no power she ever sought and she would demonstrate the usual courtesies to her last breath. "May I have custody of both, please, Aristander?"

A trace of a smile crossed his face. "Of course you may, Tetisheri. We will stop in the evidence room on our way out."

"Aristander?"

"Yes?"

She had to force the words out past the thickening in her throat. "Have there been others?"

"Other victims? Not that we've yet found, no. Why? Aren't two enough?"

Tetisheri ignored the attempt at levity and gestured at the skeletons. "Look at the weights on the feet. The older one, the top layer is sloppy, lopsided, as if when in liquid form there had been splashing." She swallowed. "As if the victim had tried to kick free and disturbed the cement while it was setting. The second weight? See how uniform, and the cement extends only just to above the ankles."

"You're saying—"

"I'm saying it looks as if the killer is getting progressively more efficient with practice. Unless this man was dead or unconscious, and yesterday you and I both thought that was unlikely."

Tetisheri heard Keren draw in a sharp breath. Aristander closed his eyes and shook his head. "Well, at least you seem to think there is only one murderer, in which I take a perverse comfort." He opened his eyes again to meet hers. "I will cause word to be spread among the fishing fleet. Any boat with divers on board will be instructed to be on the lookout.

"And," he added as if unable to stop the words, "Isis herself forbid any more are found."

And Tetisheri, the least religious person of the three of them, found herself joining Keren, that pragmatic secularist, and Aristander, that most devout worshipper of Maat, in making the sign against evil in fervent agreement.

# 9

The offices of the Royal Architect were housed in a building on a side street near the Royal Palace complex. If you squinted, you could imagine it was part of the palace complex itself, and Dixiphanes, the Royal Architect, lived with a perpetual squint. Thin, balding, in his fifties, his face twisted into a permanent sneer, he was a Greek who in his teens had taken advantage of the Ptolemies' open invitation to all scholars in the known world to take up residence in Alexandria.

In addition, Dixiphanes was a misogynist of the deepest dye and he would unquestionably have banned girls from his Mouseion classroom had not Auletes made it a condition of his employment as a teacher there. Thus it was that Cleopatra, Tetisheri, and others of their age and sex endured his lectures while never being invited into any discussion, being ignored when they asked a question, being praised for how their work looked rather than what it said, and a host of other indignities that however petty they seemed individually, collectively amounted to keeping them in as much ignorance of his subject as he could ensure.

Dixiphanes was also a man who believed all good things began and ended in his home country, and despised all of either sex who came from Rome, Numidia, Judaea, Lycia, Pontus, Thracia, Hispania, Mauretania, Germania, Britannia, or anywhere that wasn't Greece and preferably Achaea, which was, of course, his birthplace. It was educational to watch how Dixiphanes managed to ignore a royal heir because she'd been born female and in the wrong country. "Is there no one else who can teach us about architecture?" Tetisheri, exasperated, had said to Cleopatra one day after class.

"No one with his knowledge or experience," Cleopatra had replied, and laughed when she saw Tetisheri's disgruntled expression. "We will learn whether Dixiphanes wills it or no, Tetisheri. Listen to what he says about his art and ignore the rest."

So they had listened, and they had learned, and what questions this cranky old man refused to recognize or just plain ignored could be found in books in the Library or by asking other scholars in residence who were not averse to helping the clear favorite of all of Auletes' children. One thing you had to say about Dixiphanes, he clung to his prejudices without fear or favor. Later, when she gained the throne, Cleopatra had mystified many when she named him Royal Architect, but it was undeniable that the reconstruction of

Alexandria following the war was in large part due to his abilities.

Not that he would have accepted a compliment from a woman, and Tetisheri knew better than to offer him one. "Pozzolan?" he said, looking her over with disfavor. "How could you—" emphasizing the "you" "—possibly be interested in such a thing?"

Recalled instantly to the classroom of a decade before, Tetisheri resisted the urge to bring out the Eye and said in as equable a tone as she could manage, "I am commanded by our—" emphasizing the "our" "—queen to ask these questions. Shall we send to her for confirmation?"

He glared at her through watery eyes made nearsighted from years of reading architectural drawings. "Humph. Pozzolan."

"Yes, Dixiphanes, pozzolan."

His eyes narrowed at the deliberate lack of honorarium. "The man you want is Vitruvius. Vitruvius! Vitruvius, come here!"

"He's out in his workshop," a man (naturally) wearing the apprentice's sigil said, with an apologetic smile at Tetisheri he took care not to be seen by his master. "Shall I fetch him?"

"No, take me to him, please," Tetisheri said, and gave Dixiphanes the slightest possible bow. "Thank you, sir. The queen is appreciative of your help in this matter."

"What matter?" he said as she left the room. "What matter!"

"What is your name?" Tetisheri said, once they were safely out of earshot.

"Ampelius, lady."

"Have you been with your master long?"

"An eternity, lady," he said, holding a door for her. "I signed my apprenticeship papers last week."

She laughed, and repeated what Cleopatra had said so many years before. It was still true. "His knowledge and experience are unmatched in his craft."

"I am aware, lady, or I would have left the day after I apprenticed, and gone home to herd my father's goats with great good will."

"How did he settle on you?"

He made a face. "His apprentice, Dion, disappeared the day before I arrived."

"Disappeared?"

"So to speak. Everyone reckons he finally got fed up and went home and just didn't come back. Dixiphanes was most insistent he be replaced immediately."

"And you were new in town and didn't know his reputation for eating apprentices alive."

"My master is much more egalitarian than that, lady," he said in fake reproach. "I believe he is more correctly known for eating everyone alive."

She laughed. "And where do your father's sheep graze, Ampelius?"

"Near Pythia, lady."

Greece. Of course. "Pythia. My, my. Did you ever have cause to attend the oracle there?"

"I am happy to say I never have," he said decidedly. "One never knows quite what that lady means when she gives forth."

Much like a queen in that respect. Tetisheri followed him outside into a vast workshop, open to the sky and divided by waist-high fences into various cribs for different projects. The tap of hammer, the grind of saw, and the scrape of lathe competed with shouts of triumph and cries of discovery and many, many curses in Latin and Alemanni and Hebrew and Egyptian and of course Greek. Clouds of dust rose everywhere along with much sneezing and coughing, and hand-drawn carts with lengths of lumber and slabs of marble and sun-fired bricks and undressed granite bumped and banged their way through the narrow lanes separating the cribs.

Ampelius led her out of the general bedlam to a small crib filled to overflowing with shelves like ladders, with broader steps. Every level surface in this small space was crowded with beakers and bowls large and small, bags of various sizes of gravel and kinds of sand spilling onto the ground beneath, and wooden forms in adjustable squares. Many filled forms sat on the topmost shelves exposed to the sun. On the ground was a wooden barrel covered by a lid, next to which stood a slumping canvas sack from which a fine white material trickled out.

The chaos reminded her a little of Cleopatra's own work-room, where she distilled potions and unguents and other things about whose purpose it was safer not to speculate.

At the center of this scene of obscure industry stood a man covered head to foot in a fine dust.

"Vitruvius Pollio," Ampelius said, speaking in Latin, "here is the lady Tetisheri, come to discover what you can tell her about pozzolan."

"Eh?" The man looked up and blinked at them.

Patiently, as if it weren't the first time he had to do this, Ampelius repeated the introduction, this time adding pointedly, "She comes by request of the queen herself."

"Eh?"

"It's all right, Ampelius," Tetisheri said. "Could you perhaps find us something cool to drink?"

"You have but to ask, lady." He produced a stool as if by magic, dusted it off and handed her onto it as if it were a throne. Another stool was found for Vitruvius, who sat down in some bewilderment, as if not accustomed to using his backside for such a thing. In short order a pitcher of fruit juice appeared with two clean cups and a small dish of dates and almonds. Vitruvius drained his first two cups of juice without inhaling and afterward looked at the cup in surprise. "I was thirsty."

Tetisheri held out the plate of snacks and he devoured almost all of them in one continuous chew while Tetisheri nibbled on an almond to keep him company.

When the plate was clean he looked up with fully opened

eyes, saw Tetisheri, and gave a sudden smile. It was a revelation, rueful, charming, and irresistible, lighting his face from within. "My lady—?"

"Tetisheri."

"My lady Tetisheri I beg your pardon for my execrable manners. I do get a trifle, ah, wound up in my work."

She smiled back at him. Indeed it was impossible not to. "You're Roman, then," she said.

"I am, but—" an apologetic glance down at his dust-covered tunic "—what gave me away? Since I hope my appearance could not possibly have done so."

"We are speaking in Latin."

"Oh." The smile returned. "Ah. Well. So we are." He poured out the last of the juice, this time remembering what his proper Roman mother had taught him and offering her a refill first. "I thank you for your care of me."

She raised an eyebrow. "I have an ulterior motive." He grinned, and she couldn't help herself. "Sir, this isn't why I'm here, but, please, indulge my curiosity. How is it that Roman women exist to keep house and make babies and weave linen, and yet Roman men in Alexandria can be so..."

"Comfortable with women in power?"

She thought of Cotta. He had once taken hold of her without permission, but when she had called him to order he had apologized, and it was a mistake he had yet to repeat. "Well, yes, I suppose that is what I mean."

"Well, first, I wouldn't go so far as to say all Romans

feel that way. In fact, most of them are terrified of women in general and Cleopatra in particular, and the freedom women enjoy in Alexandria and Egypt is bewildering to them. Jupiter on his mountaintop, you can divorce your husbands and keep your children. The horror!" He put up his hands and hid behind them for a moment. He peeped out. "You understand that divorce is a privilege in Roman society reserved exclusively to men, the great and all-powerful patriarchs."

"I am aware," Tetisheri said dryly.

He dropped his hands. "The only answer I can give you is that some of us had mothers worthy of the name. When we visit a place like Alexandria, where a queen rules and women are allowed to be in society, in business, it feels more natural than not." He cocked an eyebrow, waiting for her response.

Cotta, with a mother. It was difficult to imagine Cotta being born in any way other than full blown from the brow of Apep.

And then she was immediately ashamed of herself for the thought. Cotta wasn't evil, he was merely a faithful servant to his general in the same way she was a faithful servant to her queen. They had the same jobs, they just served different masters. Mostly. "Are you apprenticed to Dixiphanes, Vitruvius?"

"No, by the gods, I most certainly am not. I'm an engineer by trade. I came here with Caesar's forces under Cornelius Balbas."

"Siege engines," Tetisheri said, who recognized Balbas' name.

He shrugged. "I specialized in ballista and scorpio, but yes."

"Balbas left with Caesar, didn't he? Why are you still here?"

"I asked for leave to study architecture at the Mouseion, but mostly I wanted access to the Library. I am writing a book."

"Are you? On what subject?"

"Architecture."

Tetisheri raised her eyebrows. "Does Dixiphanes know this?"

"No, and by whatever god you follow, lady, I beg you not to share this information with him. I barely managed to talk him into my having a workshop here as it was."

She kept a straight face. "You think he would take affront if he knew you were writing a book?"

With equal gravity, he said, "I think Dixiphanes reserves the right to publish on the subject exclusively to himself."

"I can't imagine why you would think that." She looked around at the overflowing shelves. "What are you doing here, exactly?"

"Experimenting with various formulas for mixing cement."

"Ah."

"Ah?"

"I asked Dixiphanes about pozzolan. He directed me to you."

"I see. Ah, indeed."

"What can you tell me?"

"Your queen is really interested in this?"

"She is. You may have noticed that much of Alexandria is under construction at present."

He sighed. "I lodge near the Heptastadion. Believe me, I noticed. Well." He took their mugs and stacked them on the tray. He crossed his arms and frowned at his feet. "Pozzolan is also called pit ash, and it's especially useful for construction in seaports because of its resistance to the salt in salt water. " He raised his eyes to Tetisheri's face and she nodded encouragingly. "The pilings for the pier at the Port of Cosa are made of pozzolan. They were poured underwater."

"Really?"

"Really, by means of a tube so the mixture would not be adulterated by the sea water, into forms that were removed when the mixture had set."

"Impressive."

"Very. Pit ash or pozzolan is commonly found near volcanoes, as near Vesuvio at Puteoli. It comes in four colors, red, gray, black, and—" He dipped a hand into the canvas sack of fine white material and let it sift through his fingers. "White. It's mixed two-for-one with lime and then enough water for a slurry. If you don't have any lime and you can afford to pound a bunch of tiles into dust—"

he stood up and located a pot on a shelf, displaying the coarse, randomly colored mixture "—you can substitute that for the lime. If you had a big, Library-sized project, say, it would take a lot of tiles, so not really a cost-effective alternative."

"I should think not."

"Unless you were going to tear down the Library and start over."

"Not quite yet."

"No." Vitruvius sat down again.

Tetisheri thought of the cement weights encasing the feet of the dead men. "It interests me that pozzolan does not deteriorate in salt water. Is this generally known?"

"Of course," he said. "It's the cement every architect and builder in any coastal community wants to use to hold his structures together."

"Like Alexandria."

"As you say."

She thought of the view through Cleopatra's window the day before, and the workman who fell. "The Pharos?"

"The Pharos is built on an island. I should think common cement would do just as well there, but that would be up to Dixiphanes, of course."

She nodded. "And just the one source, in Puteoli."

"There and a much smaller deposit on Santorin, yes."

"There are other volcanoes around the Middle Sea."

"There are, but as yet no deposits of pozzolan have been found near them."

"So you've looked."

"Oh, my, yes. We've been looking for a century or more. One day the Puteoli deposit will be depleted and we'll need another source."

Tetisheri thought again of Cotta. Or one could wait for someone else to discover a new deposit and then simply step in and take ownership. All hail the Senate and People of Rome. "A valuable commodity."

"It is that," he said ruefully, indicating the canvas sack. "I had to bribe a guard to get that much so I could continue my experiments."

"The pozzolan stores are guarded?"

"They are indeed. That bribe wiped out an entire month's pay."

"So no one in their right mind would waste it."

"No," he said. "No one in their right mind."

"Where is the store kept?"

He gave her an appraising stare. "May one ask, lady, what all these questions are in aid of?"

She didn't smile. "One may not."

"I see." He hesitated, but only for a moment. He was, after all, a guest in this city, and Tetisheri claimed to be there in the name of the queen. "At the end of Poseidon's Head, in the Royal Harbor. They built a walled compound specifically for the purpose."

"Guarded by—?"

"The Queen's Guard."

Cleopatra would not be happy to hear that her brand

new personal guard was susceptible to bribes. "In the normal way of business, if I were a builder, how would I gain access to a quantity of pozzolan?"

His eyes narrowed. "Well, first you'd need a project, with drawings, and it would have to be approved by the office of the Royal Architect."

"Dixiphanes."

"The very same. After that, it would go for final approval to the palace itself, accompanied by a detailed construction plan, including all relevant bids."

"The queen herself approves each construction project?"

"I don't know that every proposed construction project in Alexandria and Egypt passes before the royal eyes, but certainly no shovel hits dirt before it has the approval of someone in the palace."

"How many such projects are approved every year?"

He smiled. "I have no idea. You could ask Dixiphanes. He would know. Or Otho the Master of Builders, who seems be to everywhere one looks in construction these days. He's the one who pays the architects and the bricklayers and the carpenters. He would know even better than Dixiphanes."

Or she could ask the queen, who would also know and who would be infinitely more forthcoming. She hoped. "Thank you, Master Vitruvius. You have been most helpful." She hesitated. "I wonder if I might trespass further upon your good nature."

"In what way?"

"There are two samples of cement I would like you to examine."

"Your object being?"

"To discover whether they were formed of pozzolan."

"I see." He was silent for a moment. "Of course I will be happy to oblige you, lady. Where may I find these samples?"

"At the headquarters of the Shurta."

His eyebrows went up. "The Shurta?"

"You said you lodged near the Heptastadion. It will be right on your way. Ask for Aristander or Dejen. Tell them I sent you and why." She stood up and dusted off her clothes. "Do you give talks at the Library, sir?"

He gave a slight bow. "Lady, I do. It is a condition of my membership, as it is of all scholars in residence there."

"I would like to attend your next one, I think."

This time his bow was much lower. "Lady, you honor me. I am scheduled for next month, I believe. It will go up on the noticeboard in the atrium."

"What is your topic?"

"My argument is that all new construction must and should be distinguished by three qualities." He ticked them off on his fingers. "*Firmitas*, strength. *Utilitas*, utility. *Venustas*, beauty. Functional architecture will have one of these qualities. Good architecture will have two. Only great architecture will have all three."

It would be interesting to learn what he thought of the building that housed the Shurta. "Is that what your book is about?"

He laughed. "Lady, it is."

"Then I look forward to hearing you speak on it, sir."

As she passed by Dixiphanes' office she heard voices and glanced inside.

A woman dressed in a fine wool tunic and stola and a delicate pair of openwork sandals stood in close consultation with Dixiphanes. Her hair was styled in the Greek fashion, bound first by a thin ribbon behind her ears and then a wide one just over the large braid of hair coiled at her neck. It took Tetisheri more than a moment to recognize the lady Khadiga.

She slowed her steps. She must have caught the corner of Dixiphanes' eye because he looked up. "Lady Tetisheri," he said, straining for civility. "I hope Vitruvius was able to answer all your questions about pozzolan."

"A most interesting discussion, master," she said, inclining her head. "Thank you." She glanced at the other woman. She was staring at Tetisheri through narrowed eyes.

Dixiphanes didn't introduce them. He turned to Khadiga to resume their low-voiced conversation, but Tetisheri felt the lady's stare boring a hole in the back of her head until she was out of sight.

Well. Wasn't that interesting.

# 10

The sun was high in the sky as she came out of the yard just before Sixth Hour, or Twelfth Hour as she supposed they must all now call it. The street bustled with activity, a constant, jostling crowd talking at a volume that easily drowned out the noise of the yard she had just left, carts delivering and taking away again, a few people on horseback. A chariot driven by someone whose dress betrayed him as a country noble with a woman beside him whose gaudy dress proclaimed her not his wife edged through the melee without either completely tipping over the juice cart on the corner or clipping the three-year-old child who chased her cat out into the street. A victory all around.

There was a small cafe opposite and she retired to a table in the shade and ordered olives, bread, cheese, and a small beer. As she waited Dixiphanes emerged from his lair, surrounded by a dozen young men wearing apprentice badges who hung upon his every word, or pretended to.

They progressed up the street to a larger and much more expensive establishment, one that must have had extensive indoor seating. The lady Khadiga slipped out behind them and gestured, and a moment later a carriage pulled up, driven by a muscular Egyptian with a dark, closed expression. The lady looked around to see Tetisheri watching from her seat. They exchanged a long, unsmiling stare before Khadiga climbed up into the carriage. She said something to her driver, lifting her chin in Tetisheri's direction. He assessed Tetisheri with a long, cool glance and replied. Khadiga smiled and they drove off, leaving Tetisheri feeling unsettled without knowing why.

Her order came at the same time the man she had been covertly watching since she emerged from Dixiphanes' work place detached himself from the alley next to the yard and walked across the street to stand in front of her.

"Linos," she said when his shadow fell across her table. She concentrated on spreading cheese on her bread. "Join me, do. This cheese is excellent and the bread fresh baked."

There was a momentary pause, followed by the scrape of a stool. Tetisheri waited until she was sure the smile she fixed on her face would stay there before looking up.

Linos the Eunuch was thin to the point of emaciation and dark of hair and eye. In court he dressed in the brightest of silks and the thickest lines of kohl, but on the street he appeared in a simple tunic made of plain linen and a face bare of paint. He was one of Ptolemy XIV Philopator II's closest advisors, and wore the furtive look of general hoodwinkery that characterized all members of that court, most of whom were working hardest just to stay alive. Philo was known to be capricious, viciously so, and falling out of favor in his court could mean exile but could just as likely mean execution. In the pursuit of self-preservation the members of his court were willing to carry out any form of malfeasance their master required of them and much they thought up on their own initiative, including treason and murder.

They had favorite targets they liked to single out for their special attention, too, and one of them was sitting across from Linos now. "Tetisheri," he said blandly. "What a surprise."

"I could hardly believe my eyes when I saw you standing there when I arrived," she said, marveling. "What, I said to myself, what on earth would bring that most elegant, that most distinguished of courtiers to such a vulgar neighborhood as this? A place where people actually work with their hands?" She gave a delicate shudder. "It was inconceivable. Surely I must have been mistaken, I said to myself." She gave him her sweetest smile. "And yet here you are."

Nothing in either of their expressions betrayed the fact that the last time they had met, she was well on her way to being beaten to death at his master's order with his, Linos', hearty approval. "Oh, you know," he said, moving his hands to make room for the plate holding his food. "Just out for a stroll."

"A lovely day for it," Tetisheri said, approving. "Tell me, how is the king enjoying his new quarters?"

But Linos was too old a hand to betray anything like chagrin in front of an enemy. "I believe His Majesty finds them most comfortable, indeed."

"I visited Antirrhodos once many years ago," she said, assembling a thoughtful frown. "There is much to be said for island life." She smiled at him. "The onshore breezes are so pleasant, are they not?" His returning smile looked a little forced. Encouraged, she lost no time in adding insult to injury. "I know the queen spared no expense in bringing the palace into order. I was sure our good king—" kinglet, she very nearly said "—would be pleased with the care she took for her dearest brother's comfort."

Since she knew that, under the express orders of his queen, Apollodorus had overseen the remodel and that bringing the old Ptolemaic ruin "into order" had meant a heavy emphasis on the security measures he had seen fit to put into place, she was certain that the exact opposite was true. But then hers was not a noble nature.

Linos filled his mouth with cheese and bread and chewed slowly. Regaining his composure, she thought. He washed it down with a swallow of small beer. "And how was your visit with Dixiphanes, Tetisheri? I'm sure the old man was as charming as ever."

She was very nearly betrayed into a laugh and managed at the last moment to turn it into a cough, quickly smothered with her hand. "Excuse me. Indeed, the Royal Architect—"

in this context she was more than willing to give Dixiphanes the proper emphasis due his title "—was as helpful as it is in his nature to be."

His eyes narrowed. "Does the queen have some new grand edifice in mind for our fair city?"

"You surprise me again, Linos," she said, smiling. "Always."

He straightened in his chair. "She will of course consult with the king, her brother, husband, and co-ruler, before putting any major construction project in hand."

"Always," Tetisheri said again, still smiling. She drained her cup and reached for her purse, producing a coin. "Let me treat, do. Oh look, one of the new drachmas. I do love a bright, shiny, new coin, don't you? And the likeness to mother and child is so very true to life. Truly a triumph of the minter's art."

His face darkened but at that moment the server appeared miraculously, as all good servers do at the first flash of coin. "No, no, keep the change," Tetisheri said. She knotted the string of her purse and stowed it away again, and while she was so occupied she said, "You didn't tell me, Linos. What are you doing in this part of town?"

He smiled thinly and got to his feet. "As I said, Tetisheri. Just out for a stroll."

Tetisheri watched him walk away. He did not return to the alley next to Dixiphanes' workshop but continued on down the street to disappear around a corner. In the direction of Poseidon's Head, she saw, which meant he was most likely going to report to Philo on Antirrhodos. Had Linos been following her? If he had, why? Or had he been keeping Dixiphanes or someone who worked in his yard under surveillance? Again, if that was indeed what he had been doing, why?

She reviewed their conversation. No, she had said nothing of any consequence, had answered no question directly, had certainly never referred to what had brought her here. But if Philo or his minions were involved in any way in the investigation she was conducting, a measure of discretion was indicated.

And perhaps some security of her own. She must give that some thought.

Two victims. Both young men. The manner and material of death indicated that both were involved, directly or indirectly, with the building trade. The murderer had had easy access to pozzolan, enough of it to be confident it would not be missed.

Pozzolan was a precious commodity under strict control. It would seem to follow that access to it would be severely limited. A list of names of those who had such access should prove useful, if such a list existed.

It could not have been used simply because it was near to hand, which meant it had been used to send a message. Which would seem to require the bodies being found and the method of murder made known, or… or what? If the message was being sent (to whom?) to warn others off (from what?) surely Aristander of all people would have heard something of it by now. But he had looked as sick and shocked as she had felt on the beach the day before. "To be fitted with a pair of Rhakotis sandals" had been an apocryphal story, retold in the tavernas and street-side cafes by old men telling stories in hopes someone would buy them another drink.

Until it wasn't.

Tetisheri stared unseeing between the ears of the horse pulling the cabrio she had hailed. The driver stood on the step behind and shouted at anyone who thought of obstructing their progress. He made a great show of fussing with the reins, at times coming far too close to slapping Tetisheri in the face. The horse ignored him. So did she.

As much as two years separated their murders. Probably.

One of the victims followed Seshat. The other followed Ptah. Perhaps.

Her hand strayed to the purse at her girdle, feeling for the shapes of the amulets inside. Everyone in Alexandria and Egypt followed a god, or pretended to. Nearly everyone in Alexandria and Egypt wore an amulet, usually a carved pendant representing the god whose craft one labored in or whose favor one sought. Aristander wore the amulet of Maat, the goddess of truth and justice. Tetisheri wore the image of Bast, the goddess of protection. Amulets didn't have to be in the image of gods, however. Keren, who looked to the god of Judea, wore instead an image of Peseshet, a woman physician who had lived and healed in Egypt two thousand years before.

Egyptian gods came and went out of fashion as one dynasty succeeded the next. They changed names and roles and responsibilities and even appearances as an old millennium retired and a new one debuted. The deities did not dictate terms. They responded to life as it was lived every day along the Nile and the Middle Sea, reflecting the changing hopes, wishes, and beliefs of the people who lived there. Especially the Nile's rulers, who could impose their own images on whatever god's face they chose to represent in life. Alexandrians and Egyptians alike followed where their pharaohs and kings and queens spiritually led, at least outwardly, as a matter of simple survival.

Today's prevailing cult was that of Isis, whose worship had spread from Alexandria and Egypt to as far away as Rome, Athens, Persis, Parthia, and Punt, as Tetisheri knew from the witness of her own eyes. On their trip to Punt she and Uncle Neb had made offerings at a Temple of Isis in Heptanesia.

Cleopatra's first public act as the official heir to the throne was to escort the new Baucis bull across the river to its temple. Both had been in full regalia, although all present agreed that the bull, due to its sheer size, held the edge in gold leaf, and both sides of the Nile had been packed with the Egyptians who were the true object of the exercise. No Ptolemy had ever before identified themselves so openly with Isis, and nothing could have endeared her more to her Egyptian subjects. Her father, Auletes, had been abysmally ignorant of prevailing religious beliefs, and they had repaid that ignorance by relieving him of his throne. It was a lesson well learned by his daughter.

No, one did not pray to Seth when every newly minted coin showed Cleopatra and Caesarion depicted as Isis and Horus. Certainly never where Cleopatra could see you.

Otho had worn an Isis pendant, with Horus at her breast. The position of Master of Builders was of necessity a political animal, and at the moment Cleopatra was in the ascendant.

Hunefer, Tetisheri's late, unlamented husband, had aligned himself with Philo's interests. It had been the end of him, and his mother with him. But too many of Philo's friends still survived, spending their days conniving at Cleopatra's downfall. More, Tetisheri thought, to remain in the kinglet's good graces than for any real belief in the possibility of success. Philo attracted very few people of probity or ability. His court was filled with sycophants, yes-men, and enablers. To a man—and most of Philo's courtiers were men, and Greek—they despised and feared anyone who was neither. Linos for one.

*Could anyone have overheard your conversation with Cotta?* Cleopatra had asked her the day before.

No, but Nenwef had been in the Five Soldiers when she had spoken to Isidorus about Grafeas. He had placed himself—deliberately?—close enough to have heard that conversation. According to Is and Khemit before him,

Nenwef had been a friend of Grafeas. Nenwef was also a member of Philo's court, albeit little more than a hanger-on.

Nenwef went hotfoot to meet Khadiga, Otho's builder, and the very next day, Otho had maneuvered Tetisheri into his cabrio for a nice long chat, and an invitation to a social event at his house.

Like Cleopatra, Tetisheri mistrusted coincidence.

Today was... Saturday? Wasn't it? She would check the calendar when she got home. She spent a pleasant moment in imagining offering up Caesar and his calendar both as a sacrifice to Sobek. Or Tawaret, she was good with either.

The cabrio clattered to a stop and Tetisheri looked around to see that they had come to a halt before a small, square building as high as it was wide and long, the very definition of Vitruvius' functional structure. It had no portico, no windows; the exterior was whitewashed and the wooden door unvarnished, and no sign indicated who lived or worked there. It was set back from the street, surrounded by a narrow garden of papyrus and lotus watered by an artificial stream that proceeded placidly from planting to planting. There were no benches. This was not a property where one was encouraged to sit or to admire except in passing.

The walk to the door was sternly flagged with slabs of red granite, highly polished, set into white gravel the size of peas that looked as if it had been deliberately graded by hand by young maidens who were now blind.

"Is this the place, lady?" The driver sounded doubtful.

"It is." She paid him.

"Would you like me to wait?"

Tetisheri always tipped well. She looked around her. They were in the heart of the Jewish Quarter, on a side street well off the Way, on the other side of Lochias from the Palace, and at the other end of Alexandria from Eunostos. But it was still early afternoon. Plenty of time to conclude her business and be safely home before dark. "No, but thank you."

He looked doubtful, but helped her down and waited until she walked up to the door before driving off in a displeased rattle of wheels on wooden rims.

# 11

She knocked. The cover on the peephole slid back. She smiled at the large brown eye revealed there. "Hello, Nephilim. Tetisheri the Trader, here to speak with Matan."

A grunt. The cover slid closed. Tetisheri waited patiently. Nephilim did things in his own way and in his own time.

A black cat, the twin of Bast but for her amber eyes, curved around the corner of the house, greeted Tetisheri in an amiable voice, lapped up some water from the tiny stream, and made of herself a curl of fur around the roots of a flowering papyrus. Tetisheri raised her amulet to her lips. "My thanks to you, O divine Bast, for your comfort and your company." She had no idea if the goddess heard her or not, or indeed if the goddess was more than a figment of a communal cultural imagination, but it never hurt to pay one's respects. Especially to cats, who had their own methods of revenging themselves upon perceived slights.

Just to be safe, she bent to give the cat an ear rub, and was rewarded with a raspy purr.

The door opened and Nephilim stood in the opening, glowering. If a mountain could glower. "He'll see you." It was obvious he disapproved, but Tetisheri didn't take it personally. She followed him into the house, where his messy light brown hair brushed the ceiling and his shoulders nearly touched both walls of the hallway. He was truly the largest man she had ever seen, and she had been an unwilling spectator at an arena in Rome where all manner of human oddities had had at each other for the enjoyment of the screaming crowd. She remembered a Saxon twice as big as anyone else with fists the size of boulders. He had left every one of his opponents unconscious or dead in very short order. The crowd had hated having their entertainment cut so short, and the Roman running those games had had him killed for it.

Nephilim, she thought now, was twice the size of the Saxon, with an enormous musculature that forced his arms to curve out from his torso. If she ever had to fight Nephilim, she'd take care never to come within his reach. A well-placed arrow from a hundred paces, and before he got a running start, sounded about right.

They reached a door and Nephilim stood back to allow her to enter. He breathed heavily down her back. "Matan," she said, stepping into the room.

This single room took up the larger part of the interior of the building. Multiple skylights brought in the light, which illuminated a workshop packed with tables and shelves and sets of tiny tabletop drawers, so many that any possible movement between them must be conducted sideways. There were three tall tool boxes with multiple drawers, all open and spilling over with pliers, needles, tweezers, calipers, rasps, files, burrs, and other tools Tetisheri had no name for. Half a dozen small anvils were scattered around various surfaces, a set of sanding blocks were jumbled in a pile, saws of every conceivable shape and tooth size lay wherever they had last been set down, and there was a small hammer of some shape and purpose on every flat area Matan might put his hand. A thick, shiny liquid bubbled and popped in a crucible set over a miniature furnace containing a disciplined heap of glowing coals.

The walls were festooned with hanks of coral, carnelian, turquoise, lapis, and agates of every color. Strings of pearls from the palest white to rich cream fell in profusion from a hook in one corner. Here was a loop of amethysts in translucent lilac, there one of gold tiger's eye that gleamed in a stray beam of sunlight; across the room hung peridots the color of Apollodorus' eyes. A chest sat in one corner, triple locked, where, Tetisheri knew from previous visits, were kept the more valuable stones. but what the eye could see was enough justification for the presence of Nephilim, or even two of him.

The man at the center of this disciplined disarray looked up. "Tetisheri! My dear, how nice to see you!" He bustled around, behind, and between several tables, both hands outstretched, to grasp her own and beam up at her. "Thank you, Nephilim, that will be all."

The door shut behind her and they were left regarding one another. "Your friend, she is well?"

"Very well. Motherhood suits her."

His apron was covered in stains and burns. So were his hands and his arms up to the elbow, arms that were roped and sinewy from wrestling all of the beautiful things in nature into even more beautiful things to be worn or displayed. His dark eyes twinkled at her from beneath a short crop of graying curls. Matan the Goldsmith, and he was that, of course, but he was so much more. "The child thrives, yes?"

"She says he's eating for two, and possibly three."

He laughed delightedly. "The charger, she liked it?" He saw her expression and rolled his eyes. "That Cotta, he has no taste, no finesse. He wanted a lump of gold bigger than anyone else would give her, so that was what I made him."

"Some nice scenes of Alexander around the edge, though."

He laughed again. "Always so tactful, Tetisheri! What an ambassador you would have made!"

"A trader is a kind of ambassador, Matan."

"True enough, true enough!"

"What wonderful thing are you making today?"

He made a face. "A new collar for the king. Come, see." He navigated a serpentine route to the center of the room and she followed, pulling her garments in tight to her body, careful not to knock over anything too close to any edge she came near. "He wants something grand and pharaonic, as if it might be worn by Thutmose III, according to Linos, who placed the order with me."

Thutmose III had succeeded his—aunt, was it?—and spent the rest of his reign dividing his time between warring on his neighbors and chiseling her image from wherever it appeared, from Memphis to the Second Cataract. Philo hadn't slept through the entirety of his history lectures after all. He knew Cleopatra would hear of the collar, and would understand the implied insult.

The collar itself was a thing of beauty, with terminals carved in the shape of Anubis and alternating rows of gold, carnelian, and coral. The rows became longer as they descended so that the collar would lie flat upon the royal breast. Two pendants depended from the exact center of the bottom row, a white feather made of alabaster above a red heart made of coral. "It's going to weigh as much as he does," she said.

"Indeed."

"It's beautiful work, Matan."

He struck a pose. "Do I do any other kind?"

She smiled. "Indeed, and you do not."

"Yes, well. Not unless that is precisely what is ordered." It was obvious that the memory of that enormous gold plate that Cotta had ordered made to celebrate the birth of Caesarion still rankled.

An errant ray of sunshine caught and held briefly on a

translucent piece of orange gemstone. "Oh, Matan, what are these?" She navigated a route safely around a precarious pile of lapis-encrusted vases. "Carnelian?"

He joined to stare at the beautiful things. "Yes. I'm rather proud of these. At least this idiot left me alone to do my best."

They were capsa, rolls for scrolls, a set of three, each set the length of her forearm. Their heads were carved into the likenesses of Egyptian gods and goddesses, one Isis and Osiris, the second Sobek and Renenutet, the third Horus and Hathor. The connecting rods were sleek and perfectly cylindrical. "What a polish, Matan. It must have taken you days to bring up so fine a shine. They look almost translucent." She smiled at him. "You must have been terrified it would crack or chip."

"Not I!" But he grinned.

"These would make the most tattered copy of Aristotle's *Poetics* look like a first edition."

He made a face. "A more reputable use than the one he has in mind, I fear."

"What?"

"Let us just say, my dear Tetisheri, that I am given to understand the good gentleman is interested only in a certain kind of classic. One less romantic than poetry."

"Oh?" She was mystified, but only for a moment. "Oh. Oh, I see," she said slowly. "Who did you say you had the commission from again?"

"Some minor noble with more money than sense."

He looked at her, puzzled. "Why does this interest you, Tetisheri?"

"Sosigenes tells me that someone is stealing books and maps from the Library. Old books and maps, the rarest versions, the ones impossible to replace."

He looked grave. "That is very bad news, indeed. I hope steps are being taken. Guards, perhaps?"

"As Sosigenes informs me, the Library of Alexandria is the repository of all human knowledge, and their mission is to share that knowledge with everyone. Limiting access is not an option. Keeping track of visitors might answer. They're giving it a try, at any rate."

He shook his head. "Satiah's treatise on lapidary was a formative work for me, a resource I have returned to again and again. So far as I know the Library owns the only copy in existence. If something like that were stolen…"

"Hire a scribe to make a copy. The Library charges a fee but it sounds as if it would be worth it to you."

"That is an excellent idea. Now then. What brings you to me today, Tetisheri?"

Recalled to the reason for her visit, she fumbled in her purse. "I have two amulets I would like you to look at."

He frowned at them. "Huh." He gave her a quick look from beneath his curls. "Not anything that came out of this room."

"No argument there," she said with a smile. "But you've lived and worked in Alexandria for thirty years. You're the first person Uncle Neb goes to when he needs advice on a shipment of gemstones or lapidary." She nodded at the amulets. "Two bodies were discovered in suspicious circumstances. Each had only those amulets to provide any indication as to their identities. I need to know who they were, Matan."

He regarded her with a quizzical expression. "And this concerns you how, Tetisheri? The last time I checked, you were in partnership with your uncle, a proprietor of one of the most successful trading concerns on the Middle Sea. What has a trader to do with dead bodies found in suspicious circumstances?"

She met his eyes. "It may be that I am more than that now, Matan."

"How more, exactly?"

His tone was uncompromising. Reluctantly, she reached inside her tunic to reveal the Eye of Isis.

His brows came together and he stared for a long moment. The opalescent glow of the nacre combined with the rich, deep blue of the lapis seemed so lifelike as to be ready to blink.

It was a little unnerving, she thought, and raised her eyes to see that Matan looked anything but admiring of this example of his chosen art. "You recognize it?" she said, uncertain.

"Recognize it? Most certainly I recognize it! I made it, these six years ago and more!" He looked as if he wanted to throw something but he was only holding the amulets and he realized they wouldn't result in a crash loud enough to satisfy his feelings. "Damn her!" he said instead, and fiercely.

"Matan!"

"Damn her I said and damn her I meant! How could she place such a burden on you of all people, her oldest, her most dear, and her most loyal friend, the one person in Alexandria who she knows would die before she did her harm?"

Tetisheri gaped at him. Seeing it, he made an obvious effort to rein in his temper. "My apologies, Tetisheri," he said curtly, and unclenched his hand so he could look at the amulets clutched therein. He cleared a space on the table before her, laid them out with exaggerated care, and gestured at her to pay attention. "Here we have Ptah, protector of artists and craftsmen, particularly of those who labor in the tombs to make the transition from this life into the next as smooth as possible for those who can afford it. As I'm sure you know, Ptah had fallen by the divine wayside over the centuries, but the Ptolemies brought him back, to the point of having their chief priests marry into the family."

"Yes." His tone was so forbidding that she was afraid to say more.

"This particular amulet was carved from malachite, and from its appearance I would say the material came from the mines in Judea."

"It's available elsewhere?"

"It's been found in Britannia," he said. "But this is from Judea."

"How do you know?"

He shrugged, holding the pendant up to catch the light that was now slanting obliquely through the skylights. "Anyone who works with precious stones after a while begins to be able to identify their provenance." He put down the pendant and picked up a small nugget of gold that was gathered in a small bowl with others of its kind. "This nugget I can tell you comes from a particular mine in Aetheopia. See the striations? Those are copper, with which gold often occurs simultaneously. The proportion and kind of copper is also an indicator, as in other mines there will be less gold and more copper. Another mine might have gold and no copper but a significant streak of tourmaline. The more one works with precious metals and gems, the more familiar one becomes with their various birthplaces."

He replaced the nugget in the bowl and picked up the second amulet. "This was, I think, at one time a good representation of the carver's art, but it is very worn down. You see here and here, how the edges are softened? Was the one who wore this old?"

"No. Both men were young, late teens or early twenties."

"Ah. Then I suggest the possibility that this pendant was a gift or an inheritance from an older family member, worn down over the years. This figure is, of course, Seshat, the record keeper. Despite the wear you can plainly see the pen in one hand and the palm leaf rib in the other, where she tallies the years of Pharaoh's reign."

She stowed the amulets in her purse. "Thank you, Matan." She stooped to kiss his cheek.

He touched her shoulder briefly. "It is always my pleasure to see you, Tetisheri. Tell Neb it's time to throw another one of his dinner parties, and not to forget to invite me."

"As if he would."

They smiled at one another. "I'll show you out."

"I know the way, Matan."

"Ah yes, but Nephilim will never forgive me leaving anyone, even you, to wander about the shop unsupervised."

"And we must not offend Nephilim."

"As much as my life is worth."

The smiles on both sides were more genuine this time.

# 12

Outside, Tetisheri paused on the doorstep, evidently to frown at the rose bush beneath which the black cat was still curled. The cat gave a chirrup and came forward to wind around her legs. She stooped to pet it and was rewarded with shoulder dives and a nonstop purr. She crouched there for a full five minutes, blindly petting the cat, while her mind picked apart everything she had learned that day. Not enough, not nearly enough, but some things she had learned.

Rhakotis sandals had killed two people over the past two years.

Pozzolan was a valuable commodity in short supply.

The two victims were both young men of apprentice age, if not journeymen.

Both had been middle class, as witness the quality of amulets and the condition of their teeth. The broken arm was common enough to lend nothing to the one victim's story, but she would do well to remember it in case, by some miracle, she managed to discover a possible identity and that man had had a broken arm in his past.

It was likely that both had either been in trades associated with building or had had family members who were.

There was a slight chance that the amulets indicated they were Egyptian, but no certainty. The city teemed with students, scholars, and soldiers from everywhere in the known world, all worshipping their own gods and adopting native ones with abandon, without interference from the authorities, a tolerance enforced by the Ptolemies from the day Alexander had scattered the grain to form its boundaries. A tolerance, it might be said, continually tested by the Egyptian population. Auletes had lost his throne too many times to count and not only because he had had too many children who wanted to take it from him. Cleopatra had an enormous job in front of her, and yes, Matan was right in that the queen used every resource she had to get it done, including her own person, never mind her friends.

It did not necessarily follow that those friends loved the realm any less than their queen, and weren't prepared to sacrifice for it.

The black cat butted her hand and purred.

Where next? She should take a look at the store of pozzolan to confirm Vitruvius' information.

Otho, now, there was someone whose activities would bear closer observation, in part because he had forced himself upon her notice, but much more so because of his chosen trade. Builders were by profession practical and ruthless, and Otho wasn't just a builder, he was the Master of Builders. A man in such a position could with a word turn Rhakotis sandals from myth to reality.

Khadiga. Connected to Otho, if the craftsmen working on his house were to be believed, by more than a professional relationship. And she knew Dixiphanes, but then what contractor would not know the Royal Architect? A woman contractor, moreover, to whom Dixiphanes was willing to speak to with civility, in itself worthy of notice.

Nenwef must be interviewed as well.

It would be difficult to check up on Linos' activities, as Philo would not tolerate anyone in his court who was on speaking terms with anyone in his sister's court. She wondered if Linos' coat was susceptible to turning, and dismissed the notion instantly. Impossible to trust someone so closely in the confidence of the kinglet.

But it would benefit the Eye of Isis to have an ear in Philo's court, she thought. Nenwef, now, might be a different story.

And then there was Cotta, all atwitter with nervousness that Cleopatra might develop her own source of pozzolan, thereby cutting into Rome's monopoly. Was that all that was going on there? It was a given he was acting in Caesar's interests. He was Caesar's cousin and Caesar's man. The difficulty here was that one never knew with Cotta until it was too late.

Of course, one could say exactly the same thing of Cleopatra Philopator, Seventh of Her Name, Lady of the Two Lands, Isis on Earth, et cetera, et cetera.

One thing only seemed certain: that this looked like being a long, tedious investigation with no certainty of a satisfactory conclusion at the end. She sighed, gave the cat's ears a farewell scratch, and rose to her feet. In the way of cats it fussed around, getting underfoot and obstructing her progress, until at last it ran ahead with a meow that sounded amazingly like Cleopatra's "Tcha!" of the day before. Excellent, she'd annoyed Bast. What fresh horror awaited her around the corner could only be imagined.

She walked briskly toward the distant sound of hustle and bustle that betokened Alexandria in the full of a busy afternoon. The shadows had lengthened during her visit with Matan and as she neared the Way, the street filled with slaves and servants laden with baskets and boxes and loaves of bread tucked under their arms. Harried maids with long tails of children kept stopping to count heads just to make sure. Jewish elders in skullcaps bowed courteously and made sure the skirts of their gowns did not touch the skirt of her stola.

Someone jostled her from behind and threw a curt apology over his shoulder as he hustled on his way. He at least knew where he was going and what he was doing next. She envied him. She dodged a woman balancing an enormous bundle tied up in a brilliant yellow scarf on top of her head and reached the corner, threading her way through the usual cluster of boys standing ready to be dispatched on messages for the busy citizens of Alexandria. She recognized one of them, Babak, the slim Nubian from the day before. She smiled at him and he smiled back, and then his smile faded into a look of increasing horror as he looked behind her.

She prickled all over goosebumps and started to turn, too late, as she was enveloped in a length of cloth that smelled of paint. It was all that was allowed to register before she was swept from her feet, her shout of outrage muffled by the cloth, and dropped unceremoniously in a vehicle of some sort. She tried to scramble to her feet and was rocked backwards into a hard surface as the vehicle lurched forward.

A large weight settled onto her face that she realized was someone's foot and she was furious and tried to fight her way free of the cloth, to no avail. Another heavy weight, a second foot, was pressed hard against her legs. "Be still," a rough voice she did not recognize said. A man's voice. Greek, with a heavy accent. One accustomed to giving orders and being obeyed.

The vehicle turned a corner, hard, and she was slammed against one of the sides. The feet keeping her down slacked in pressure for a moment and instinctively she tried to move from beneath them, to free her hands at least. The pressure was immediately increased, harder this time. "Now, now," the voice said. "Fear not, lady. All we want to do is fit you with a nice new pair of sandals. All you ladies love new shoes, and we're going to give you a pair for free."

*A nice pair of sandals.*

A series of images flashed through her mind. The table

in the Shurta. The body on the beach the day before. The slurry of cement slowly thickening around their legs. The splash. The last gulp of air, the burning lungs, the sting of salt water in nose and throat and lungs. The long, slow descent through the water from light into darkness.

They went over a curb or a loose tile and the vehicle shuddered and creaked. The man swore fluently, in Egyptian this time.

She had been kidnapped.

The enveloping fabric entangled her limbs and smothered her face. She tried to breathe in and only succeeded in sucking the rough cloth into her mouth. She coughed and struggled and the foot on her head shifted to her throat and pressed down hard. "None of that now."

Her lungs screamed for air and her mind swam. As if from a great distance she could hear the hustle and bustle of the Way, the shouts of vendors, the haggling of housewives, the chattering of children. It was inconceivable that this was happening to her, Tetisheri of House Nebenteru, beloved niece, valued advisor, successful trader and the queen's own Eye. This could not be happening to her.

But it was.

Her mind struggled to grasp that one fact. It was slippery and elusive and determined to avoid close examination, until, suddenly, Isidorus' voice rang in her head like the bell in a Roman bath.

*"Remember your most important weapon is between your ears."*

She clung to that statement. What else had he said?

*"You are not large, Tetisheri, and you're a woman, which means you will never be able to build up the kind of muscle necessary to go toe to toe with a man, or men. I can teach you the basics and I will drill all three of you in them until you beg me for mercy, but surprise will always be your strength. Watch. Wait for the moment when your opponent drops their guard. Give them reason to believe you won't fight. Disarm them by making them think you're weak and afraid."*

*"And then what? If I'll never be strong enough to fight them, then what do I do?"*

*"Disarm them, disable them if you can, even if you only manage to throw them off balance. And then run away."*

*"Run away!"*

*"Yes, run away. If you can't win, and the odds will ever be against you in that regard, you can always run. As fast as you can. We'll be working on your wind and speed, too, all three of you."*

The carriage jolted again and the fabric over her face shifted, just a fraction, but it was enough. She took a great, greedy gasp of, no, not the salt water of her imaginings but of glorious, free Alexandrian air, muffled as it was by what she would not allow to become her shroud.

Her brain began to work again. The paralysis that had come with terror faded, to be replaced with a warming, welcome rage at this insult to her person and more, to her status. Who dared lay hands on Tetisheri of the House of

Nebenteru? Who dared offer this insult to the Eye of Isis, to the eyes and ears of the Lady of the Two Lands?

The insult would not go unanswered. With a forcible effort of will she relaxed, going limp, making sure it was felt by her captor. She was rewarded by a lessening of pressure on both her head and her legs. She forced a whimper.

"If you scream I will break your neck." The voice was low, certain, and studiedly indifferent as to her choice of action. She didn't believe him for a moment. If he'd wanted her dead he could have struck her down in the street and left her there. No, they must believe that she had answers to their questions, whatever those questions might be, so she was to be at least delivered alive.

How long she would remain so afterward was anyone's guess.

But with the lessening of pressure she could breathe again, and she took in more great gulps of air, and concentrated. The cloth restraining her resolved itself into a thin burlap before her straining eyes. It was a close weave but she could still see the shift of light as they moved past various buildings. That large shadow was surely the Library. She listened intently to the sound of the hoofbeats pulling the vehicle. Swift, sure, metal shoes striking stone, a horse, not a mule. She heard the slap of reins and saw another shift of shadows. Her captor was using his feet to hold her down and his hands to drive. Very probably he was alone.

The elation resulting from that realization cleared her head further, to assimilate more details. Babak. Babak had witnessed her abduction. The boy knew who she was and where she lived. He might, he just might alert her household, especially since Nebenteru had tipped him so well the day before.

More shadows passed. She strained to see. The Dicosterium. The Soma, perhaps. Others. They were moving swiftly now, with fewer stops and starts, indicating a lessening of the crowds thronging the Way. Suddenly she was thrown against the far surface of the cart and her captor's feet slipped.

He swore in fluent Egyptian. Ah. "Make way for your betters, you greasy little vagrant, before I drive right over the top of you!"

There was a flurry of return insults from the street, young voices, male and female, mocking, insulting, profaning all the gods there might be, and in Alexandria that was more than a few.

The man came halfway to his feet. "Out of the way, you mangy little beggars!"

His feet lost their purchase on her throat and legs and it was enough. She brought her feet together and her knees to her chest and kicked out as hard as she could. She smacked into something and was rewarded with a thud and the sound of flesh on wood and, hopefully, a crunch. The man who held her captive gave a bellow of outrage and pain. Now was not the time to discern which and she pushed herself to her feet and flung herself over the side head first, trying to roll as she fell. She landed hard on her shoulders but continued rolling forward to scramble to her feet. She made to throw off the burlap and found other hands there before hers. The first face she saw was Babak's.

"Hurry, miss, before he comes!"

She didn't need telling twice and found herself running for a side street surrounded by Babak and a group of other boys and girls. Around the first corner she stopped. "Wait!" she said. "Wait!"

"Agape, keep watch!" A ragged but clean girl detached herself from the group and went to stand at the corner, peering around at the street. "Lady, we must keep going. He may follow!"

"I don't think so. I think I hurt him." The street they had led her down was well chosen, too narrow to admit a cart or a chariot and, for the moment, deserted. She looked back at the boy. "Can you find me a cabrio? I want to follow him."

He looked startled. "Lady? But you just got free of him!"

"I need to know who he was and who he reports to." He hesitated. "There is a fee in it for you." She looked around at their faces. "For you all."

Babak smiled. "Agape! Roshanak! Did you hear?"

At the corner Agape turned her head. "He has given up the chase and is leaving. The lady was right, he is limping. If you want me to do something, say so now."

Another girl, just as ragged but with a bit of a swagger, looked Tetisheri up and down. "I see no coin."

"There will be coin enough for all," Tetisheri said. She

groped at her waist and, unbelievably, found her purse right where she'd left it. She gave it a shake, resulting in a jangle that brightened eyes all around. "All of this and twice again if you help me follow that man and find out who he is."

Everyone looked at Babak, who was clearly in charge. "Agape, follow him and don't lose him."

"And be careful!" Tetisheri said, belatedly realizing what she was asking. The payment for her delivery, alive, would not extend to these children.

The girl spared a moment for a scornful look and vanished around the corner without a word.

"Roshanak, follow Agape. Lay back but don't lose her! Narses, Bradan, find a cabrio. Quick about it now!"

The two boys disappeared after the girls.

"Babak," Tetisheri said, "you are a wonder. It was you and your friends who rescued me?"

"Lady, so far as I could see you rescued yourself." The grin lit up his thin face. "It was most efficient."

She rubbed her shoulder. "Not to mention graceful."

He laughed.

"Nevertheless, you created the opportunity for me to do so. I won't forget it."

"Babak!" One of the boys stood in the entrance to the street, waving.

Narses and Bradan waited by a cabrio with a grizzled elder at the reins who looked as if she'd been around since Ptolemy V. A plump, sedate mare with a clean coat, freshly brushed, stood patiently between the shafts. "Where to?" she said.

"I don't know," Tetisheri said, climbing in. She looked down at the boys. "Babak, could one of your people go to my house and report to my uncle as to these events?"

"Of course, lady." He spoke in an undertone to Narses.

She pulled the amulet of Bast over her head and held it out. "Here. Take this to show them I sent you. And wait there for us."

Narses accepted the pendant, looked at Babak for confirmation of his orders, and at his nod took off at a run, in the right direction, Tetisheri was relieved to see.

A marked clearing of throat came from their driver.

"Babak, will you and your friend come with me?"

From the expression on the boys' faces, a ride in a cabrio was a rare event in their lives. They jumped up next to her with alacrity.

"Where," the driver said patiently, "to?"

Tetisheri turned to look her full in the face for the first time. She was older, yes, with gray hair pulled into a neat knot at the back of her head. She wore a workmanlike tunic of tanned linen, and the cabrio badge that fastened her palla at the shoulder looked reassuringly worn and had been shined that morning. The hands that held the reins were clean and firm in their grip on the reins. "What is your name?"

"Rhode, lady." The driver mistook the meaning behind the question. "I am a member in good standing of Cabrio

Alexandria and my dues are paid up through the end of the year. Where were you wishing to go?"

The best of the cabrio drivers of Alexandria were human maps, the older ones especially holding the ever-changing rat's nests of Alexandrian side streets and rapidly emerging neighborhoods between their ears, updating and revising as new construction dictated. The worst were the youngest, who would stop at every intersection to ask the way, which would double the time of transit and the fare along with it.

Rhode carried herself with dignity and met Tetisheri's eyes without fear or favor, waiting for an answer. "Babak?" Tetisheri said.

He pulled himself to his feet, put two fingers in his mouth, and gave forth with a loud whistle. The horse shifted but stilled immediately when Rhode's grip tightened. Another good sign.

"There, lady," Babak said.

The other three craned their necks. The cabrio stood just beneath the Western Aqueduct where it ended at the Way. Tetisheri followed Babak's pointing finger and saw Roshanak waving vigorously at them from where the bridge spanned the course of the Nile Canal that led from Kibotos south and east to join with the great river. She gestured exaggeratedly at the street that paralleled the canal on its eastern bank.

"That way, Rhode, please," Tetisheri said but they were already in motion.

"Where are we going?"

"We are following someone."

"Who?"

"I don't know."

"What is he or she driving?"

"I don't know." Tetisheri ignored Rhode's impatient huff and looked at Babak.

"A small carriage, painted black, no house insignia," the boy said readily. "One horse, a gelding, a roan."

"What did the man who—what did the man driving it look like?"

"He was Egyptian, lady. Older. A serving man, at a guess some lord's personal bodyguard or servant. He has that ex-soldier look about him. He wore a dark blue tunic that had no house insignia, either. He had dark hair and eyes. He looked—" Babak hesitated.

"Yes?"

"Unhappy."

"Angry," Bradan said. "If he had been able to catch us he would have killed us, I think."

"Was he armed?"

Both boys nodded vigorously. "He wore a gladius and a dagger, lady."

"And wrist and shin guards," Bradan said. "Well used."

"Watch for the girl," Tetisheri said to Rhode. "Follow where she leads but stay well back. I don't want the man we are following to spot us."

"May one ask what this is all about?"

"Only after I find out," Tetisheri said. "You will be well

paid. I am Tetisheri the Trader, partner in Nebenteru's Luxury Goods."

"Ah." Rhode let up on the reins and the mare moved forward. "I am familiar with the firm."

Theirs was a dizzying route, threading a very crooked needle through side streets and back alleys. They might have passed the Serapeum. Tetisheri held on to the sides of the cabrio to avoid being thrown out and tried not to clench her teeth against the roughness of the ride, afraid she would chip one of them. The boys hung dangerously over opposite sides, pointing at Roshanak whenever she bobbed up to indicate a new direction. The Nile Canal appeared and disappeared from view.

Apart from one near collision with a vendor selling pomegranate juice, who raised her fist and screamed curses after them, and a temporary check caused by an enormous dray filled with gravel spilling over the sides, they managed to avoid outright mayhem.

When the traffic became almost entirely heavy carts loaded with stone and brick and mud and clay and gypsum and disassembled cranes and wooden forms and pile drivers and scaffolding, with bricklayers and stonemasons and carpenters and plumbers and roofers and landscapers on foot carrying the tools of their trade over their shoulders or pushing them in carts before them, Tetisheri knew they must be in Rhakotis. Everyone moved briskly and with purpose and no one looked hungry, slave or craftsman, in itself a comment on the state of the industry. A fine dust was incessantly kicked up into the air to form a permanent yellowish fog, and Tetisheri found herself on the verge of one continuous sneeze.

At the next cross street Agape and Roshanak waved them down. "He drove into the stables belonging to a house in the next street, lady."

Tetisheri climbed down to the street. "Please wait, Rhode. You will convey the lot of us to my home when we conclude our business here."

"I will?"

"She will?"

"Show me," Tetisheri said to the girls.

# 13

On the other side of the teeming street sat a square bulk behind a high brick wall that looked as if it might successfully withstand assault by a Roman legion. The crowns of date palms planted behind the wall formed a living hedge along the top, and the roof of the building it enclosed supported a small forest of its own. Towers with wind catchers stood at all four corners of the building and narrow slits lined the walls beneath a modest cornice. There was a doorway at street level, the double doors made of plain ironwood hanging from bronze hinges. Guards, large men and well armed, stood on either side of the door. They didn't look bored.

Next to the house and dwarfing it was an immense yard, also walled and equal in size to Otho's. It might even have been busier. Double doors were folded back to allow for near constant traffic in and out. Inside she glimpsed some representation of every part of the builder's trade being energetically pursued. The din was deafening and the smell of fresh sawdust overwhelming. Pyramids of logs belted to flat carts went into the gates and newly planed planks of lumber came out in neatly stacked bundles on other carts, bound for a building site somewhere in the city. Enormous carts hauled by equally enormous bullocks yoked six at a time and laden with stone chipped raw from some distant cliff rumbled into the yard, and carts filled with precisely stacked, perfectly planed, exquisitely dressed blocks of pink granite from Syene and white marble from Petraea trundled out again. Four-sided carts heaped with raw clay went in and piping in every diameter came out. Over it all the shouts and curses of the foremen rose in an infuriated wave of sound that on occasion drowned out the rasp of saw on wood and the ring of chisel and hammer on stone. As they watched someone screamed and a few short moments later two men hustled out of the gate with a stretcher between them, carrying a man bleeding profusely from his left thigh.

No, construction in Alexandria was definitely not a job for the faint of heart.

"Where did the cart go?" she asked the girls.

They pointed to what appeared to be a small stable joined to the house on the left and the construction yard on the right. She moved as if to step out into the street for a closer look and they held her back. "No, lady. Stay in the shadow. You can see him from here. Only look."

She did as they bade her. As she blinked the dust from her eyes the scene across from the busy street came into focus.

The stable was recessed from the two buildings on either

side, forming a small, empty courtyard. The two doors were only half open but she could see a man clad in a neat tunic and kilt. He looked vaguely familiar. She stared, frustrated for a moment not to be able to place him, and then she had it. Khadiga's servant, the man driving her carriage that morning.

So. Tetisheri was pleased to see that Agape was right and he was limping, heavily. And she was pretty sure she knew who owned the house and yard.

He untacked the horse and led it into a stall, pitching an armful of hay in after it. He dipped a leather bucket into a tun and carried it dripping to the stall and closed the stall door. He left the stable and went to a door inset into the wall of the house.

His shoulders rose and fell on a deep breath. The portrait, Tetisheri thought, of a man about to report a failed mission to his employer.

He knocked. The door opened immediately and he was admitted.

She led the way back to the cabrio. "Babak, you're known to my house. I would like Rhode to take you there so you can tell them where I am."

"Just me?"

"All of you but one. I need one of you to remain in case. Your choice."

He didn't hesitate. "Agape."

The girl nodded. "Good," Tetisheri said. "Rhode, can you find your way back here?"

"Certainly I can," Rhode said. "Although I've yet to be paid for coming here once."

"Babak, will you mind Rhode's horse for her for a moment?"

Babak looked thrilled at the very idea, Rhode less so, but she waited for Babak to take hold of the mare's cheek strap and stepped down to the street to follow Tetisheri, who stopped just out of earshot.

"Lady, I don't know what—"

Tetisheri reached into the neck of her stola and pulled the Eye out just far enough for Rhode to see it. "Do you know what this signifies?"

Rhode gaped for a moment.

"Sorry," Tetisheri said.

In her time as a cabrio Rhode had evidently paid attention to the language she heard every day in the streets of Alexandria, and she gave voice to it all on one extended exhale. When she ran out of breath she just glared. Tetisheri waited her out. "I really am sorry, Rhode, and I promise you will be paid and handsomely. The queen does not forget her friends."

"I would very much rather that she did," Rhode said with feeling.

I know just how you feel, Tetisheri thought, but said soothingly, "The Lady of the Two Lands will see that you do not suffer by your service to her." She replaced the Eye inside her bodice. "My command to you is not onerous. I require that you take Babak and his friends to my home. Tell them that it is my wish they remain there until I return, and to be shown the hospitality of the house."

"And then I'll be paid?"

"And then you will return here to await me, to bring me home. And, ah, Agape."

"And then I'll be paid?"

"Do you doubt the ability of the queen's coffers to meet your demands?"

She could hear Rhode's teeth grinding together. "No, lady, although I do worry that working with the Eye of Isis herself will leave me little time to enjoy my reward."

There was that, but Tetisheri could not allow it to be a consideration. "Please do as I say, Rhode, and then return here to this exact place and wait for my return."

"As the Eye wishes." This was said with immense sarcasm but in a nearly inaudible voice as she was returning to her cabrio, so Tetisheri decided to overlook it. And really, how could she blame the cabriador for saying out loud what she had so often thought herself? And she wasn't even a year into the job.

*How could she place such a burden on you of all people, her oldest, her most dear, and her most loyal friend, the one person in Alexandria who she knows would die before she did her harm?*

She shook off the memory of Matan's words, because really, what other recourse had she, and beckoned to Agape as the cabrio began to clatter off behind them. "I need to know who lives in that house."

Agape, a too-thin sprite whose eyes were too old for her face, said, "As you wish, lady. How, exactly?"

"I want you to wait here. I'm going to reconnoiter." Agape looked blank and Tetisheri said, "I'm going to walk around the house and yard to see what I can see."

"But you are known to them, lady. The man who took you is in that house. What if he sees you?"

Tetisheri glanced up at the sky and then at the lengthening shadows cast by the buildings beneath. It was coming up on Tenth Hour, or Fourth Hour by Caesar's reckoning. More workers were beginning to leave the yard than enter it. "Wait here. If I'm not back by full dark, have Rhode take you to my house and have them send Apollodorus to find me." She thought of the body on the beach and repressed a shudder. "But I will be."

The girl's eyes widened. "Apollodorus?" Her voice rose into a squeak. "Lady—"

"Quiet." Tetisheri's tone silenced the girl, although her expression was mutinous. "Tell them—" She paused. "Tell them I said to come quickly."

She pulled her palla over her head and draped it so that her face was hidden, and set out across the street with much more confidence than she felt.

There were two guards at the doors of both the house on the left and the yard on the right. The ones in front of the house looked idle, in contrast to the ones who guarded the entrance to the yard, who challenged everyone on the way in and checked all bundles, boxes, carts, and wagons on the way out.

Tetisheri dodged through the traffic, angling her way toward the house, and slowed her steps, trying to remember how Cleopatra moved her hips whenever she was around Caesar and making a good faith effort to copy it. The effort threw her off balance and she didn't have to pretend to stumble. She uttered a muffled oath in a vexed tone and bent to dislodge a nonexistent stone from her sandal. The guards both took notice, as how could they not when she was aiming her behind right at them. "Are you in a difficulty, pretty lady? May I help?"

His partner, an older man, was sitting on a three-legged stool, a knife in one hand and a piece of wood in the other. He gave Tetisheri an appreciative look, and went back to his whittling.

She gave a poor imitation of a breathless giggle—this flirtation business was not her forte—and replied in the most dulcet tones she could, "That is most kind, sir. I'm afraid I'm late for my appointment with—"

She paused artistically and, well, he was only a man showing off for a pretty girl and as such inclined to be loquacious. "Are you a friend of Khadiga, lady?"

She pushed her palla back a little and did her best to twinkle at him. "Why, yes, I am, and I'm afraid I'm late."

He looked at her face and brightened. "It's quite all right, lady. The mistress is in the yard at present, attending to business," he said, gesturing next door. "She should return momentarily."

"She may have forgotten our appointment," Tetisheri said, pouting.

He leered. "Impossible, lady."

Having learned what she wanted to know, she was about to make some excuse and extricate herself from a situation that could go sideways at any moment, when behind her there was an approaching rattle of hooves and wheels and a large wagon pulled in before the stable. It was drawn by two oxen and piled high with large canvas sacks. Two men sat before them, one of them on the reins and both of them armed. They carried themselves with the lazy arrogance of legionaries and she was sure they were former soldiers in the Roman army, although not Roman themselves. One was tall and fair, a Saxon. The other, the one holding the reins, was broad-shouldered and dark of hair and eye; from Hispania, she thought.

The guards distracted, she slipped across the street and behind a food cart doing a brisk business in rolls of flat bread filled with spiced minced goat and grain. She could smell the mint in it from where she stood and her stomach growled. The vendor cast her a quizzical look but said nothing. A few minutes later he passed her half a roll. She contrived to drop a drachma on his cart, which disappeared as fast as the roll did.

Meanwhile, the Saxon dropped down to the ground

and trotted around to the door Tetisheri's abductor had closed behind him. He knocked, and then hammered when there wasn't an immediate answer. The Hispanian shouted something at him and he shouted something back. They both looked hot, dirty, and impatient, as if at the end of a very long, very tiresome day, and when the door opened the Saxon shouted shouted at whomever was standing behind it. The noise of the street blocked out the words, and then the door opened wider and Tetisheri's Egyptian abductor stood revealed.

He shouted something at the Hispanian and the Saxon moved into the street to direct traffic as the Hispanian, with a maximum amount of swearing, backed the recalcitrant oxen, who looked hot and tired, too, so that the laden cart reversed into the stable.

Tetisheri took advantage of the minor uproar to ghost up the street and around the opposite side of the yard. No one saw her and she took a moment to be pleased with herself before continuing to skirt the wall. There was very little space between the wall surrounding the yard and the wall of the building next to it—a warehouse, she thought—and little light filtered down. She paced forward carefully, with each step feeling for debris or rough ground, anything that might cause a trip and fall. She wondered why the guards didn't make an hourly perambulation around the perimeter, and indeed why Khadiga hadn't bothered with lanterns to light its length, and concluded that the height and thickness of the wall must be deemed enough of a deterrent to those who might be unwontedly interested. Such as herself.

She also wondered about the buildings nearest the wall, and how it came about that none of them had windows facing this alley. There were lots on this street where remained only the ruins of previous houses or businesses. She wondered if she investigated their owners who those owners might prove to be, although she thought she could make a pretty good guess. This street and its surroundings, including the vacant lots and derelict buildings that isolated it, had the feeling of being carefully constructed so as to ensure an absence of oversight.

She came to the end of the north-facing wall and peered around the corner. The alley was walled off between the wall around the yard and the house next door, but it was an old wall made of wood that had dried out and shrunk so that there were large gaps between the boards. She put her eye to one and retreated precipitately, her heart thundering in her ears. The wagon had been backed into the stable now and through it to the alley, which appeared to be in use as a storage area.

What was in the wagon—and the boxes, bags, and kegs crowding both sides of the alley for that matter—that could not be unloaded in the yard on the other side of the wall? In full view of anyone passing? With the knowledge of the craftsmen working there?

The tailgate had been let down. The men were unloading

the bags with swift, silent efficiency, although the weight of each bag caused their legs to bow.

"Is this the end of it?" she heard someone say.

"Yes."

"Good. Tell them to head upriver immediately and to stay in Syene until I send for them again."

"Ma'am, Minius is insisting on a break. He says his crew hasn't—"

"Sobek take Minius and his crew straight to hell! They're getting their share and ten times what they are worth at that." A brief pause. "Tell Minius I said the queen is starting to sniff around and that if he wants to explain to her personally what we've been doing for the past two years I'll be happy to leave him to it."

"The queen?" The apprehension in those two words was plain.

"One of her people. What she knows, the queen knows. Tell Minius I said to stay there until he hears from me. His crew can take their break in Syene."

A whispered colloquy. A clearing of throat. "I think the two of us will travel upriver with Minius this trip."

"A very sound idea." The woman's voice was very dry.

"What about me?"

This voice was fearful, too, fearful, and... familiar. Tetisheri put her eye again to the gap.

She saw a clump of people outlined by the last of the day's light as it slanted in through the stable doors from the street outside. A stocky figure she recognized as Khadiga's stood facing away from her, draped in a rich red stola that brushed the ground with a disregard for the worth of the fabric only a very rich woman could display. Her black hair was knotted in a much more elaborate style than last seen, a testimony to the employment of at least two personal maids. Her voice was deep and vibrant with contempt. "What about you, little worm?"

"What shall I do? Where shall I go?"

Nenwef? Tetisheri dared another glimpse. The fading light outlined his slender figure, glowing with rich fabrics and gems as tasteless as they were expensive.

"I've served you well, lady. I brought you word of things no one else heard or could have."

"And you were well paid for it."

The whine was more pronounced this time, with just the hint of an underlying threat beneath it. "But what will I do if they question me? What will I say? You know what the queen is like, you've heard the stories. I can't promise I—"

"Taki, Goyo," the woman said.

The rest of what Nenwef was saying ended in a muffled squeak. Tetisheri risked another look just in time to see Nenwef bundled into what was likely the same length of burlap she had been caught in herself and tossed just as unceremoniously into the wagon.

"What are we supposed to do with him?" the Saxon said.

"He has become a nuisance. See to him for me, please." The sound of a heavy purse being caught.

"At your command, lady."

"Tell Minius I said not to take the *Cameli* on the canal. Yes, I know he has been doing so on the return trips, against my express orders I might add, but this time tell him I said not to."

"He won't like that."

"I doubt he would like being boarded by one of the queen's customs agents, either. Tell him I said to take the delta, and that if I discover he has disobeyed me not to bother returning."

"As you wish, lady."

The two guards were up on the seat with the oxen immediately in motion. The Egyptian had the stable doors closed in the next moment. Khadiga had gone inside the house. He followed her, silhouetted against the lamplight inside for just long enough for Tetisheri to see that he was still limping before the door closed behind them.

Tetisheri backed up a few noiseless steps until she judged herself far enough out of earshot, and then turned and moved rapidly back the way she had come. By the time she reached the street again the wagon was rumbling out of sight around a corner. At that moment she heard Rhode shout, "Shove over, you son of a harpy! You damned Romans always think you own the streets!"

There was a fearful crunch and Rhode's cabrio lurched through the narrow gap and clunked over the street stones behind a mare that was considerably wider of eye than she had been the last time Tetisheri had seen her.

The older guard on the door of the house had stopped

whittling long enough to look over his shoulder at the commotion and Rhode shouted at him. "Keep your eyes to yourself, old man, this woman drives as she pleases!" and thumped and banged her way past and around a corner and out of sight.

Tetisheri stifled a laugh and slipped from the alley, crossed the street and walked swiftly after Rhode. The guard who had flirted with her noticed and whistled. "Hey, gorgeous! Oh, come on, honey, be Venus to my Mars and make all my dreams come true! Come over here and share wine with a lonely man, do!"

Tetisheri managed a breathless giggle and put on speed.

His fellow guard slapped the back of his head with the flat of his hand. "We're not paid to pick up girls, you idiot. Keep your mind on the job." But he, too, gave Tetisheri an appraising look before she whisked herself around a corner and saw Rhode's cabrio outlined against the light of a lantern set next to a door, Agape peering at her over the side. She broke into a run and tumbled inside.

Rhode slapped the reins against the mare's back and they were off. "I presume I now have the extreme good fortune of taking you home and leaving you there?"

# 14

Tetisheri took her first full breath since leaving the Jewish Quarter, and met Rhode's eyes. Maybe it was the effect of a very long, very fraught day. Maybe it had something do with the exhilaration of escaping her own pair of Rhakotis sandals. Maybe it was just the mere fact of being alive and free. Whatever the reason the cabriador's indignant expression struck her as uproariously funny. She burst out laughing and couldn't stop. Helpless, she lay back in the seat and laughed loud and long and the more she laughed the more indignant Rhode became and the funnier Tetisheri found it.

When at last she ran down she gulped and choked and managed to say, "I'm sorry, Rhode, but no. We need to follow that wagon. The one that just left."

The outrage in Rhode's expression set her off again. By the time Tetisheri managed to regain some semblance of composure they had emerged from the warren of streets in Rhakotis and had crossed the Canopic Way. The

Heptastadion was visible on the right. Tetisheri guessed that they were close to the Gate of the Moon. "Do we have them in sight?"

"I haven't lost them." Rime formed on the cabriador's words.

"Good," Tetisheri said, feeling the hilarity beginning to bubble up again beneath her breastbone and repressing it with a stern effort of will. "I don't want to approach them, I just want to see where they are going."

There was no rejoinder. Tetisheri resigned herself to a frosty journey, and concentrated on stopping the hiccups her laughing fit had inspired. She had to find a place to relieve herself, too, and soon.

*Tell Minius I said not to take the* Cameli *on the canal.*

*Cameli* must be the name of the boat and Minius the name of its master. The Nile Canal, besides providing a water view to those lucky enough to own property on it, like Otho, was a waterway of immense importance to the city, routinely cleaned of debris and dredged of silt and with its own body of supervisors, regulators and engineers. Careful note was made of its traffic by customs agents and tax assessors. Entering the city with a cargo, the scrutiny of city officials could not be avoided. If your ship was empty, however, it would be the quickest route back upriver and if this Minius was anything like every ship's captain she had ever met, time wasted taking the sea route from the city to the delta was money lost. Not to mention the additional danger from pirates who waited in the Middle

Sea to pick ships clean of cargoes for resale and crews for slaves.

Goyo must have had excellent night vision because the dray eeled its way through the Gordian knot of Rhakotis' streets to emerge unscathed on the Canopic Way, where it turned left. Rhode paralleled their route on the first street south of the Way, keeping far enough behind to stay out of sight and hearing.

"You're very good at this," Tetisheri said, hoping a little admiration of the cabriador's skill might not come amiss.

Rhode grunted.

They passed beneath the Gate of the Moon without incident, the guards on duty waving both vehicles through with only a cursory challenge as to their identities and destination. All impulse to laugh was quenched when Tetisheri realized they were headed to the same area to which Aristander had called her the day before. The wagon disappeared into the jumble of homes and businesses lining the beach very near to where the body had been recovered.

"Wait here," she told Rhode and Agape, and stepped down from the cabrio. It was easy enough to slip from shadow to shadow. There was the aroma of a hundred dinners wafting through the air and the sound of talk and laughter through open windows. She ducked beneath all the windowsills, narrowly missed tripping over a child-sized chariot, blundered into a trellis of peas where she stopped briefly to pick a handful, got tangled up in a carpet some industrious housewife had hung to beat and left there to obstruct the footsteps of unwary Eyes, wet herself to the knee in a communal fountain, accidentally kicked a cat who put up an indignant howl, and staggered out from an alley barely wide enough to permit her passage onto the beach. It was dark enough by now that she knew this first by the sand clumping between her wet toes. Stealthy she was not and it could only have been by the intervention of the divine Bast that she hadn't alerted every wrongdoer in the entire city to her presence.

Low voices alerted her and she crouched behind the nearest large object, which proved to be a coil of hempen rope as thick as her wrist.

"What in the name of Geri and Freki are we supposed to do with him?"

"We could wait till we're outside the harbor and put him over the side."

"By Odin's remaining eye! He's the son of some nobleman or other; they'll have our hides if we touch a hair of his pwecious widdle head."

"We've already done more than that." A mutter of Hispanian in a dialect unknown to Tetisheri. "She told us to see to him. What do you think she meant by that? Gods above, you've seen how she treats her own daughter. What do you think she'll do to us if she thinks we've disobeyed her?"

A muffled squeal and some agitated squeaks. Nenwef, who undoubtedly knew exactly what Khadiga had meant.

Overhead the stars were beginning to wink into existence.

As her eyes accustomed themselves to the diminished light, she saw the wagon and the oxen with the two guards standing next to it. They stood at the land end of a, what was it, promontory? She squinted, willing her eyes to come into focus. Everything came together all at once and she knew exactly where she was. "Hathor's sacred cow!" For a moment she was afraid she'd said it out loud but the two men didn't flinch. Her heart thundering in her ears, she crouched down behind the coil of rope and listened with both her ears.

"We could take him to Syene with us." Taki, she thought.

"I don't fancy listening to him whine all the way upriver." A pause. "But you're right, Taki. We didn't sign on as assassins, we signed on as guards. Much better to leave that kind of thing to Tamir. It's what she hired him for."

Tamir. An Egyptian name. Khadiga's personal servant?

A sigh. "Fine. Let's load him in. But I'm leaving the gag on him until we're well out of the city."

"You can leave it on him as far as Syene as far as I'm concerned. What do we do with the cart?"

"Leave it here. If she wants it she can send someone to fetch it."

They looped the leading rein around a bollard and left the oxen and wagon where they were. The Saxon slung Nenwef over his shoulder and both men trotted down the ramp connecting the dock to a single small slip, next to which, now that she looked for it, she could see a boat bobbing. A lantern flashed on deck and was as quickly hidden. A rumble of voices, a thud of feet on deck, a dip of oars, and a rustle of sailcloth. The black shape of the ship parted from the slip and melted into the darkness.

Through trial and error and an accidental intrusion into a romantic tryst between two lovers she was fairly certain were not married to each other, Tetisheri made her way back to the cabrio. By some miracle, Rhode was still there, waiting. Fulminating, too, but waiting nevertheless. Agape was crouched in a corner, arms wrapped around her knees.

Tetisheri climbed up beside her and held out her hand with an ingratiating smile. "Peas?"

Tetisheri was allowed one knock before the door was yanked from her hand. There stood Keren, Phoebe, Nebet, and Nike, with Uncle Neb looming up behind, all with anxious expressions on their faces. Bast wove between their feet, giving voice to her thoughts, which didn't sound at all complimentary.

"Tetisheri!" They surged forward in a body and buffeted her with embraces and admonitory slaps against any portion of her anatomy nearest their hands. "Thank all the gods!"

"What did you mean by sending us those messages, you atrocious girl! Frightening us all out of a day's life, I never!"

"Tetisheri, you will get yourself inside immediately and give us an accounting of your behavior!"

Nike merely scowled but Uncle Neb's roar could have been heard at the Palace. "I was ready to call out the Shurta, girl!"

Behind them she saw Babak and Company shrink a little. She reached out to pat his arm when she was allowed to move of her own volition. "They're not dangerous, just loud. Stay for something to eat, and for a night's rest under cover. I have work for you this evening, and I want to talk to you in the morning, too." She looked at Nike as she spoke.

Nike gave Babak and Company a disapproving once-over but saw them installed in the kitchen with a full plate before each of them. Tetisheri waved off her anxious family, who surrounded her like twittering birds, and went to her office. There she wrote two notes, supervised by Bast, who was also pleased to continue to offer her commentary on Tetisheri's behavior. "Yes, yes, I am properly chastised," she said, trying not to scribble in her haste. Demotic was difficult enough to read without the writer being sloppy, but it was less common in written form than Greek and afforded some protection in case the notes went astray.

The first note was by far the longest, the second only a few lines. When she had finished the first two, she wrote a third, this one in Latin. It took longer to write than the first two but she didn't know this correspondent well and wanted to make herself perfectly clear. She sealed all three notes with wax, a security measure she seldom employed, and went to find Babak. Between a full belly and the warmth of the kitchen fire his four friends were already dozing off on the hearth rug. He looked a little sleepy himself, but he woke up when he saw her. "Lady?" he said in a low voice.

She beckoned him out of earshot of his friends. "Take this one—you see here, with the double crown drawn next to the seal—to the Royal Palace. Ask for Charmion. Deliver it into no one's hands but hers, do you understand?"

His eyes widened, both at the mention of the palace and the stern note in her voice. "I understand, lady."

"Do you know where the Five Soldiers is?"

He grinned. "Everyone knows where the Five Soldiers is, lady."

"Good. Take this one there. Ask for Isidorus. Again, into no one else's hand, do you understand?"

"Lady, I do."

She held out the third note. "This will be more difficult. All I know is that he lodges near the Heptastadion. This late you will have to knock on some doors to find it."

He contrived a creditable bow. "It shall be done, lady."

"You're not afraid to travel across Alexandria after dark?"

"The work goes quicker in the dark, lady. No crowds to contend with. And I am fleet of foot."

"I saw that earlier." She looked him over, and again she liked what she saw. Intelligent eyes, a quick mind, a determinedly professional appearance, or as near as one could get to it living in the streets. He had blue-black skin and long limbs and was tall for his years. A Nubian, like Nike, she had no doubt. "If Charmion has you wait for a reply, wait. Otherwise, return here when you have delivered all three messages. Come round to the back. I'll tell Phoebe to leave the kitchen door unlocked." She looked over his shoulder at the four other children piled together in front of the fire. Bradan snored, and Roshanak drooled. Or perhaps it was the other way around. "Always together, you and these friends of yours?"

His shoulders stiffened and he looked her straight in the eye. "Lady, we are. We are a company."

All or none, then. She nodded. "Very well. I have an idea in mind for you and your friends that will benefit us all, if you are willing."

"And what might that be?"

She shook her head. "At the moment you have work to do. Let us meet tomorrow in my office after you break your fast." He brightened, no doubt at the thought of another free meal, and no wonder. "We will discuss it then." She quirked an eyebrow. "Of course, all depends on the speed and efficiency of your completing the tasks I have set for you now."

He smiled his answer and was gone in a rush that raised dust from all four corners of the room. "We are going to rename you Hermes," she said to the empty air, and went in to join her family at dinner, not without some trepidation, which, as it transpired, was fully warranted. For one thing, Rhode had joined them at table. "Ah," Tetisheri said after a beat, "I'm glad you could join us, Rhode," and reached for the cucumbers and yogurt.

The dishes circulated around the table, plates were filled expeditiously, and Tetisheri hoped mouths filled soon thereafter.

But not for long, and certainly not long enough for Tetisheri to eat her fill and escape. She was very hungry indeed, having eaten nothing but a handful of peas since that kindly vendor had given her half a roll, and she had yet to clear her plate of her first helping when Uncle Neb cleared his throat.

"Tetisheri."

Not Teti, not Sheri, not "light of my life," not "daughter of my heart," but her name in full. Oh dear.

"Rhode—" he inclined his head toward their guest, who inclined hers as graciously back—"Rhode has seen fit to inform us where you spent your time these hours past." His stare sharpened into a glare. "When you were casting your household into disarray with multiple messages informing us that you were fine, just fine and not to worry but that you might be late for dinner."

She scraped up the last of the kofta and luxuriated in the taste of ground lamb, garlic and onions. She reached for the medames and ladled a generous portion onto her plate. The beans looked lonely so she took the last piece of bread.

She became aware of the silence around the table and looked up.

"When was the last time you ate?" Keren said.

She chewed and swallowed. "A real meal? Breakfast, I think." She stared down at her plate, empty again, and debated whether to refill it, but the simmering outrage radiating from the head of the household advised against it. She dipped her hands in the water bowl and dried them on her napkin. "I'm sorry, Uncle. I was a little preoccupied there for a few moments. You were saying?"

He swelled up like a Nile toad, and then, unexpectedly, Rhode stepped in. "Have you not told them?"

Uncle Neb looked even more thunderous. "Not told us what?"

"Don't—"

"This is your family!" Rhode was aghast. "They don't know?"

"Know what?" Phoebe said.

Rhode stared accusingly at Tetisheri.

Tetisheri had seen this coming ever since she accepted the queen's commission, but she had been hoping to put it off just a little longer.

Bast chose this moment to leap up on the table and sit down next to Tetisheri's plate, where she curled her tail around her precisely placed feet and fixed Tetisheri with an unwinking blue stare. She might be proof against her family but never against Bast.

"As the goddess wills," she said, only half in jest. She looked around the table. "That business with the missing coin? I looked into it at the queen's request, and afterward she was pleased to name me the new Eye of Isis." She pulled out the Eye and held it up.

There followed a long silence. Tetisheri bowed her head before the oncoming storm.

"Is that all?" Keren said. "I guessed that when you asked me to look at Khemit's body."

Tetisheri's head came up.

"Was this meant to be some big mystery?" Phoebe said, rising to begin stacking the serving dishes. "All this toing and froing between here and the palace. Of course Cleopatra has you working for her. Who else can she trust?"

"Apollodorus," Uncle Neb said, frowning at her.

"Well, Apollodorus, yes, and perhaps Aristander, but you know as well as I do, Nebenteru, that there are people lining up all the way around the city wall to subvert and suborn the queen's rule. And that doesn't even include her nasty little brother and that bunch of malcontents he keeps close by him at his court."

"No one is supposed to know," Tetisheri said weakly. Everyone laughed, and Bast, with a look of infinite superiority, began washing her ear. "Uncle Neb?"

"I guessed, but I do not approve, Tetisheri. The business suffers when you are away."

"Did it suffer today?" she said.

Really, she had not meant to be pert, but Keren turned a laugh into a cough and made a show of studying the juice inside her glass.

Neb ignored them both with lofty dignity. "And while I

understand why you made this choice, I am not happy when it puts you in danger." He glared around the table. "And causes your family anxiety!"

Tetisheri digested this in silence for a moment. So Aristander knew, and all of the Five Soldiers knew, and Matan knew, and Rhode knew, and now her entire household knew. "I'm sorry, Uncle," she said at last. "I'm sorry, everyone. I'll try not to do so again."

"See that you don't. Did you discover who it was that laid hands upon you?"

"Ah—"

"You cannot say. Very well. No doubt the queen will know how to deal with such persons. And if she doesn't, I most certainly do." Neb rose to his considerable height, put his nose in the air, and sailed out of the room, the pearl at the point of his beard quivering with wounded dignity.

Keren met Tetisheri's eyes. "Inevitable," she said. "And at least your skin is still whole."

A snort drew their attention to the other end of the table. Rhode stacked her cup on her plate and rose to her feet. "I do not know how I allowed myself to become part of this—this—"

"Cabal?" Keren said blandly.

Tetisheri hid a laugh. "Rhode, truly you have been most inconvenienced this day, I agree, but for this night, please accept the hospitality of our house. Your horse and cabrio have been accommodated in our stable, have they not? Good. It is far too late for you to go home, and besides, there is something I wish to discuss with you tomorrow morning. Phoebe?"

"I'll make up a bed."

Rhode would have protested but she was looking as tired and grubby as Tetisheri felt and made only a token protest before following Phoebe out of the room.

"Keren, I forgot to mention this this morning, but you and Neb and I have been invited to a party tomorrow."

"Where?"

"Rhakotis."

"Who invited us?"

"Otho." At Keren's look of bewilderment she elaborated. "The Master of Builders."

Keren whistled.

"Exactly."

"Something to do with—"

"Yes, but I don't know exactly what, yet."

Keren said shrewdly, "And with the little matter of your abduction today?"

"Again, yes, and again, I don't know what." But she was beginning to have an idea.

"Have you informed Apollodorus?"

"No. Not yet."

Keren's eyebrows went up. "My recommendation? Before you do, remove yourselves to several leagues beyond the city walls."

Out of nowhere came the memory of Apollodorus strolling into Philo's court two months before. Supremely casual, utterly confident, and undeniably deadly. "He's not here tonight," she said, and the words sounded forlorn even to her own ears.

"And thank Hashem for it," Keren said. "If we were upset can you imagine his reaction?"

Tetisheri was unable to repress a shiver. Of fear? Or anticipation?

"Uh-huh," Keren said. "Have you informed Neb about tomorrow's festivities?"

Tetisheri shook her herself back into the present. "In the morning. You know he'll come; he loves a party. Will you attend?" She smiled sideways at her friend. "Bring Simon, if you like."

Keren flicked a bean at her.

# 15

Babak was there the following morning with replies from all three of her correspondents. She read through them quickly, and looked back up at Babak, standing more or less at attention before her.

He and his friends had risen with the rest of the household and broken their fast around the kitchen table. Everyone ignored the fact that the five of them ate as much as a cohort of legionnaires. As hungry as they were, their manners were surprisingly good. Tetisheri noted that their language was less foul than the average street urchin's— although she had fond memories of some of the choice epithets hurled at Tamir as they'd thwarted yesterday's kidnapping attempt—and though their clothes were ragged it was obvious they had made some attempt to keep them clean and mended.

"Bring your friends," she said. "I have a proposition for you."

They assembled willingly enough. Full bellies and a warm

night inside did amazing things for one's attitude. "Babak, let me begin with you."

Babak was ten years of age. His father had been under arms in Auletes' service, and had been killed in the Battle of the Nile. His mother had sickened and died not long afterward and Babak had been thrown onto the streets. There he had lived since, sleeping in alleys and abandoned buildings and begging scraps from back doors and running messages, earning enough to survive, just. It was not an unfamiliar story in Alexandria. "You've had some schooling," she said.

He looked surprised. "Why, yes, lady. Before she married my mother was nursemaid to a noble's daughter and she learned with her charge as she was tutored. She in turn taught me." His brow creased. "How did you know?"

"You were able to read the names on the notes I sent out last night. Do you read more than Demotic?"

"Well. Some Latin. Greek, of course." At her look he shifted on his feet and color ran up beneath his skin. "Enough to understand an address on a message, anyway."

She nodded. "How many languages do you speak?"

"Greek, lady, and Latin. Some Egyptian. A few Nubian oaths."

The stories of the other four were much the same. Agape, the youngest, had been on the street the longest, four years; Babak, the eldest, almost two. Agape spoke Alemanni, Narses Parthian, Roshanak Egyptian, and they were all fluent in Greek. Three of them were illegitimate, cast off by their families as soon as they could walk out of the house. Better than sold into slavery, which was what had happened to Bradan, who had escaped his master, although he refused to give any details other than that he had arrived in Alexandria as a stowaway on a trading vessel. Tetisheri was about to inquire further when she saw Babak give his head a tiny shake.

So instead she said, "It happens that I may have a use for you."

"All of us?" Babak said quickly.

"All of you. In my work I have need of fast, reliable runners, to carry messages back and forth across the city." And perhaps one day outside the city as well, she thought. "This is what I propose: That in exchange for providing me that service, the five of you will be housed, clothed, and fed, and earn one drachma each per week."

"Only one drachma!" Roshanak, naturally. "We might as well be in the hands of pirates!"

But she didn't stomp off in a dudgeon, and Tetisheri hid a smile. "One drachma per week. You will undoubtedly be offered tips and those are yours to keep as well." She fixed them with a stern eye. "There is one rule, ladies and gentlemen, and one rule only. You are never, ever, to speak of my business to anyone except me, not without my authorization. Do you understand? You may not brag to your friends about your new situation, or to anyone you might meet while at work, or to a random stranger on the street. If the queen herself asks, you will refer her royal majesty to me."

She paused, meeting their eyes one by one. "If you break

this rule, you will immediately be terminated from my employment, all five of you, and shown the door. Are we understood?" They nodded, their faces serious, and their expressions encouraged her to confide in them, just a little. "This is not only because I am jealous of my privacy, but because it will be safer for everyone in this household that my business not be generally known."

"What harm comes to a trader?" Narses, silenced by a gesture from Babak, who said, "Board and room and clothing, a drachma a week, and we get to keep our tips."

"Correct."

"Where will we live?"

"There are living quarters over our stable. You'll take your meals in our kitchen. You, Babak, appear to be the leader of your company." She waited but no one contradicted her. "Very well. It will be up to you to arrange your shifts. One of you must be on duty every hour, day and night. There may be times when I will require all of you to run messages or errands at once. Your work schedule is likely to be erratic." She sat back. Bast, supervising the negotiations from her perch on the desk, gave an inquiring chirrup.

"Well, Babak, do you and yours accept my commission?"

Uncle Neb was standing in the hallway with a bemused expression on his face, watching the flow of street urchins around him and back toward the kitchen. "What's all this?"

"Meet our new pages."

"Ah." His face cleared. "Excellent, more men in the house. I was beginning to feel outnumbered."

"Well—"

His smile faded. "What?"

"I was thinking that our stable has been empty since we went to Punt."

With foreboding, he said, "Yes?"

"I was talking to Rhode this morning. If we made her an offer I think she might be agreeable to coming to work for us. I told her she could have one of the apartments over the stable for her own."

"And you are reserving the other, I suppose, as a dormitory for our new pages? Are we quite sure Rhode wants to live across the hall from a lot of rambunctious youngsters?" He shook his head in mock reproof. "Pages, our own cabrio— what next? None of this is going to come cheap, Tetisheri."

He spoke severely but he was only pretending, and his mind was clearly elsewhere. "Uncle? Was there something you wanted to discuss?"

"In my office, please."

She followed him back into the house. His office was against the back wall, the one shared with their warehouse. It was larger than hers and needed to be, as it was crowded with choice items brought back from his voyages, most of which were set aside until he could bring himself to part with them to a buyer. He sat down behind his desk, a large square of cedar sanded to a golden finish, whose gorgeous surface was obscenely obscured by papers, tablets, styluses, pens, bottles of ink, a pair of life-sized shelducks carved from lapis, an antique chaturanga board with a complete set of pieces made from black, green, red and yellow jade, and a large onyx owl with a reproachful expression on its carved face, which might have had something to do with how close he was to the edge. Tetisheri moved him back to a safe distance and sat down across from her uncle.

"I've decided to buy another boat," he said. "In fact, two."

She was surprised but not unduly so. "Have you?"

"I want you to try to talk me out of it."

She laughed.

His expression lightened and he smiled at her. "But, seriously, Tetisheri."

"But, seriously, Uncle Neb," she said, still laughing. "Have you looked at the books recently?"

"I have. We are in excellent balance, Tetisheri, much due to the trip to Punt and your inspired purchase of that noble's estate—what was his name?"

"Her, and it was Roxana."

"Ah yes, now I remember. She was some kind of queen, I believe?"

"What passes for one in Punt, and her children were squabbling over their inheritance when her brother swooped down from the mountains, killed them all, and put Roxana's personal belongings up for bid in one job lot."

"Nothing but junk was, I believe, my professional assessment."

"I believe it was, Uncle."

He shook his finger at her. "Never mind taking that modest tone with me, young lady. You insisted on bidding and I was soft enough to go along with you, and—"

"And I believe the ruby you gifted the queen upon her return remains one of her favorite pieces of jewelry. I've seen her wear it often."

"Doesn't stop her inspecting every load I bring into port to see if I have any books on board."

"To be fair, Uncle, she does pay us for them." She reflected. "Sometimes."

"Sometimes." They smiled at each other. What Alexandrian traders called between themselves "the book tax" was a small enough price to pay for the good will of the port authorities.

"Why two new boats, Uncle?"

He spread his hands. "We need the tonnage. I could have filled the *Hapi*'s hold twice over in Rome with luxury goods going and, yes, books coming back had I not contracted for that load of pozzolan." He made a face. "I hate shipping that stuff. It gets into everything, including up your nose and in your ears. The crew hates it, too, especially the cleanup afterward."

"It is profitable, though."

"Oh, Isis above and below, is it ever. It is the only reason I can see for its existence, to fill our coffers to overflowing. But—"

"But it isn't much fun."

He beamed at her. "Exactly." He sobered again. "All I know is I had to leave at least two full loads sitting on the dock, and that someone else got paid for bringing them to Alexandria." He frowned. "Now that the war looks like really being over, shipping will get back to its normal level. There will be more competition."

"Hence the Nebenteru Trading Fleet."

He smiled. "Hence."

"What boat did you have your eye on?"

"Well..." He unclasped his hands and sat back in his chair. "I was thinking of building them new." He saw her expression and said hastily, "I did look at the books, Tetisheri, truly I did, and unless we want to go into moneylending we need to begin investing some of our profits back into our business. The only way to expand our trade is to enlarge the amount of tonnage we can ship."

"So far, so good, Uncle, but what's wrong with a used boat? Euphemia must have twenty caiques that would suit us for sale in her yard right now."

"Yes, yes, I'm sure she does, but..."

Tetisheri, suspicious of the furtive expression on Neb's face, said sternly, "What are you up to, Uncle?"

"Well, I—I don't know if I—what I meant to say—well, and Tetisheri, I have no wish to upset you, but—"

"Uncle Neb! What?"

In a rush he said, "Laogonus invited several of us on a day trip on the *Thalassa*."

It took Tetisheri a moment to recover her power of

speech. Into this vacuum Uncle Neb rushed, heedless of how very close he was to ending his life as he knew it. "I know you traveled on the *Thalassa* yourself earlier this year and Laogonus says you were quite impressed—"

"Uncle Neb."

Something in the tone of her voice stopped the words in his mouth.

"The *Thalassa* is a fine ship with an extraordinary crew, beginning with Laogonus, but it is not a trading ship."

"But she flew like a bird, Tetisheri! We went round the delta to Pellusium and were back before dark!"

"I take it the wind was blowing?" Tetisheri's voice could have cut glass.

"Well, of course—"

"And I'm sure Laogonus explained that if the wind doesn't blow, the boat doesn't go," she said remorselessly.

"Well, yes, but—"

"Did he also tell you that we were becalmed on our return from Crete? Which made us easy prey for the pirate ship that attacked us?"

"But he showed us the—"

"Yes, of course, the ballista. Did you notice how much of the hold it occupied? Not to mention the ammunition for it? Did you happen to wonder how much cargo that might displace?"

Neb crumpled a little beneath her glare. "Well, of course, Tetisheri, if you feel so strongly about it..." His voice trailed away.

She knew she was glaring and she took a deep breath and let it out very slowly. He looked so much like a sulky schoolboy denied a sweet cake because it was too close to dinner that her sense of humor was inadvertently tickled and she had to cough to disguise a sudden laugh. "I have no objection to building new, Uncle Neb, but I would prefer that we stick to the tried and true designs, preferably ones with oars and a crew to man them."

There might have been a mumble about how costly such manpower was and the overlarge budget it took to feed a freedman crew but she ignored it. The *Hapi* had twenty rowers a side, free men all, and had made and was still making their fortune for them. He knew it as well as she did. "First, why don't you go down and talk to Euphemia? See what she has in stock. If you truly see nothing you like, then go talk to Demetrius. His ways are always full but you know he'll make room for you if he can."

He'd brightened when she'd said she had no objection to building new, and she was overcome by a rush of love for this man who had offered her a home and employment and above all security at the moment in her life when she'd had none of them. Even more important, he'd taught her how to love, a thing neither her mother nor her husband had been able to do. Not that either of them had tried. "I think increasing our tonnage is an inspired idea, Uncle," she said. "You're quite right, it's also necessary if we don't want other traders picking up the freight we miss because we don't have any room for it." And then, because she was well aware of what his reaction would be, she said casually, "I met the Nomarch of the Black Ox in the Emporeum last week. He was shopping in the livestock market, and he spoke bitterly about the quality of the fleeces of the sheep for sale. I wonder if—"

"No. Absolutely not. No livestock. Animals don't run from only one end. We'd have to burn the boat and build another because we'd never be able to scrub out the smell." He snorted. "Pozzolan is bad enough, and once we have our new ships, Tetisheri, we will dedicate one boat to construction supplies alone. But no livestock!"

"Whatever you think best," she said mildly. He gave her a look of deep suspicion. She laughed and went to the door. She had another thought and looked over her shoulder. "Uncle, you delivered the pozzolan to the royal docks, didn't you?"

"I did. Why?"

"And Cotta was there."

"Yes. I told you this before, Tetisheri."

"Was this pozzolan delivered for any specific project?"

"Not that anyone told me."

"Who unloaded it?"

He sat back in his chair and regarded her with a frowning look. "Two apprentices attended, with half a dozen laborers. The first one, he was Dixiphanes' apprentice, not Dion, the new one. Apollonius? Imperius? Ampelius, that was it. Pleasant fellow—Ampelius kept count of the sacks as they were unloaded, the other scribe as they were loaded into wagons. When they were done they compared their counts and split the stick and gave me my half so I could present it for payment. All much as usual."

"I see. Thank you, Uncle."

"I suppose this has something to do with your, ah, other job."

She smiled at him. "Also, Uncle, we've been invited to a reception this afternoon, you and I and Keren. In Rhakotis."

Uncle Neb was above all else a social animal and he brightened at this news. "Excellent! I'll be able to wear my new silk tunic. Where in Rhakotis?"

"At the home of the Master of Builders."

He raised his eyebrows. "Well, that should be interesting."

You have no idea, Uncle, she thought.

"By the way," he said. "I took a turn through the Emporeum before breakfast and fell into conversation with Theron."

Theron, a local papyrus merchant, was one of Neb's oldest cronies. "And?"

"And he does occasionally trade in old scrolls and books on the side. All legitimately obtained, of course."

"Of course."

He gave her another suspicious look. "I asked him if he knew who was operating at the high end of the business. He couldn't say outright, but he did say there have been rumors." An eyebrow quirked. "You won't believe it."

"Don't keep me in suspense, Uncle."

He said one word. "Calliope."

"Calliope? *The* Calliope? The hetaira?" He nodded, and she pursed her lips in a soundless whistle.

He nodded again, the mischief fading with his smile. "Be careful how you go, Tetisheri. She has many friends."

"Thank you, Uncle."

"Where are you off to?"

"The Library. I must speak to Yasmin. But I'll be back in time to dress for the occasion."

"Tetisheri…" He pawed through the detritus on his desk, clearly wanting to say something else and as clearly uncomfortable with it.

"Yes, Uncle?"

"It would be good to travel together again."

"It would indeed, Uncle."

His hands stilled, and he raised hopeful eyes. "Do you think—"

She thought of the Eye, at present safely locked away in its hidden compartment in her bedroom. "The queen would have to give me leave, Uncle, and we probably couldn't go as far as Punt again, but yes. I do think."

This time Uncle Neb's smile was a wonder to behold.

# 16

S he left him spreading out his vast store of maps of the Middle Sea and the Eastern Ocean, arguing with himself over the most profitable routes for his nascent fleet. She paused long enough to retrieve her palla and the Eye before dodging friends and acquaintances through the Emporeum and hailing a cabrio on the Way. There was little traffic at this hour of the morning and in short order it had deposited her in front of the Library. Inside she found Sosigenes missing but Yasmin very much present.

"Tetisheri!" Yasmin came forward to exchange a warm embrace.

"You've missed Tenth Day dinner twice in a row now," Tetisheri said, stepping back. "Uncle Neb is ready to send out the Shurta."

"But we're not meant to call it Tenth Day any longer, by order of the divine Caesar," Yasmin said, adopting a solemn mien belied by the twinkle in her eyes. "So how am I to know what day I am ordered to table?"

"You are ordered to table any day you care to show your face but you'd better show it soon before it's forgotten." Tetisheri dropped the mock reproof. "We are alone?"

Yasmin's smile faded, too. "We are. Sosigenes is attending a lecture on Eratosthenes' biography of Arsinoë."

"I thought all copies of that had been destroyed by Agathocles, trying to cover his tracks."

Yasmin rolled her eyes. "Silly girl. Know you nothing of scholars and their ability to argue over anything, or for that matter nothing at all?" She smiled when Tetisheri laughed.

"Yasmin, there is something—"

"You are the Eye of the Isis," Yasmin said, and smiled at Tetisheri's expression. "What Sosigenes knows, I know. He fears that if he dies suddenly the Library will collapse for want of someone who knows where all the secret rooms and the keys to them are."

"Apparently everyone knows—" Tetisheri started to say with some asperity, and then stopped. "There is more than one secret room?"

Yasmin would only smile in reply.

She was a slim, vibrant woman some ten years Tetisheri's senior, with warm olive skin, bright brown eyes, straight black hair pulled into a severe knot from which some errant wisp was always straying, and a bold nose with a hint of a curl to the end of it that announced her heritage to anyone who'd ever been to Persis. She had, with help, fled a husband, three co-wives, and twenty-four children (sure to be more by now, as she herself was sure to have been replaced) to find sanctuary in Alexandria and, also with help, employment in the Great Library. She was dressed neatly and with propriety in tunic and palla in sober hues, enlivened by the ink stains where she'd forgotten and wiped her fingers. "How may I help you, Tetisheri?"

She indicated a stool and found one for herself. "You knew Khemit, then," Tetisheri said, keeping her voice low.

Answering in the same low tone, Yasmin said, "Of course. Sosigenes introduced us when he took me on. The Room of the Eye is in my charge."

"Did she, perhaps, ever discuss her—her work?" Tetisheri still didn't know quite what to call it.

"Not often," Yasmin said thoughtfully. "In fact—yes, Timo?"

Tetisheri turned her head to see a young woman in the anonymous linen chiton of the scholar hovering at the door. "I beg your pardon, Yasmin, but—"

"A moment, Tetisheri." Yasmin got up and went out in the hall to confer. A few moments later she was back, shaking her head.

"What?"

"Alexandria is a marvelous city, full of wonders in art and science, the greatest repository of scholarship in theory and in practice in the entire world. And yet when the scholars and the students flock here, seeking knowledge and enlightenment, they bring with them all their own prejudices and use them to color everything they see and everything they do."

Tetisheri regarded her. "You sound just like the queen at her most exasperated."

Yasmin let out an impatient huff. "It's nothing that doesn't happen every day in this institution. Timo is teaching a class in literature, focusing on how women are portrayed in the classic Greek plays. She restricted the students to women. Some of the male students are making a fuss."

"What did you tell her?"

"To tell Aniketos—a self-important little twerp—to form his own class, to which he can invite anyone he chooses." She sighed. "It's hard for the women students. Well. Harder. Alexandria is the only place where they're allowed to openly study what they wish, but that doesn't mean they don't come up against the baked-in biases imported by citizens of countries where women exist to cook dinner, feed the chickens, and make babies."

"That sounds like a class the queen might be interested in auditing."

Yasmin raised her brows. "She would be most welcome, and her presence would stop Aniketos' whining, certainly." She noticed one of the ink stains on her palla and gave it a futile rub. "It has been a while since we've seen her here. We used to see her often."

"She's been busy."

"True enough." Yasmin gave up scrubbing at the ink stain and folded her hands on her knee. "You asked me if Khemit had ever discussed her investigations with me."

"Did she?"

Yasmin hesitated. "A few times."

"You're not in trouble here, Yasmin. So far as I can tell she confided in no one else. Her weaving business was kept entirely separate from her, ah, official, activities, and she had no family. Myself, I'm just glad to know she had someone safe to talk to here." Tetisheri smiled. "As I do now."

Yasmin's brow cleared. "I see. Well, I don't, actually. What is it you want to know?"

"Did she mention anything about a young scribe who had gone missing? His name was Grafeas. Son to Archeion, owner and proprietor of the Hall of Scribes. His mother's name is Eirene."

"I don't—"

"This would have been two years ago. The queen was in exile, and Arsinoë would have been on the throne."

Yasmin's expression darkened. "Not a good time, that. There was much to distract."

A masterpiece of understatement, Tetisheri thought.

Yasmin brooded for a few moments before her brow cleared. "Wait. I do remember Eirene."

"She came here?"

"She came asking for Khemit."

"Khemit did interview them both. It's in her report."

"Well, somehow Eirene knew to come here to try to get in touch with Khemit. I expect it had something to do with the fact that she once served at court."

"Eirene, mother to Grafeas, served in Cleopatra's court?"

"Yes. Well, Auletes and Cleopatra's court. She was one of the queen's personal maids before she left to marry Archeion. You didn't know?"

"No, I didn't, and it explains Khemit's interest in the case, which puzzled me. Did you send Eirene to Khemit?"

"It is forbidden. One knows nothing of such a thing as an Eye of Isis here."

"Ah. What did Eirene say?"

"Nothing. She wept, and then she left, still weeping." It was clear that Yasmin had been less than impressed. Not the motherly type, Yasmin.

"And Khemit? Did she say anything to you of the young man's disappearance?"

"Something, yes," Yasmin said, her brow creasing. "Yes, I remember now. Eirene's son—Grafeas—left work early, she said, and disappeared between work and the Five Soldiers, where he was meant to meet friends for a scheduled class."

"And?"

"And she could not understand how he had disappeared in plain sight so completely, at a time of day when the streets are full, and on that day in particular."

"Why that day in particular?"

"Pompey was on his way, and Arsinoë and her idiot brother had ordered all the soldiers into the streets as a show of force. Marching up and down and making a nuisance of themselves, and then running like frightened children at the first glint of the sun on a Roman shield."

Tetisheri ignored the editorializing. "Did she say anything else?"

"She intimated that there was something off about his betrothal." Yasmin's brow wrinkled. "Or with the betrothed? Or with the betrothed's family?"

"She says in her report that his friends had indicated that the marriage wasn't his idea."

Yasmin snorted. "As if any marriage is ever the idea of the two involved, especially when property is involved. As you and I well know, Tetisheri." Their eyes met in an acknowledgement that was more than a little grim. Yasmin sat back. "But why do you want to know? This was two queens, a king, and nearly two years ago now. In what way does this matter concern the queen?"

"I don't know that it does, but there are these coincidences involved and now I've just stumbled across another." She stood up. "You will send for me if you remember anything else?"

"Of course." Yasmin rose to her feet. "Where are you off to now?"

"I think I should pay a visit to Grafeas' parents."

"Have you found him then, Tetisheri?"

"I'm very much afraid that I have." She saw Yasmin's look of concern and changed the subject deliberately. "Sosigenes told me of the thefts."

Yasmin's brow darkened. "Yes. We took your suggestion, Tetisheri. We have posted people at the doors of the most valuable collections, and told them to tell anyone who asked exactly what they were doing and why."

"Good. Additionally, if I may suggest, change those people frequently."

Yasmin nodded. "Yes. I can see it. A thief, outwardly respectable, befriends one of our staff, and it won't be long before a coin changes hands and eyes are averted as another book or scroll vanishes into someone's satchel." She closed her eyes briefly. "How I hate this, Tetisheri." She raised her hands, palms up. "This is a place sacred to knowledge. When a book is stolen, it isn't only the Library that is robbed, it is every student who comes here seeking information."

"Yes. Yasmin, what do you know of Calliope?"

Yasmin's eyebrows went up. "*The* Calliope?" Tetisheri nodded. "I know what everyone knows. The most famous hetaira of our city and possibly of our time." She sat back, hands folded on her knee, eyes bright. Tetisheri recognized the pose. Yasmin was a born storyteller. "She came to Alexandria from Rome in something of a hurry as I hear the tale, although I have no idea if it's true."

"Do tell."

Yasmin smiled. "The tale is that she was tried for impiety before the Senate."

"Really." Tetisheri was impressed. "What did she do?"

"There the rumors multiply. She profaned the gods, she conspired against the republic, she robbed the treasury, take your pick."

"As prudish as Romans are known to be, I wouldn't

think robbing the treasury would come under the heading of impiety."

Yasmin shrugged. "There are a dozen more. Where the rumors dovetail is in how she got off." She paused dramatically. "Her patron had her disrobe before her judges."

"She stripped in front of the Senate of Rome?"

"So say some. Those some also say that the delicacy of her beauty overcame the jurors, to the point that they wept real tears, and unanimously found her innocent and set her free on the spot."

"Uh-huh."

Yasmin smiled. "Whatever the truth of the matter is, she disappeared from the City of the Seven Hills, shortly thereafter to reappear here in Alexandria."

"She's a hetaira, as I understand the term."

Yasmin nodded. "Not a Phryne."

"She's still a prostitute."

Yasmin considered. "If you mean, she takes money for sex, yes. But she generally keeps one patron at a time, and those patrons are known to be men of culture and refinement."

"And wealth."

"Cynic. Yes, and wealth. She is predominantly known, however, for hosting events to which are invited the brightest scholars, the most promising artists and writers, visiting heads of state, captains of industry, anyone within the walls of the city she deems worthy of interest." She raised an eyebrow. "It is possible the queen herself attended one."

"Really."

The eyebrow remained raised. "Really. It was when Caesar was still in residence. Calliope sent him an invitation to one of her receptions. Of course he accepted."

"Of course." Tetisheri felt a smile spread across her face. "And Cleopatra went with him."

"Indeed she did."

"Well done, O most high."

"Indeed," Yasmin said dryly, "and no one could accuse our queen of being incapable of recognizing a threat when she saw one."

"She has had some experience. Tell me, among all these rumors, true or not, have there been any of Calliope dealing in stolen goods?"

Yasmin's eyes widened. "Do you mean like books?"

"Perhaps."

The other woman drew in a breath, a frown creasing her brow, and expelled it on a long sigh. "If there are such rumors, none have come to my ears."

"Is she a patron of the Library?"

"She is that. She's in here at least once a week, but all that proves is that she is a reader, and perhaps a scholar herself. She attends lectures and exhibitions, but again, all that proves is that she is a citizen of Alexandria."

Tetisheri made a humming noise. "Who was her patron? The one who allegedly defended her before the Senate?"

"Oh. Maecenas."

"Cilnius Maecenas? Gaius Octavius' friend? My, my. Our Calliope does walk the rarefied heights."

Yasmin leaned forward to put a hand on Tetisheri's knee. "She does, and she has many, many friends on both sides of the Middle Sea. Be careful how you go there."

"Always."

Yasmin rolled her eyes and sat back. "Tell me the news."

"Since you haven't been home lately, you ingrate, you haven't heard the latest. Uncle Neb is in the mood to buy more ships and is already laying out trade routes for them."

"The Nebenteru Trading Fleet?"

"Exactly what I said." Tetisheri shrugged. "He made a good case for it. Expand or sink. Financially, at least. Since the peace, anyone with so much as a reed boat is renting him- or herself out to transport goods. Our last time up the river we bought a cone of sugar off a woman who was floating down the current on a raft made from lotus stalks tied together. We had to tow her to shore before she made of herself an offering to Tawaret."

Yasmin smiled broadly. "You're right. It is long past time I was home for Tenth Day dinner."

"Sunday, now." Tetisheri leaned forward to kiss Yasmin's cheek. "We are your home, Yasmin. There is a meal and a bed waiting whenever you wish."

Yasmin hugged her. "I do know that, my dear."

"Mistress—"

Timo was back. She looked miserable.

Yasmin sighed. "Yes, Timo, what is it now?"

Tetisheri escaped.

# 17

It was mid-morning as she descended the steps of the Library. This time there was no Apollodorus waiting for her. She paused on the bottom step, scowling into the distance.

He had not sent word excusing his absence at dinner the night before. Of course, he was not required to account for his whereabouts to anyone but the queen. He didn't know where she had been yesterday, either. And a good thing, too, as Keren had pointed out.

Still, she was very much afraid she was developing something perilously near a pout and she rearranged her features into what she hoped was a smooth, impassive mask. There was work to be done, after all, and none of it would be accomplished by a silly girl mooning after her lover. Very well. It was possible that she might have identified the first of the dead men fitted with a pair of Rhakotis sandals. She needed to interview Archeion and Eirene, Grafeas' parents, to be sure. She hailed a cabrio and directed him to the Promenade.

Grafeas' betrothed, Raia, and her father, Muhandis, might also have useful information. She still had to visit the store of pozzolan to confirm Vitruvius' story of how he acquired his, too. She felt a little guilty about Vitruvius, as he was at present very probably cursing the fact they had ever met.

Is's note had assured her the task she had set him was well in hand. If he pulled it off she might have an ear in Philo's court, which would be very useful indeed.

She was pretty certain by now that she understood the motive behind the deaths of the two men. She knew who one of them was and her next interview would confirm it. The second man's identify would need confirmation but at least she had a name.

Cleopatra's reply had come early that morning. The queen had agreed to Tetisheri's idea, with a few refinements.

Of a surety, Cotta would be present, as he was present at every major social event. She wondered how Cleopatra meant to navigate that dangerous shoal. Caesar's legions had put Cleopatra back on her throne. Cotta was Caesar's legate in Alexandria, and he was watching the queen's every move. One letter on a fast boat to Rome, assuming Caesar had finally reached it and had survived all the rumored assassination attempts, and Caesar would demand an accounting for whatever Cotta chose to bring to his attention. Tetisheri had no illusions, as she was certain Cleopatra had none, that Caesar was so lost to love that he would ignore peculation of any valuable resource without retribution. Egypt already grew the grain that fed Rome, and that was more advantage than many an aspiring autocracy would allow.

Her driver cleared his throat loudly, and she became aware that they had drawn up before a small house set back from the street. "The home of Archeion, lady."

She reached for her purse. "Thank you. Could you wait for me, please?"

He huffed. "I'm coming to end of my shift, lady, and I'm hungry."

She tossed him another drachma and he agreed without enthusiasm. She hoped very much to return home to find Rhode in residence over the stable.

The house of Archeion and Eirene was small but well appointed in an understated way. Two columns framed the front door with an entablature adorned with a frieze of repeating figures of Seshat, stylus in hand, inscribing something on a palm leaf. They glowed with beautiful color applied by an artist's hand. There was a narrow strip of garden in front to the left and right of the door, and bean plants with green and purple pods had been encouraged to climb a series of decorative supports, which, upon closer inspection, proved to be overlarge styluses made of hammered bronze.

Tetisheri felt for the outline of the amulets in her purse. She was not looking forward to this interview.

A servant with the proud carriage of a freedwoman answered to her knock and bowed her inside. Her master was at his place of business but her mistress was at home, if the lady were pleased to wait. The lady was and the servant installed Tetisheri in a small but richly furnished parlor and bowed herself out.

Tetisheri wandered around the room while she waited. The couch and chairs were carved of ebony, with lion's paws for feet and leopard skin upholstery. A niche in one wall displayed a small figure of Seshat in ivory with palm leaf and stylus carved from tourmaline. Everything was to scale and the figure looked ready to step down from her pedestal at any moment. It looked like Matan's work. The scribe business must be doing very well indeed.

A noise caused her to turn. In the doorway stood a woman, middle-aged, with thick brown hair graying at her temples, bound at her brow by a silver circlet and caught behind in a knotted braid in the old Greek style. Her eyes were widely spaced and dark brown, framed in thick lashes. She would have been stunning when she was young but age and grief had carved deep lines in her brow and at the corners of her mouth. She wore a cream-colored stola clasped at one shoulder with a silver brooch in the shape of a papyrus blossom, and simple leather sandals. A typical Alexandrian matron, settled, secure, certain of her place in the order of life, but one who had seen her share of sorrow.

Her straight dark eyebrows came together to create a puzzled frown. "Lady?" she said. "May I help you?"

Tetisheri bent her head briefly. "I am Tetisheri. I work with Aristander."

"Aristander? The head of the Shurta?" A hasty step

brought the matron into the room. "Bring you news of my son?"

"It is Eirene, wife of Archeion, is it not?"

"Yes, yes, but do you bring news of my son, Grafeas?" A hand clutched at Tetisheri's arm.

Tetisheri had never brought the news of the death of a loved one to his nearest relations before. She repressed the impulse to blurt the news and run from the room. "Here," she said gently, taking Eirene by the hand and guiding her to the couch. "I will sit with you." Eirene wouldn't let go of her hand and so she let it rest there for the moment. "Your son was Grafeas, a scribe."

"Yes." A tear slid down her cheek.

"He went missing two years ago."

"Yes."

"Did he perchance break his arm at some point in his life?"

Another tear. "Yes. His right arm. He fell from a scaffolding on a building site."

"Did he wear an amulet?"

A second tear followed the first. "He did."

"One of Seshat?"

A silent sob shook Eirene's shoulders. "Yes. It belonged to his grandfather. His father gave it to him when he apprenticed as a scribe."

Tetisheri took a deep breath and freed her hand to reach into her purse. The Seshat amulet nestled into her palm. She held it out.

Eirene grasped Tetisheri's hand in both of her own and broke, head curling down to her breast, ugly sobs tearing out of her throat. "Yes," she managed to say. "Yes, that is my son's amulet."

Tetisheri looked up to see the servant standing in the doorway, with a few more heads peering over her shoulders. "Your mistress is overset. Please bring something cool for her to drink."

A pitcher of chilled pomegranate juice and two glasses appeared, and, thoughtfully, a length of worn linen for Eirene to dry her face. Tetisheri poured her a glass and encouraged her to drink it all, sip by sip. When she was done she had regained something of her composure and Tetisheri felt safe enough to say, still gently, "I am so very sorry to bring you this news, Eirene, but I believe the body of your son has been found."

"How? How did he die?"

"The Shurta believe he was drowned." There were limits. Apply red hot coals to the soles of her feet and Tetisheri would still not reveal to this grieving mother the grisly details of her son's death.

Eirene's head came up. "Drowned?" she said blankly. "Drowned? Are you sure?"

"Quite sure," Tetisheri said. She cocked her head. "Why? What surprises you about that?"

"He could swim like a fish. Grafeas." As if she had had another son who had died two years before. "I—it is surprising to me that he could—" She looked up and saw the servant standing in the doorway. "Narcissa, send a message to Archeion. Convey my apologies for disturbing him at work but ask him please to return home at once."

"It is already done, mistress."

A wan smile. "Thank you, my dear. The house will be in some upset for a while, I'm afraid. Tell the servants to begin preparations." She looked at Tetisheri and spoke with some dignity, although her lips were trembling. "I am to suppose that our son's remains will be returned to us, so we may undertake the funerary rites and see him properly into the next life?"

"When the investigation into his death is concluded, yes."

"There are questions?"

Tetisheri thought how best to put it, but there was no best way. "I'm afraid your son's death was not accidental."

Eirene's eyes widened. "He was murdered?"

"I'm so sorry to have to bring you this news, but yes, that is the Shurta's finding."

Tetisheri had braced herself for an outburst, but instead a glaze seemed to come over Eirene's eyes. "Someone killed him, you say?"

"Yes."

"I—see." She took a long, shuddering breath. "When will the investigation conclude?"

"I'm sorry, Eirene. I don't know. As soon as possible. The queen herself has commanded it."

Eirene's head came up and her eyes narrowed. "The queen?" She hesitated. "Khemit—are you—?"

Tetisheri said nothing.

"Yes. Of course." She sat up, her shoulders straight. "Please convey to the queen my gratitude and my husband's gratitude for her attention to this matter."

Tetisheri bowed her head briefly. "It will be my privilege."

"I have sent for my husband," Eirene said unnecessarily.

"Thank you," Tetisheri said. "As distressing as this time must be, I have questions for you both."

Narcissa brought a tray of bread, soft cheese, and olives. Neither of them were hungry. "You served the queen," Tetisheri said, tentatively.

Eirene stirred, drawing her gaze back from some image far in the past that only she could see. "I did." A ghost of a smile. "Grafeas was nearly a man by then and the times were so unsettled that it seemed wise to have someone in the family close to power. My father had served her father and he put my name forward."

"It must have been difficult in those days. So many heirs. So many courts. So many competing factions." And a weathervane for a king, she could have added, but didn't.

Eirene shrugged. "My father told me to smile and bow whenever anyone in the royal family spoke to me, but to obey only Cleopatra."

It sounded like good advice to Tetisheri. "And did that work?"

"For the most part." Another faint smile. "She was a force with which to be reckoned even then."

"And now."

Another smile. "And now. But I had very little to do with the queen herself personally. I served behind the scenes."

Which explained why she and Tetisheri had never met.

The front door opened and closed and they heard voices in the hall.

Both women rose to their feet as a man appeared in the doorway, out of breath. "What is it? What's wrong?" He stepped forward and Eirene went into his arms with a rush. He held her for a moment, his face creased with worry, his cheek pressed to her hair. He grasped her shoulders and pushed her back so he could look into her face. "My dear, what is it?"

He was tall and thin in an ink-stained tunic and a toga of fine wool with embroidery around the hem. His remaining hair stood up in gray tufts, some of them stained by the same ink that blotted his fingers and his tunic. His face was lined and his eyes dark and deep-set and concerned. He looked over his wife's head at Tetisheri. "And you are?"

Eirene stepped back and gave Tetisheri an embarrassed smile. "I'm sorry. Archeion, this is the lady Tetisheri. She brings news of Grafeas. He—" Her voice broke.

Archeion pulled her to him again and she buried her face in his shoulder. "Tell me."

"I represent the queen, who has taken an interest in this matter," Tetisheri said. "I'm very sorry to have to tell you this, but your son's body has been found, and the Shurta suspects that foul play was involved."

"Foul play?" he said blankly, and then his face darkened. "You mean he was murdered."

It wasn't a question. "I'm afraid so, yes."

Eirene raised her face and the eyes of husband and wife met for a long moment. "Let us sit down, my dear." He guided her to the couch. "Please to be seated, too, lady—I'm sorry, what was your name again?"

"Tetisheri," she said. She repeated what she had told Eirene and showed him the amulet.

His face contorted with grief but he otherwise maintained his composure. "Yes, that was my father's token. I gave it to Grafeas when he began at the Hall of Scribes. May we see him?"

"I don't recommend it, sir," she said carefully. "It would be best to remember him how he was when you last saw him."

"I—see." He was silent for a moment. "He will be returned to us?"

"As soon as the investigation is complete. It is hoped that will be soon." She hesitated. "I wonder if I might ask you a few questions."

"You're a friend of the queen," he said formally. "We are honored by her interest in this matter of our son." His voice trembled a little on that last word. "Please. Ask your questions. We will do our best to answer."

"Do you remember your son having any arguments with his friends or co-workers?"

He drew himself up proudly. "No, most certainly not. He

knew being the son of the owner of the business left him open to accusations of nepotism. It only made him work all the harder. He was a son to be proud of."

Which made his loss all the more acutely felt. "He had no enemies?"

"How would he go about making any?"

That would be the question, Tetisheri thought, because someone hadn't liked him very much at all.

"He was always a quiet, studious boy," Eirene said. "He grew out of the usual child's mischief early on." She smiled in fond remembrance. "I remember one of his friend's mothers saying he was a good influence on them, that he kept their own mischief in check."

"He had two particular friends, I believe?"

"Ahmose and Nenwef." Archeion exchanged a glance with his wife. "We didn't care much for Nenwef, I must say."

Eirene shook her head. "So spoiled, and selfish, but Grafeas saw something in him."

"He was trying to save him from himself, I think," Archeion said. "I don't know that he thought of Nenwef as so much of a friend as a reclamation project." He looked at Eirene and they smiled at each other.

"And Ahmose?"

"A goodly young man, came from a family in the building trades, I think. Very athletic. Wanted to be a soldier but his parents apprenticed him to the law before he could enlist."

There was a brief silence. "Grafeas was to be married, I understand."

"Er, yes," Archeion said, with another look at his wife.

"Raia, daughter of Muhandis," Eirene said without enthusiasm. Tetisheri raised her eyebrows invitingly. "Oh, she was a fine young woman. I'm sorry, is a fine young woman. Pretty, modest, well-trained. Like Grafeas, she was an only child, and had trained in her parents' business from when she was only little. She would have been welcomed into our family."

"Grafeas was looking forward to his marriage?"

They exchanged another glance. "She was more fond than he," Eirene said, "but he liked her well enough and he was prepared to do his duty."

An arranged marriage. Isidorus had intimated as much. "Is Muhandis a scribe by profession?" She wasn't expecting an affirmative answer. Muhandis was an Egyptian name, and the Greeks of Alexandria had so far kept a stranglehold on the business.

"Isis above, no." Archeion looked somewhere between shocked and amused. "Muhandis is—was, I'm sorry to say—a builder." He added, almost mournfully, "A very successful builder, in fact. His death was an enormous loss to the Hall of Scribes. Grafeas handled all his work."

"Muhandis is dead?"

"Yes. He died shortly after Grafeas—disappeared."

"How did he die?"

"He—" Archeion glanced at his wife. "He disappeared, too."

"Like Grafeas?"

"Not exactly." He hesitated. "I have no wish to speak ill of those gone beyond the reach of everyday cares, you understand."

"Of course not. And?"

Tetisheri's tone was inexorable and he flushed a little with embarrassment. "And there were rumors of him from upriver. That he had abandoned his wife and child and his business here in Alexandria for a mistress in Napata."

"Was he seen alive elsewhere after his disappearance from the city?"

He reflected, his hand absently running up and down his wife's back in a comforting gesture. "I never saw him again myself, but for at least a year afterward there was one story after another of him being seen at a ceremony in Memphis, overseeing the building of a tomb in Thebes, on a pleasure barge before the First Cataract. Always he was said to be in the company of a beautiful woman covered all over in jewels. There was even a name for her. The Nubian Aphrodite." He looked up to meet Tetisheri's eyes. "I always thought it had less to do with the truth and more to do with how much everyone disliked his wife."

"Indeed," Eirene said, a flush rising into her cheeks. "She was known to be always interfering in her husband's business, making deals behind his back, submitting bids, breaking contracts." She looked up at her husband. "She wrangled over every bill we ever submitted for payment. It was no wonder people were happy to repeat any story that might hurt her."

"Did Muhandis' business collapse after his, ah, disappearance?"

Archeion looked startled. "Why, no, it is still one of the largest building concerns in the city."

"There are no hard feelings between the two families?"

He was bewildered now. "Why would there be?"

"I don't understand why Raia would change clerks."

His brow cleared. "Oh. I see. Raia didn't inherit because Muhandis' wife survived him to inherit the business. She runs it now."

"Ah."

"Khadiga." Eirene spat the name like a curse.

"Khadiga?"

"Eirene," Archeion said, but his wife was too angry for tact.

"She did not approve of the betrothal. She didn't think Grafeas was of high enough station to marry into their family. Egyptians! Pharaoh worshippers, the lot of them. Thinking they were above marrying into our family, when our line goes back to Herodotus!"

# 18

The pozzolan was secured behind a very recently assembled stakewall, the smell of sap strong enough to make the eyes water, erected at the end of Poseidon's Head. A length of canvas stretched between the wall and two posts driven into the ground provided shade, and two stools sat beneath it on either side of a square drawn in the dirt. Two men in Queen's Guard regalia sat on the stools playing dice. They looked up when the cabrio approached.

Tetisheri smoothed her hair and resettled her amulet in the exact center of her breast, and smiled what she hoped was the same dazzling smile that had ensnared the guards in front of Otho's house the day before. "Gentlemen."

Gratifyingly, they straightened as young men do when faced with even a marginally pretty woman. They were both very young, both Egyptian, and both so obviously new to their office that they had barely worn out the creases in their uniforms. When they managed to get their mouths closed they leaped to their feet in unison and jostled each other to be first in line to assist her in the onerous task of descending from the cabrio.

"I am the lady Tetisheri," she said, with just enough grandeur in her manner to engender respect but not enough to intimidate.

They bowed, clumsily. "Khufu, lady, and this is Menes."

She smiled upon them both, doing her best to radiate charm. "Ah, members of the queen's new guard, isn't it? And you come from upriver, unless I miss my guess."

Khufu smiled shyly. "The Nome of the Bow, lady."

"Really. They say the name comes from the fact that the Nome of the Bow produces Egypt's finest archers. Is that true? Does Nekhbet guide your eye?"

Menes said proudly, "In our village we learn to shoot from our mother's knee, lady."

She allowed herself an admiring glance. "I must say you look very fine indeed in your uniforms. I know the queen is proud that so many of her people who live upriver have answered the call to man her armies."

Khufu looked awestruck. "You know the queen, lady?"

"We have met," she said modestly.

They both looked dazzled to have come this close to royalty. It was shamefully easy to talk them into unbarring the gate and giving her a tour of what was inside the stakewall, which consisted of heavy canvas bags stacked head high and so closely together it was difficult to pass between the rows. At least half of them bore the customs stamp of Nebenteru's Luxury Goods. She listened with flattering attention punctuated by gasps of admiration as the two young men vied with each other to pretend to know everything there was to know about customs stamps, while she studied the various bags with an outwardly disinterested eye, and reflected on how difficult it was to forge a government stamp. It was one thing for a forged stamp to pass muster once, at the entry of the goods into the country when they were part of a larger shipment, one of many shipments during a day, and the agents were being run off their feet. A second, more careful examination must surely discover the blurred lines and the imperfect cartouche of the counterfeit.

But then smugglers were always in a hurry, and it was always their downfall.

Near the gate she saw one bag sitting apart, half empty. A tiny stream of white powdery substance spilled down the side; it looked familiar. They were persuaded to scoop a double handful into a small leather bag—she thought it might have been a purse belonging to one of them cannibalized for the purpose—and presented it to her as if they were handing over the lost treasure of Adjib. They were only too eager as well to use their knives to cut the section from an empty bag bearing a customs stamp. Mementoes of a delightful visit, she told them, and, distressingly, they swallowed it whole.

She waved as she drove off and then faced forward, torn between the elation of confirming a source's story and worry over how to report this honestly to Cleopatra without getting both of those poor boys executed.

Elation won. What was luck for if it was never to be tested? "Driver."

"Lady?"

"With your kindness, I must make one more stop before my final destination." She tilted her head and smiled at him upside down as he stood on the step behind her. "I'll double your fare."

He shook out the reins with enthusiasm and the horse between the shafts moved into a smart trot.

For the first time it occurred to Tetisheri to wonder how she went about being reimbursed for her expenditures in service to the queen.

Or if she would be. She had not seen any records of cash accounts in the Room of the Eye.

It so happened that the cabriador knew the way to her destination, although the glance he gave her was speculative in the extreme. It was a small house on a short, quiet street just off Lochias, across from the Promenade. Quite an exclusive neighborhood.

The house looked very plain from the outside, white stucco walls with a flat roof, a modest front door reached by three granite steps and framed by two pilasters topped with a cornice and a pediment. The pediment was broken by a finial, a small but beautifully carved marble figure of a nude woman holding a robe, head turned, smiling slightly. Aphrodite. Tetisheri laughed out loud.

The door opened at her knock and she was greeted by a gaunt woman with thinning gray hair pulled back so tightly the mottled skin over her cheekbones looked as if it might tear. She had dark eyes set deep in heavy folds and a nose that looked like the battering ram on a trireme. If she'd had three heads she could have stood guard at the door of the Underworld. "Yes?"

One had to admire how much menace she managed to infuse into a single word. "My compliments to the lady Calliope, and could she spare me a few moments of her time?"

She was subjected to a thorough inspection and found wanting. "And you are?"

"The lady Tetisheri, of House Nebenteru."

The forbidding expression did not change, but something seemed to shift behind the dark eyes. She stepped back and pulled the door wide. "I will see if my mistress is at home to callers."

She was shown into a small parlor that was richly furnished without being in any way vulgar. There was a marble bust on a pedestal in every corner, a collection of sculptures on a side table, and the couches and chairs were the opposite of ornate while at the same time conveying the impression that the frame was of the finest ebony and the fabric covering the cushions of the finest silk. Two large windows with broad, upholstered sills looked out on artful riots of blooming shrubs. The floor was covered in a brightly colored mosaic that—Tetisheri tilted her head—yes, that told the story of Zeus and Europa. The bull was startlingly well equipped, which would explain the five children. One could only pity Europa. One could also wonder why the stories of women in classical mythology on the north side of the Middle Sea were invariably told only in relation to the male figures in their lives, men or gods. Not always so in Egypt. Some scholar at the Great Library was probably writing a paper on the topic at this very moment.

Another shelf stood opposite the first, this one partitioned into a dozen levels of as many squares each. Inside each square was a scroll. A space in the center of the unit held a pair of mahogany capsa.

She heard footsteps approaching and turned to greet her hostess.

For such a storied hetaira she had been expecting the living embodiment of Aphrodite herself. Instead she was confronted with a slim, almost boyish figure, slight of breast and hip. Her long limbs gave her the impression of being taller than she actually was. Her skin was clear and smooth and the color of honey and her hair was an indeterminate light brown brushed to a to a sheen and bound into a braid as thick as her upper arm. Her eyes, large, wide-spaced, and thickly lashed, were her best feature, some changeable color between gray and green. They met Tetisheri's own without apprehension.

She was dressed in a simple linen peplos of fine weave dyed light blue, with a zoster of embossed leather worked in some colorful design resting just above her hips, which were so insubstantial the zoster looked in danger of slipping to the floor at any moment. The pins at her shoulders were small bronze representations of the tyet, inlaid with turquoise. Like her room, the lady's appearance was understated but expensive.

"The lady Tetisheri? I am Calliope. I don't believe we've met." Her voice was unexpectedly low and yet seemed to ring from the walls of the room. The hetaira had presence.

Tetisheri bent her head in return. "We haven't, lady, and I beg your pardon for this uninvited intrusion into your day, and I thank you for taking the time to speak with me. Cerberus there seemed uncertain as to whether you were receiving visitors."

"Cerberus?"

"Your servant. The one who answered the door."

Calliope's lips twitched, and Tetisheri liked her the better for it. "Ah. Yes. Phryne. She can be very protective."

"Phryne? Her name is Phryne?"

"Yes."

Tetisheri struggled not to laugh as the human hyena marched in with a tray holding a pitcher, glasses, and an assortment of savory pastries. "One must always be at home to a member of the house of Nebenteru."

Must one? Tetisheri thought, as Phryne departed.

"A little carava, perhaps? Or would you prefer wine?"

"Carava would be most welcome." Tetisheri waited as the hetaira filled two cups made of clear blown glass. She held hers up. "From Judea."

Calliope smiled, revealing white, even teeth. She had eaten well her entire life. "You know your glassware."

"I visited a glassworks in Shalem the last time I accompanied my uncle to Judea. They are doing some amazing work there. Amazing, and precious." She sipped. The carava was almost as exquisite as the glass that held it, just the right amount of tamarind for tart and not too much honey for sweet. "I must be careful not to drop it."

"Please," Calliope said.

There was something about the eyes that caused the image of the coltish adolescent to recede into the reality of a woman of years and experience. Tetisheri thought she saw some wariness in the straight gaze as well, enough to endorse her decision to come here today. "This is a lovely room."

"Thank you. I do host the occasional event, and I like to showcase some of our younger artists."

Tetisheri was fairly certain that the bust of Aphrodite rising from a cockleshell sitting on a pedestal in the northwest corner of the parlor was attempting to be a portrait of its owner. "Very kind of you to draw attention to their work. So helpful to new artists." She indicated the bookshelf. "You're a great reader as well, I see."

"Many of our local poets and playwrights are kind enough to gift me with copies of their work."

Tetisheri set her glass down carefully on the polished ebony of the little table between the chairs. "I understand you are a patron of our Library as well."

Calliope smiled. It was a delightful smile, revealing dimples in both cheeks. "Isn't every single person between the Sun and the Moon? And if not, they should be."

"You and I agree there. However." Tetisheri sighed. "I am very sorry to report that our Library has been subjected of late to a series of thefts."

The dimples disappeared. "You don't say so? An abomination, a sacrilege, even! A loss not only to the city but to knowledge itself!"

She sounded absolutely sincere, but then it was a quality in which her profession would have allowed her infinite practice. Tetisheri gave a grave nod. "And sorry am I to report it." She clasped her hands on her knee and leaned forward, infusing earnestness into every line of her body and the very timbre of her voice. "I have been tasked by the authorities to reach out to those good citizens known to be patrons of the Library, in hopes that they will spread the word among the other good citizens of our fair city to be on the watch for these scrolls, books, and manuscripts to surface." She indicated the bookcase with a wave of her hand that was far less graceful than her hostess'. "Perhaps someone offers to present you with the gift of a rare volume, with no mention of how or from whom it was acquired. Or you hear of a friend or acquaintance purchasing such a thing. Possibly a vendor informs you that he or she has acquired the works of Socrates, or Eratosthenes, or the collected works of the great Homer in an edition never before heard of in a private collection."

"Authorities?" Calliope said, narrowing her focus to the single word in Tetisheri's peroration that could reasonably be constituted a credible threat to her personal well-being.

Tetisheri glanced to the north and lowered her voice. "The very highest of authorities."

If Calliope's skin had before been the color of honey it was now the color of marble. "Ah." She looked down and realized that she was holding an empty glass, and set it on the table with less care than she might have. "While I myself have never heard of such an abomination, if I do, of course any help I can give I will give gladly."

"I knew you would," Tetisheri said with perfect truth. She unclasped her hands and smoothed the fabric over her knees. "And if you could, perhaps, repeat this story to those of your friends who might be interested."

"But of course. I am sure each of them will be as shocked as I was to hear of such an affront to the greatest institution in Alexandria."

"All know Calliope for a dedicated patron of the arts and artists." Tetisheri rose to her feet. "I'm afraid I must go. I have a reception to attend in Rhakotis, and if I don't return home in time to change my dress I will disgrace my household."

"Otho's reception?" Calliope said, looking immediately as if she wished she hadn't.

"Why, yes! Will you be in attendance as well? How delightful! I believe it is meant to be the premier event of the social season."

"I had received an invitation, yes."

"Then I look forward to seeing you there." Tetisheri shook her head. "I always find these events to be so intimidating, the rooms filled with so many people I don't know and to whom I don't know how to talk. It will be a relief to find a friendly face there."

She turned to go.

"Lady Tetisheri?"

Tetisheri turned. "Yes?"

Calliope's fine eyes held a speculative expression. "How many, ah, friends of the Great Library have you approached so far on this particular topic?"

Tetisheri met the hetaira's unwavering gaze with as bland an expression as she could manage. "You're the first."

They stared at each other for a long, silent moment, and then, unexpectedly, Calliope laughed. If she had been charming when she smiled, she was irresistible when her face was lit with amusement. "I see," she said. "I see, indeed."

Tetisheri inclined her head slightly. "I was sure you would. Thank you again for your hospitality. Good day."

She arrived on her own doorstep at the same moment as Babak and his four friends, each carrying a pitifully small amount of personal belongings. "Ah," she said. "Babak and Company. Well met."

"You said we should come today," Roshanak said accusingly.

"You said we could move in over the stable this morning," Narses said, no less so.

Tetisheri was reminded, yet again, that every promise ever made to these children, implied or overt, had been broken multiple times. That they were here this promptly was evidence, as if she needed it, that they were still suspicious of their good fortune. She had some suspicion herself that the main reason they were here was Babak's role as their leader. As the one with the least time served on the streets, he was more willing to take something on faith, at least initially.

"And it is morning, more or less, and here you are," she said cheerfully, and led them to a small yard beside the house with a well surrounded by a low, stone wall in the middle of it. A small house at the back of the yard contained a stable below with a narrow staircase leading up the outside to a landing between two rooms. An assortment of tack had been neatly stacked in one corner of the stable, and upstairs the door on the left was ajar, through which she could see bundles and bags in a pile in the middle of the room. Rhode had taken the smaller room, Tetisheri was relieved to see. She opened the door opposite. "Come in."

They filed past her. The room was square and spare. Nike and Phoebe and Nebet had been hard at work this morning because it had been scoured clean. There was a long, low table against one wall with pitchers and bowls above and buckets below. There were two broad windows with wooden shutters overlooking the yard in front and the warehouse in back. Five mats with bedding were rolled and neatly stacked in one corner. "The well as you saw is out front. The privy is in back. You'll take your meals with us, and don't be afraid to ask Phoebe for a snack when you get hungry between meals."

"Anytime we want to eat, we can eat? For free?" Bradan said.

"No, not for free. It's part of the salary you receive for your work."

"Plus one drachma a week," Agape said quickly. "Each."

Tetisheri smiled at her. The girl didn't smile back, not yet, but it was early days. "And one drachma each per week. There are shelves for your belongings. Get settled in and then go to the kitchen, where Phoebe has your lunch waiting. Afterward, Nike will take you to the baths, and you will be issued new clothes."

"We have clothes," Roshanak said.

Tetisheri looked them over critically. "Indeed, and I would ask you to wash them and keep them by. They may come in useful in your work for me."

"You mean we'll have something to wear when you decide it costs too much to feed us and you kick us out again."

Tetisheri looked at Roshanak, who glared defiantly back. "No. That isn't what I meant, Roshanak. Let's take a little time to get to know one another before we have our first fight, shall we?"

Babak elbowed Roshanak in the side and bestowed upon Tetisheri a beatific smile. "At your command, lady."

Roshanak snorted, but Tetisheri left them quarreling over who got to roll out their bed next to the windows. She wondered how long it would take them to get used to sleeping beneath a roof again.

She beckoned to Babak and he followed her to the landing. "I have a job for you this afternoon. Two, in fact."

Tetisheri descended the stairs and entered the stable to find the other newest member of her household currying her horse. The mare was nearly moaning with pleasure. "Lady."

"Call me Tetisheri, please, Rhode. We are going out this afternoon, Uncle Neb, Keren, and I."

"I was so informed."

"Good. I'm glad you decided to join us."

Rhode eyed her over the horse's back. "It won't be boring. Will it."

Tetisheri laughed. At the rate she was acquiring dependents, a larger fleet wasn't an aspiration, it was a necessity. She went into the house with a light heart. Phoebe was making lamb kebabs to feed what she darkly described as a ravening horde. She saw Tetisheri's expression and she smiled. "It's fine, Tetisheri, don't worry. Nike needs the company of other children so she can learn how to be one herself, and Nebet and I like Rhode."

"It's a lot more work for you on very short notice."

"We should hire a maid."

"Or two, or even three. I leave it to you."

Phoebe handed her a kebab. "Eat up. You know you won't be able to eat anything at the reception."

True enough. There was always someone talking at you at these kinds of events, and this one would certainly be no exception. Munching on the juicy, tender lamb seasoned with rosemary, she went to her office. No messages had arrived, for which she rendered gratitude to Bast, who was curled on her usual corner of the desk and accepted it as only her due. There were still at least two hours until they had to leave for the festivities. Possibly three, as fashionably late was always more desirable, as later more people would be present before whom one could parade one's entrance. She put the time to good use, writing up her findings over the past week in chronological order, assembling her conclusions, and listing the questions she still had. Chief among these was the identity of the second victim, although she was was almost certain she knew, and two more questions that Babak would, hopefully, find the answers for in time.

Again, her imagination returned to her first sight of the first body on the beach outside the Gate of the Moon. How many more bodies lurked beneath the waves of the Middle Sea, waiting to be found? It was a question that might never be answered.

She raised her head and stared out the window into the rose garden. They were red and white and pink, some of the blossoms the size of Neb's fist. A gentle breeze bearing their sweet scent slipped into the room. As always, the tang of the salt sea was subtly present. She could hear the rumble of wooden wheels, the curses of stevedores, the snap of sails, but under it all she could also hear the eternal slap of the waves against the pilings and the hulls of the ships moored to them. The sea was life every bit as much as it was death.

And then she sighed and looked down at her work. It had organized her thoughts to write it all down, even if her penmanship was far messier than Khemit's neat hand. Demotic degenerated far too easily into a scrawl, and she wondered if in future she should write her accounts in Greek. Or Latin, even, although the thought of Aurelius Cotta getting his hands on the records of the Eye of Isis and being able to read them sent a shudder down her spine.

She wondered if she was too old to learn cuneiform.

And then she laughed at herself. Khemit had woven a clue to her last investigation into a tapestry, but Tetisheri was no weaver. A written report in a common tongue was the best she could do.

She tidied her desk, put the report under lock and key, and went to her room to see what Keren had decided she should wear to Otho's reception, only to discover that her attire had been sent from the palace itself, accompanied by a note, read out loud by Keren in dramatic accents, with gestures. "'The queen would be pleased if you would wear this to the event this afternoon.'"

"Signed by Charmion," Tetisheri said, reading the note over Keren's shoulder. "I could have ignored it if it had been signed by Iras."

"No," Keren said, putting away the clothes she had previously chosen in the wardrobe and closing the door behind them. "You couldn't."

# 19

The fountain in front of Otho's was functioning today. It sprayed each cabrio, carriage, and chariot entering the half-circle driveway with a light mist of water that smelled faintly of lavender.

Rhode pulled to a stop at the exact center of the marble staircase. She was wearing newly bought livery, as yet without a house crest, as Nebenteru and Tetisheri had yet to devise one. The carriage was nevertheless immaculate. Her mare, coat brushed and hooves polished, stood still as a statue as the three of them descended. Once they were safely on the ground, she moved smoothly back into motion, to be immediately replaced by a much larger and grander carriage drawn by a pair of horses.

"My word," Uncle Neb said, staring up at the house. "He does do himself proud, does Otho."

"He's either Greek or he wishes he was," Keren said.

"I feel as if I'm taking part in a bad play," Tetisheri said.

"Aren't we?" Keren said with a grimace.

"I wonder if the food and drink on the inside matches the outside?" Nebenteru winked at the two of them and offered his arms. "Let's find out, shall we?"

They ascended the staircase and passed between the double row of columns into the atrium. It was the largest atrium Tetisheri had ever seen, with an impluvium featuring the twin of the fountain out front. The room was filled with a chattering crowd made up of Alexandria's richest and most influential people dressed in their best clothes, looking—and sounding—nothing so much as like a flock of exotic birds.

There was no wall space left unadorned. Brightly painted statues of gods from all the pantheons; marble busts of poets Persian, Greek, and Roman; a bejeweled bow with a quiver full of arrows fletched in amber; a coral cup with jade handles carved in the likeness of laurel leaves; a Greek vase exquisitely painted with scenes of Minoan bull-leaping; an amphora as tall as Tetisheri with a glaze as blue and as deep as the Middle Sea itself. It was an army of art arrayed on a row of columns standing to attention against all four walls, daring any other collection to match it in battle.

She saw Otho immediately, although he was nearly eclipsed by the woman standing next to him. She blinked and saw that it was Khadiga, whose dress was elaborately tucked and folded and by some alchemy of the dyer's art appeared to be made of hammered copper. The fillet that bound back her dark hair was also of copper, as were the earrings that touched her shoulders, the collar that covered her breast, and the double set of armbands she wore at wrist and upper arm.

Behind her was a slight figure, a young woman who looked enough like the woman in copper to be recognized as her daughter, but shorter and slimmer. Her stola and palla paled to a kind of faded pink, she wore a ribbon around her forehead instead of a fillet, her earrings were single pearls, and an amulet made also of pearl hung at her throat.

One could imagine that her youth and inexperience could preclude her from the more elaborate costume of her mother. If one had a nastier turn of mind, one could imagine that she was being kept deliberately in the shadow of the older woman.

Uncle Neb, still staring at the woman in copper—Tetisheri wasn't sure he'd even registered Otho's presence at her side—took a deep, appreciative breath. Before he could rush forward to introduce himself to someone so obviously meriting his undivided attention, Tetisheri held him back, and Keren, too. In a low voice she said, "Remember what I said. Keep me in sight at all times. When you see me signal, leave at once. Do you promise?"

"I heard you the first time, Tetisheri," he said severely. He resettled his new tunic (a wonder of the weaver's art in leaf green and amethyst) and strode off to make his bow to his host.

Keren was laughing and trying her best to hide it.

"This isn't funny!"

"Oh yes, it is, Tetisheri. Oh yes, it most certainly is." She looked over Tetisheri's shoulder, and smiled. "Ah, there is Doris and her husband. I haven't seen her in ages."

And Tetisheri was left alone, but not for long. She felt his presence at her back before she heard his voice.

"So here you are."

She turned and smiled up at Apollodorus.

He ran a warm and appreciative eye over her stola and matching palla, white linen embroidered with silver thread. "You look even more beautiful than usual."

He, too, was attired in a formal tunic and toga, his also made of white linen and embroidered with silver thread. "Did the queen send you that to wear?"

He looked down at himself. "She did."

She tried to sound stern. "Where is your gladius, sir?"

He raised the toga a little. The hilt appeared and disappeared again almost immediately. Looking unarmed and being unarmed were always two different things for Apollodorus. "I have a gift for you."

She tried not to gape. "A gift?"

He produced a band of silver, wide but delicately made and so highly polished she could see her reflection in it. "Oh," was all she could say, and watched as he slid it slowly over her hand, wrist, and arm, to seat it firmly halfway between elbow and shoulder. He ran his finger around the edge. His hands were rough and warm and rasped deliciously against her skin. "It fits perfectly. I thought it would."

She blushed, at his tone and at his touch, and his smile turned wicked. "Whatever can you be thinking about, lady?"

She willed back her blush, and deliberately let her eyes drop to his mouth. "I don't know what you can possibly mean, sir."

He caught her hand and raised it to his lips, kissing it and at the same time contriving to tickle it with his tongue. "I missed you last night."

It took her a moment to catch her breath. "Good."

He held out his arm and placed her hand on his. "Shall we see what's on offer in the way of food and drink?"

"I think we must first greet our host."

He sighed. "As you say."

They strolled around the impluvium, the large square pool filling the center of the room, exchanging nods with Cotta, who, being ubiquitous, was of course present and talking to Linos. Linos pretended not to see them. Dixiphanes was there, too, which could be no surprise given how important his favor was to Alexandria's builders. He, too, contrived to ignore her. Ampelius, at his side, sent her a smile behind his master's back.

"Who is that?" Apollodorus said.

"Ampelius, apprentice to Dixiphanes."

"Ah. Poor bastard."

Next to Ampelius stood Vitruvius, although it took Tetisheri a moment to recognize him. He was attired in the dress tunic and cape of a Roman legionary, with a beautifully worked bronze cintus around his waist. Unlike Apollodorus, he'd left his gladius at home. He smiled and gave a slight bow. She inclined her head.

"And who is he, pray tell?"

She smiled up at him. "An architect. He's writing a book."

"And you would know this how?"

He was jealous. A tiny frisson ran up her spine. "We met during the course of my recent investigation."

"Ah."

A bit farther on stood Calliope, attired in an elaborately draped chiton, her hair done up in a braided edifice that looked too heavy for her slender neck to hold up. She wore long earrings inlaid with gold and lapis, with a girdle and sandals to match. The epitome of elegance without elaboration. Tetisheri could only admire her taste.

The hetaira was surrounded by men but the one whose arm she was on looked familiar. He was a Roman, not quite portly, dressed in a toga over a tunic. His hair had been dressed with some kind of oil and stood up in curled locks all over his head. The oil was heavily perfumed and the odor wafted all the way over to Tetisheri. She could feel a sneeze coming on.

And they were standing before the same bookshelf Tetisheri had seen in Calliope's parlor just hours before. It, or its very twin.

Calliope caught sight of Tetisheri and nodded, smiling, dimples flashing. The men around her might have sighed in unison.

Tetisheri, smiling, nodded back. Oh well done, she thought, well done indeed.

"And how do you come to know the most famous hetaira

in Alexandria?" She started to answer and he held up a hand. "Let me guess: You met during the course of your recent investigation."

Tetisheri stifled a giggle. "No, this was something different. Who is she with?"

"Don't you recognize him? You saw him at the Five Soldiers the other afternoon. Titus. The social-climbing aspirant to the blade."

"Oh. I didn't recognize him without all the sweat."

"And blood."

"And blood." At heart Alexandria really was a small town.

They came to the crowd clustering around Otho and waited their turn. Nebenteru had established himself next to Khadiga. He was fingering the cloth of her dress, Tetisheri hoped with her permission.

"Ah, Tetisheri, how lovely to see you," Otho said, reaching out to take her hand between both of his. "I'm so glad you accepted my invitation. Your uncle has just been regaling us with tales of your adventures across the Eastern Ocean."

"Well met, Otho. Thank you for inviting us to your lovely home."

He beamed. "It is my very great pleasure! Of course I've been living here for the past year, but the docks were finished some months ago, and the column paintings on the porch were completed barely in time for today. Magnificent, aren't they?"

"Magnificent," Tetisheri said. "You know Apollodorus, I believe?"

"We have not met formally, but of course all of Alexandria knows of Apollodorus."

The men exchanged a brief grip. "Otho. Well met."

Otho's eyes darted between the two of them. "You came here together?"

The deep voice was imperturbable. "No, but I intend to leave with her."

Otho threw back his head and roared out a laugh. "A man after my own heart!" Still chuckling, he said to Nebenteru, "Excuse me, old fellow, I must introduce my new friend to my old friend. Apollodorus, the lady Khadiga. Lady, you'll know of Apollodorus, of course."

Khadiga's smile was meant to be friendly and it was if you didn't meet her eyes. Her gaze was fixed and unnerving, rather like a crocodile estimating whether your body fat would be worth the effort of fetching it off the sandbank. Tetisheri waited for Apollodorus and Khadiga to finish their pleasantries and then stepped forward, fixing a smile as bright as it was insincere to her face. She hoped it didn't look as off as it felt.

"Ah yes, and the lady Tetisheri, my dear," Otho said with an expansive gesture. "I'm sure she must be known to you as friend to our good queen."

"Known to me, of course, but we haven't met, have we, lady?" It was the voice she had heard in the alley, deep and decisive, the voice of someone used to giving orders and having them obeyed. And of exacting swift and sure retribution when that obedience was delayed.

Tetisheri smiled into the eyes of the woman who had tried to have her murdered only the day before. "No, but I believe I am acquainted with an associate of yours."

The thick, straight eyebrows raised. "Oh?"

"Yes, one..." Tetisheri frowned, trying to remember. "Ah, yes. One Tamir, isn't it? An Egyptian, I believe."

Khadiga's expression remained politely inquiring. "Tamir? Tamir? No, I'm sorry, the name isn't familiar to me."

"My mistake. I must be thinking of someone else."

Message delivered, and to more than one person. The young woman standing behind Khadiga looked puzzled. Otho looked uneasy, sensing an undercurrent he couldn't identify. "Khadiga is one of my closest associates," he said. "In fact, she contracted to do much of the construction on this house. I beg your pardon, but General Thales is waving at me. Please, there is food and drink. Go, go, enjoy yourselves!"

As they strolled away Apollodorus said in a voice meant only for her ears, "So the lady Khadiga was Otho's contractor?"

"It appears so."

"I wonder who his architect was." He squeezed her arm. "Dixiphanes, do you think?"

Yes, that was exactly what she thought.

A rectangular marble table stood against the back wall on legs carved in the likenesses of the Muses. Translucent alabaster pitchers of wine and juice were constantly being refilled by slaves in new kilts, and the array of delicacies on offer would put Phoebe to shame. Candied almonds, honey tarts, dolmas, lamb kebabs, and—

"Look." Apollodorus' voice held a slight tremor. She followed his pointing finger.

In the center of the table stood an almond pastry birdcage covered in white icing. It sat on a thick, square cake that was even now being cut and served. There were three levels to the cage, and—

"No," Tetisheri said, and moved closer.

But yes, in each level there were live birds, pigeons in the bottom, doves in the middle, and desert larks at the top. Every one of them was busily engaged in pecking at the bars of their cages, which appeared to be encrusted with pistachios.

She looked around at Apollodorus, whose shoulders were shaking. She snatched up two cups of something and they retreated around the impluvium to a corner near the door. There they sipped what proved to be a decent red wine and recovered their composure.

Aristander chose this moment to arrive, striding into Otho's atrium in dress nemes, tunic, and kilt, very much on his dignity. His attire was made from the same linen she and Apollodorus were wearing, with the very same silver embroidery. He frowned reprovingly at Tetisheri, who was flushed with laughter and unsuccessfully trying to hide it.

All temptation to laugh was instantly quenched at the sight of Aristander's companion, however. "Why, Nenwef," she said, recovering her voice. "What a surprise. I had heard that you'd gone on a little... voyage."

Nenwef, attired in his gaudiest silks and draped with what appeared to be most of his jewels, glared at her, but it was a half-hearted effort at best. He was frightened, and trying – and failing – not to show how much.

She raised an eyebrow at Aristander, who nodded, allowing a faint smile to disturb his dignity. He took Nenwef by the elbow and moved off.

Just in time to make way for the rattle of sistrums, the beating of tambours and the blaring of trumpets that preceded the entrance of Ptolemy XIV Philopator, brother and husband of Cleopatra and co-ruler of Alexandria and Egypt. He didn't arrive at once, of course, because first there had to be a parade of dancing boys and girls strewing flower petals, followed by two standard bearers, a jumble of courtiers, and a small orchestra. It became painfully obvious they weren't accustomed to walking and playing at the same time.

And then came the kinglet himself, draped in cloth of gold and wearing a heavy gold cobra that was just that little bit too large for him, as it kept slipping down over his right eyebrow. Hard on his heels was a company of soldiers in full armor, sweating heavily.

The king paused before the atrium and looked about him with a regal air. Well, he tried, but he wasn't a very prepossessing creature, Philo. "Greetings, my loyal subjects," he said, waving what appeared to be a flyswatter made of golden thread. Of course, to match his attire. Even his sandals were gold.

Fortunately everyone knew what was his due and bowed from the waist. Some present may have bowed less low than others. Otho surged through the crowd to bow lowest of all, his forehead nearly touching the floor, an impressive feat for a man of his age and girth. "Majesty, what an honor! To have you grace my humble affair is more than I could have hoped for."

"Oh, get up, Otho, do," Philo said in a languid voice, and gave Otho his hand, a signal honor, because everyone knew Philo had a horror of contracting disease from the unwashed.

Otho straightened, took the offered hand with tender care, and bowed low over it. Philo gave him a tap on the shoulder with the flyswatter and he straightened with a smile on his face that looked a little forced. It could have been the panic of any host faced with a large number of uninvited guests— *How am I going to feed all these extra people?* It could have been something else entirely, too, but all he said was, "I will have a couch brought at once, majesty."

Another swat from the fly catcher, and if the infinitesimal wince Tetisheri saw cross Otho's face was an indication, this one carried enough force to sting. "Yes, yes, but give me your arm, Otho, as I greet my loyal subjects."

Another signal honor and one that could not be refused. As luck would have it Philo turned right to begin his progress and the first people he saw were Tetisheri and

Apollodorus. Otho had barely paused when Philo dug his fingers so tight into Otho's arm that Otho gasped, and the two passed by without stopping. Tetisheri made sure to keep her head bent until the two were well and truly past. Conversation, which had halted at the king's entrance, resumed, although at a much lower volume. Some present were titillated by Philo's appearance, others shocked, and some were outright frightened. One never knew which way an unstable personality like Philo would lean but they were all painfully familiar with the ensuing havoc he could wreak when he did.

She straightened. "Did you know he was coming?"

"No. I wonder if—"

What he wondered was drowned out by a sudden increase in volume of the conversation, followed by absolute silence, followed by everyone in the assembly dropping first to their knees and then to their hands, presenting their foreheads to the floor and their collective backsides to all the gods above and more importantly to the living one in the doorway.

The sole exception was Philo, who remained standing, glaring at the door with a slowly reddening face. Otho, next to him, had made it to one knee but Philo refused to release his arm so he could make it all the rest of the way down. Otho remained suspended halfway, an agonized expression on his face that could have come from the pain of Philo's grip (unlikely) or from fear of what would happen to him if he didn't pay proper respect to Philo's sister (much more so).

In the doorway there stood a single figure clad in a simple white stola, bloused over a slim belt worked in silver and plain leather sandals. Her palla was white as well, but as she moved the light caught the silver threads worked into the weave. A silver brooch pinned the palla to one shoulder, and a silver fillet circled her brow to contain the fall of dark, shoulder-length hair. She wore no other jewelry.

She was the picture of elegance and dignity. By contrast, Philo looked as if he'd been dressed by a four-year-old playing in her mother's jewel coffer, and Khadiga like one of the women who worked nights on the Bruchium waterfront.

Tetisheri sought out and found Keren and Nebenteru, and gave her head an infinitesimal jerk. The two of them, she was pleased to note, began at once to move slowly but steadily toward the door.

Cleopatra's voice was warm and friendly and easily filled the room. "Rise, please, my people. It is impossible to greet you properly when I can't see your faces."

The crowd rose to its feet as one, and this time all wore the same expression: A deep apprehension. One Ptolemy was bad enough, but two...

"Otho, my dear friend." Cleopatra waded through the crowd, which perforce melted away before her. She reached out both her hands. By sheer force of will Otho wrenched his arm free of Philo's grip to place his hands in hers. "Well met, dear sir. But I must admit I'm hurt. My invitation to this most festive gathering, with all of Alexandria present—" she sent a smile around the room that rivaled Helios for brightness and Calliope for charm "—must have been lost somewhere between here and the palace."

If possible, Otho's face went even whiter but he made a manful effort at recovery. "Majesty, you need no invitation. You are always welcome."

"You are too kind." She turned to Philo. "I give you good day, brother. Long it has been since we met." Simple words, but if one closed one's eyes, one could hear a lion growling.

Philo definitely heard it, and so did the crowd, which took an involuntary, collective step backward. "Sister," he said, or rather spat, which might have sounded more impressive if his voice hadn't broken on the word. The unspoken "Not long enough" was also plain.

"My husband, the divine Caesar, sends his kindest regards, and his hopes that his greeting finds you flourishing."

There was a muted murmur of commentary at this, which all recognized to be nothing less than provocation.

"Caesar writes to me himself," Philo said through his teeth. "We have no need of an intermediary."

The murmur became less muted and a little frantic, especially toward the back of the room where the refreshment table was. Apollodorus' shoulders began to shake again. Tetisheri followed his gaze. "Oh dear."

The almond pastry had not held up to the test and the doves and larks and pigeons were launching themselves into the air with a tremendous flapping of wings and shrill cries of alarm. In vain did the slaves attempt to catch them, although they did manage to knock what was left of the cage from the table. It fell to the floor with a mighty crash and smashed into bits. Meanwhile the birds darted between the guests, depositing their opinions of the event on a toga here and a headdress there before ascending in a frantic flurry of wings up out of the compluvium and into the free air and sunshine. Tetisheri nearly cheered.

Everyone else was more than happy to be offered an additional excuse to vacate the premises at speed and made for the door, dividing around the slender figure of the queen as a swift-running stream does around a pillar of granite, which might in this instance have been more yielding. Safely past, they streamed down the steps where they could be heard shouting for their cabrios, carriages, curricles, and chariots. Some of them were in such haste or so impatient of the traffic jam that they left their personal vehicles behind and walked home, no matter how far the distance or how insubstantial their footwear.

Dixiphanes, Ampelius, and Vitruvius with his attendant acolytes in tow swept past. Tetisheri touched Vitruvius' arm as he passed her. "Wait," she said in a low voice.

He raised his eyebrows but obediently dropped back and came to stand next to her. "What's going on?"

"Your testimony may be required shortly."

"'Testimony?'" He raised his eyebrows. "Is there to be a trial?"

"Something like that."

As more people left and the flow outward lessened, Babak managed to wriggle his way inside. He went directly to

Tetisheri and whispered in her ear. She listened, nodding. She asked him two questions. He handed her two ragged patches of material, which disappeared inside her palla. She patted him on the shoulder and motioned to him to stand next to Vitruvius. He smoothed down the front of his new tunic and then caught sight of the queen.

His eyes goggled and his jaw dropped. His head swiveled around to Tetisheri. He pointed, his finger trembling.

Vitruvius closed his hand over Babak's and forced it down to his side, and then raised his hand again to the boy's chin and gently shut his mouth.

Khadiga and her daughter were almost to the door when Aristander intercepted them. She looked like she might still try to make a run for it, until four more shurta appeared in the doorway in front of her. She glared at them. They didn't move. Her face flushed a dark, congested red. Aristander took her arm in a firm grasp and escorted her to the side.

Her daughter stood rooted in place, watching all this with wide eyes. One of the shurta, stern-faced, escorted her to join her mother. She went without protest, looking bewildered but as yet unafraid. She said something to her mother, who ignored her.

Calliope and Titus passed near enough to Tetisheri for Calliope's dress to brush Tetisheri's own. She nodded in passing, maintaining an unhurried pace. It appeared her hand on Titus' arm was the only thing that kept him from breaking into an undignified gallop.

A few minutes later only a few remained, Cotta and Linos and Philo among them.

"Leave us," Cleopatra said.

Even Cotta was not proof against the iron in that command, but for a moment he stood in the doorway, looking back, until two of Aristander's shurta, respectful but firm, escorted him the rest of the way.

Philo and his entourage only remained.

"Brother," Cleopatra said.

He snarled at her.

She smiled at him.

He snarled again and stormed out after Cotta. His dancing troupe, his musicians, and his guard scurried after him.

"The members of your household should leave us as well, Otho."

The slaves standing along the walls didn't wait for confirmation from their master and evaporated. No one knew what was about to happen in this room but no one wanted to be present for it.

Cleopatra, Tetisheri, Apollodorus, Vitruvius, Aristander and his men, Otho, Khadiga and her daughter, and Babak remained.

"Close the doors."

The doors, front and back, were duly closed. The thuds, echoing each other, sounded ominous, even somehow final, as if the doors would never be opened again.

# 20

"Apollodorus, Aristander, attend me, please." Aristander and Apollodorus came forward to stand behind the queen.

Cleopatra smiled again at Otho, who tried and failed not to cringe. Facing down a trio composed of the head of the Shurta, the legendary Apollodorus, and the Lady of the Two Lands with anything resembling composure was not something for which he had been prepared, on this or any other day. "I believe there was some mention of a chair being brought for my brother. Perhaps I could be extended the same courtesy."

"Of course, majesty, yes, majesty, certainly, majesty." Otho scurried from the room, accompanied by one of the shurta, and returned in short order with a chair that was more like a throne, no back, wooden arms carved into furled ferns, and a green and gold tapestry upholstery. Otho helped carry it in with his own hands.

"My very own chair, majesty," Otho said eagerly, and then, too late, thought better of it.

"Fit for royalty."

"Oh no, no indeed, majesty, I would never dream of—"

Cleopatra took what was now her chair, back straight, hands placed lightly on the armrests. "The Eye of Isis will come forth."

Her voice echoed from deep inside the very walls of the new house, or perhaps it only sounded that way to Tetisheri. She closed her eyes briefly, passing the dizzying activities of the past four days in quick review, and then produced the Eye of Isis from beneath her palla and centered it on her breast. There were several gasps from around the room. She walked forward, past Apollodorus, to take her place at the queen's right hand. The light from the compluvium streamed down to illuminate their figures, three standing equidistant around the one seated, all in white and silver. Why, it was almost as if it had been staged.

Before them were arrayed Khadiga and her daughter, and Otho. Khadiga stood with her shoulders squared and her broad face expressionless. Her daughter looked confused and terrified. Otho's knees were shaking so hard his tunic vibrated in harmony.

Grouped at a little distance were Vitruvius, Babak, Nenwef, and four of Aristander's shurta (one was Dejen, who winked again at Tetisheri). It would not be comforting to anyone present that the queen wished to keep what was about to pass in this room limited to as few witnesses as possible.

"Nothing of which passes here today will be spoken of outside this room, on pain of death," the queen said, still in that inflexible tone, and waited for a moment to let the message sink in. "Begin, my Eye."

The face of the woman sitting at her left could have been carved from stone. This was no longer her friend; this was Cleopatra Philopator, Seventh of Her Name, the Lady of the Two Lands, the might and majesty and history of Alexandria and Egypt in human form, Isis Herself stepped down to Earth to render judgement. What was said in her presence could never be unsaid. What was heard in her presence could never be unheard. What happened here would have consequences, real, immediate, and very probably unpleasant for someone.

Tetisheri looked at Apollodorus. He smiled, letting her see his confidence and pride in her. She took a deep breath.

"Majesty. Two days ago, a body was discovered offshore, west of the Gate of the Moon. His feet had first been encased in cement, after which he had been thrown into the sea to drown.

"I was called to the scene by Aristander, who informed me that this was the second body to be found in such circumstances. The first had been discovered nearly two years before. His murder remained unsolved. Both bodies were later determined to be young men. Very few identifying marks remained, but both wore amulets. One had suffered a minor fracture to his arm not long before he died."

Raia gasped, her hand flying to her mouth.

"Upon hearing my report, majesty, you tasked the Eye with determining the circumstances of their deaths.

"Discovering their identities was my first priority. As I said, the only possession either had retained was their amulet. I took these to Matan the jeweler, who could tell me which god the amulets represented and what they were made of, but no more.

"I spoke also to one Vitruvius, present here today, a Roman engineer and architect, at present resident in the city conducting experiments under the patronage of the office of the Royal Architect. He advised me on the properties of the various kinds of cement in hopes of tracing the kind that was used for the murders. At my request, he examined the bodies and identified the cement used in the murder of the two men as pozzolan. It is relatively rare – it comes from Italy – and is ideal for use in buildings on or near the sea, as it does not deteriorate under the influence of salt water as other cements do. As such it is much in demand, and there is never enough supply to meet it.

"During the course of my investigation, I must have betrayed myself to the murderer, because yesterday I was kidnapped, after which I was informed that I was to be fitted with 'a new pair of sandals.' Thanks to the quick thinking of one of my household who witnessed the event, the attempt was foiled. I then followed my kidnapper back to the house of his employer."

Khadiga's shoulders became ever so slightly less defiant.

"His employer was overseeing the offloading of large bags of such weight that it took two guards to move them from the cart. More significant was that it was moved by a small group of trusted employees, under cover of approaching darkness. It was obvious that the contents of this shipment were meant to be a closely guarded secret.

"I overheard some little conversation that took place between the two men who delivered the freight, the man who kidnapped me, and his employer, who ordered them to take the ship that had transported the freight to Syene and to stay there until further notice.

"I followed the two men—"

The slump to Khadiga's shoulders was more definite now, and her face looked gray beneath its customarily high color.

"—through the Gate of the Moon to a small pier under construction on the coastline west of the city. There they boarded a boat and departed." Tetisheri cleared her throat. "It should be said that, under the orders of their employer, they took someone with them, against his will."

"A second kidnapping victim?"

"So it seemed to me, majesty. When I returned home, I dispatched notes to the following people: One to the palace to apprise you of current events and one to Apollodorus, asking him to retrieve the unwitting, ah, guest on board the ship."

"And the third?"

"The third was to Vitruvius."

"Ah. And?"

"I found the location of the pier to be curious and possibly relevant to my inquiry, majesty."

"How so?"

"For one thing, it was very near to where the second body had been found. For another, since I had learned from Vitruvius of the efficacy of pozzolan in building along waterfronts, I wondered what kind of cement they were using there. I asked him to determine that for me."

"And?"

Tetisheri motioned to the Roman. He stepped forward briskly, nodded to Tetisheri, and bowed deeply to Cleopatra. "Majesty."

"Well met, Vitruvius. The crown appreciates your help in this matter. Did you visit the pier our Eye described?"

"Majesty, I did."

"And what did you discover?"

"The driven pilings, the temporary ones, are of course made of timber, majesty. The permanent pilings, the ones that replace the temporary ones, were poured from pozzolan cement."

There was a moment of silence. "I see," the queen said. "You are certain of your facts, Vitruvius?"

"Majesty, I am. I chipped out a sample and tested it in my workshop. It is pozzolan cement."

"I see," the queen said again. "Well, then, all I can do is thank you for your service to my realm, Vitruvius. Be sure I shall speak kindly of you when next I write to my husband, Julius Caesar."

"It was my privilege and my pleasure to serve, majesty."

He bowed again, and returned to his place.

"Continue, my Eye."

"Your majesty would know better than I if the current plan for public works includes construction of a new pier outside the city."

"To my certain knowledge it does not," the queen said. "We have yet to complete the repairs to the Pharos, which is by far more important to the future of our city and country and indeed the Middle Sea." She paused. "Whatever would be the point in building a pier outside the city?"

Tetisheri said woodenly, because Cleopatra knew perfectly well what the answer to her question was, "One incentive could come from the notion that goods shipped from that pier would depart from outside the city walls, and thereby be exempt from city taxes."

A sound that was somewhere between a sigh and a groan came from Otho.

"An interesting, if foolish notion." Another brief, painful silence. "But we stray from the main point at issue, my Eye. What of the bodies discovered by the Shurta?"

"I believe the matters are connected, majesty."

"How so?"

For the first time, Tetisheri looked at Raia. "I believe the daughter of Khadiga has information that will aid us in finding out the truth, majesty."

"Is that so?" Cleopatra looked at Khadiga's daughter. "Stand forward, Raia."

It was to her credit that Raia did so without hesitation, ignoring the hand half raised to her by her mother. She stopped before Cleopatra and prostrated herself.

"Stand up, Raia," the queen said impatiently. "I can't talk to your backside."

Raia stood up, shrinking, hands clasped tightly in front of her.

"Continue, my Eye."

"Majesty." Tetisheri took a step forward. "Raia of Rhakotis, you are the daughter of Muhandis, are you not?"

"I am."

"And the daughter of Khadiga?"

"Yes."

"Two years ago you were betrothed to Grafeas, son of Archeion, scribe of this city, and his wife, Eirene?"

"I was." Her voice trembled only a little.

"But the marriage did not take place."

"It did not."

"Why not?"

"He—disappeared."

"Disappeared?"

"He left work one afternoon and was never seen again." Raia blinked back tears.

"Did he talk to you of his work?"

Raia raised her chin. "We spoke together of the work we both did. I am an only child, too, and the future of the family business rests in me, as his family's did in Grafeas."

"My investigation has shown that he was serving as scribe for half a dozen different clients when he disappeared."

"I believe so. I don't—"

"Was one of them your father?"

Raia stared at Tetisheri.

"Was one of—"

"Yes."

"What did it concern?"

Raia looked at the queen, who stared back at her. No help there. "It involved a case of construction fraud."

"An accusation against him or a complaint he was making?"

Raia seemed to gather her courage. "A complaint my father had against the Royal Architect."

"What was his complaint?"

Raia swallowed. "His complaint was that the quality of cement authorized by the Royal Architect was not of the kind necessary for his current project."

"Which was?"

"The rebuilding of a pier destroyed in the war, lady."

"Where?"

"In the Great Harbor. Located somewhere between the Heptastadion and Poseidon's Head. I don't know exactly where. I never personally visited the site."

"Did Muhandis, your father, have some notion that Dixiphanes had access to the kind of cement he needed for his project?"

Raia looked surprised, Tetisheri thought genuinely so. "But yes, lady."

"Even in the middle of the war?"

"But the war interfered very little with traffic on the Great River, lady. The Great Harbor was blockaded, yes, but there was always the Canal."

"So the cement Muhandis questioned came from somewhere up the Nile?"

"Yes."

"Majesty," Tetisheri said, choosing her words carefully, "there has as yet been reported no discovery of pozzolan cement in Egypt. Therefore, such cement as was shipped downriver to Alexandria must perforce have been cement of a different kind, and as such unsuitable for salt water construction."

A brief silence. "Your reasoning is sound, my Eye."

Tetisheri faced Raia again, pity in her heart. "Is it possible, lady, that Grafeas knew this, too?"

Raia stared at her. "Lady, I—" Her voice faded away.

The queen stirred. "Do you know what has happened here, my Eye?"

"I believe I do, majesty."

"Explain."

Tetisheri took a deep breath and let it out slowly. She turned to face the queen. "I believe that someone—" she didn't look at Otho or Khadiga "—found a deposit of cement somewhere near Syene. It wasn't as good as pozzolan but it looked enough like it that it would pass a cursory examination, so long as no one sampled the finished product once it was poured and in place." Or later checked to see if it had begun to dissolve upon contact with salt water. "I believe that this someone began swapping out the substandard cement for the real pozzolan imported from Puteoli in order to use the genuine pozzolan on their own projects. I believe Muhandis discovered this substitution and told Grafeas, who wrote and submitted his complaint before the court."

"And?"

Tetisheri looked at Raia. Raia wasn't looking at her. She had turned to stare at her mother. Khadiga continued to look straight ahead, meeting no one's eyes.

"And I believe," Tetisheri said, "they were both killed for the knowledge of this conspiracy by people who wished for it to continue."

"Muhandis is dead?"

"It is said that he, ah, eloped with his mistress. There have been rumors that place him in various locations upriver."

"You do not believe these rumors."

"Majesty, I do not. His disappearance was entirely too convenient. It led to his wife, the lady Khadiga, assuming control of his contracting business, where she has been in sole authority since his disappearance." She gestured at Otho. "Otho himself said today she built this house. Earlier today, an agent of mine discovered a store of pozzolan, still marked with the insignia of the trader who shipped it to Alexandria, in one of the storehouses on this estate." She produced two swatches Babak had brought her. "These bear the customs stamp of a well-known trader of the city, one Nebenteru." Her voice was very dry. "They were found in one of the warehouses on the property shared by this house."

This time Otho groaned out loud, a long, drawn out sound of pain and fear. "Majesty, believe me, I did not know, I did not—"

"Silence."

Otho wrapped his arms around his belly and sagged forward, his breath coming harsh and fast. One could almost hear the terrified judder of his heart in his breast.

"What happened here, my Eye?"

"Majesty, as I understand from Vitruvius, pozzolan is shipped to Alexandria from Puteoli, after which it is parceled out to builders for projects approved by the crown. It is my belief that the pozzolan was picked up for one approved project and delivered to another, unapproved project."

"And then?"

"And then an inferior cement mined from a site upriver was delivered to the approved project."

Cleopatra sat very still, her face a mask clothed in golden skin. "And used in its construction."

"Yes."

"Beginning with Muhandis?"

"That I cannot be sure of, as Muhandis cannot be found to be questioned. If you were to ask me to speculate, I would say no. If he had been swapping out ordinary cement for pozzolan, he would not have accused the Royal Architect of doing so. It would have brought attention to his own illegal activities."

"I see. And Muhandis' charges against our Royal Architect?"

Tetisheri tried not to choke over the words. "It seems obvious that Muhandis suspected him of the thefts, but the truth was that the thief was much closer to home."

"Is it true?" Raia's words were barely above a whisper. "Is it true, Mother?"

Khadiga stirred. Her head came up, her shoulders went back, and she looked the queen straight in the eye. "My daughter was wholly ignorant of these things. I claim all responsibility."

"Including the murder of Grafeas?"

"That I know nothing of."

"And the other man?"

"I don't even know who he is."

"And the murder of your husband?"

Khadiga shook her head. "Muhandis ran away with his mistress. There were enough reports of him being seen with her from here to Syene to convince me. So far as I know he is still living, majesty."

*All we want to do is fit you with a nice new pair of sandals.* "Majesty," Tetisheri said, "if the lady Khadiga's servant, one Tamir the Egyptian, could be found, his testimony might contradict these protestations of innocence."

Khadiga didn't even bother looking her way.

"Aristander," the queen said.

Aristander came forward. "At your command, majesty, this morning I sent someone to look for Tamir the Egyptian, at the lady Khadiga's house, here, and the three building sites the lady's business has in hand. He was nowhere to be found."

Lawless and murderous, Khadiga certainly wasn't stupid. Against her will Tetisheri felt a grudging respect. Otho—she glanced at him and looked away again immediately. It felt almost indecent to witness his terror.

"Mother! Is this true!"

"Hush, child." The queen's voice was firm but kind. "Do I understand that you have been acting as your mother's second-in-command at Muhandis Construction?"

Raia turned to look at the queen. She seemed dazed, and no wonder. "I—yes, majesty. I am responsible for all the day-to-day operations. She has even recently begun to allow me to write bids."

The queen nodded. "Good. I would hate to be responsible for putting so many people out of work. Tetisheri, is there any other evidence you would like to offer?"

There was Nenwef's testimony but she judged him to be at best an unreliable witness. She had only wanted him there to show Khadiga that she had no hope of pleading innocent to Tetisheri's claims.

And this had never been about the murders, anyway.

"My Eye?"

"This concludes my report, majesty." Which was a lie and everyone in the room knew it.

"Very well. Lady Khadiga."

There it was again, that commanding voice. "You will be taken from this place to be put to the question. I want a full accounting of every building site where ordinary cement was substituted for pozzolan, and the names of everyone who conspired with you to do so. I recommend that you answer truthfully. It will be far less painful for you. Aristander?"

He beckoned to the two shurta and Khadiga was removed. She made it all the way out of Otho's atrium without having to be carried. Impressive.

"Lady Raia, your have our condolences on the loss of your father and your mother. Be about your business."

Raia took a moment to understand that she was free to go. She dropped to her hands and knees and made obeisance to the Lady of the Two Lands, a wise show of fealty, and departed.

Cleopatra did not watch her go. "Otho."

"M-m-m-majesty." Otho's legs finally gave out and he crashed to his knees. Tetisheri winced when she heard the crack of bone meeting marble.

"You were affianced to the lady Khadiga, were you not?"

"M-m-m-majesty, I—"

"I would hesitate before I found anyone guilty merely by association, but you must admit that in this case I have cause for suspicion."

"M-m-m—"

"I am disposed to be lenient, however, because of the service you have given to our city and country over the past two years. Repairing the Heptastadion in only seven days. Your people still labor on the Pharos; indeed, I can plainly hear them at work from the palace."

"M-m—"

"And then there is the esteem in which you are held by your peers. They have deemed you worthy of the title Master of Builders. A rare honor, indeed." The queen meditated on this for a moment.

Otho remained on his knees, no doubt in part hoping to engender sympathy, but Tetisheri believed mostly because his legs had lost the ability to hold him upright.

"All this must weigh in the balance against what is only, after all, circumstantial evidence that you conspired with Khadiga in this theft of our property. As my Eye properly reports—" Cleopatra carefully did not look in Tetisheri's direction, perhaps fearing the expression she would see there "—it appears that the guard around our store of pozzolan is so lacking that the substitution was easily orchestrated. This will be remedied."

Tetisheri thought of the two young guards at the pozzolan store, and hoped they would survive the impending purge.

The queen rose to her feet and walked further into the atrium. "This is a very handsome house, Otho." She looked at him over her shoulder. He stared dumbly back. "And, as you proved today, suitable for large gatherings. There is the added convenience of water access via the canal, and such extensive docking, too. Yes, I think it will do quite well."

"M-majesty?"

Cleopatra returned to her seat and placed her hands on the armrests in a formal pose. "I am annexing your house to the royal estate, Otho. Oh don't worry, you'll be suitably compensated. In fact—Tetisheri, have you a drachma?"

Stone-faced, Tetisheri produced a coin.

"Oh, and it's one of the new ones. Such a good likeness, don't you think? Even if I shouldn't say so." She held it out to Otho, who perforce managed to fumble to his feet to come forward to accept it in a shrinking palm. He stared down at it dumbly. It meant he would live, even if he didn't quite believe it yet.

"And please, don't inconvenience yourself. There's no hurry, Otho," the queen said with an airy wave.

"Tomorrow morning will be quite soon enough for me to take possession."

# EPÍLOGOS

There had been so much interest in Vitruvius' lecture that Sosigenes had moved it to the Pan Amphitheater. It was a small, exquisite structure at the corner of Pan and Lochias, faced entirely in marble, columns, flagstones, seats in ascending tiers, staircases, and proscenium. It had been one of Auletes' flightier fancies, because he wanted a suitable venue in which to play his flute. It would explain why the acoustics were so good here and why every syllable Vitruvius spoke rang from the marble surfaces of the theater so clearly.

Tetisheri was seated in the middle of the last tier, which was otherwise empty, the only one to remain so. She hadn't even looked around when someone took the seat next to her shortly after Vitruvius began speaking.

He was reading from his book. "Architecture depends on Order, Arrangement, Eurythmy, Symmetry, Propriety, and Economy."

Otho had sold most of his slaves and moved into a modest

house inland from the canal. He had not inquired as to the whereabouts or well-being of the lady Khadiga. Thus far, he remained Master of Builders. Tetisheri was certain that Khadiga had been the driving force in their partnership, and she wondered how long it would be before the builders' guild voted him out in favor of someone else.

She was equally certain Khadiga hadn't built that house for Otho, she'd built it for herself. The dock alone would have been much more convenient for smuggling than her own house. When one succeeded at smuggling one item, one was only emboldened to smuggle more.

"Order gives due measure to the members of a work considered separately, and symmetrical agreement to the proportions of the whole."

Raia had wasted no time in mourning the loss of her second parent. From all reports she was meeting the business' contractual obligations. Tetisheri had heard that Raia's bid for the remodeling of Otho's house into a public building had been awarded to her, and detected the queen's hand at work. Muhandis Construction employed upwards of a hundred craftsmen, all of whom lived in Alexandria and spent their money there. Raia was making a significant contribution to the local economy, and would be encouraged to continue to do so.

"Arrangement includes the putting of things in their proper places and the elegance of effect which is due to adjustments appropriate to the character of the work."

Tamir was still missing. Tetisheri suspected that his

body was currently keeping company with Muhandis at the bottom of the Middle Sea, his feet encased in cement, his body feeding the fish. Khadiga had been every bit as ruthless at ridding herself of encumbrances and threats as was her queen.

Although the queen, in her determination to keep Dixiphanes' name free of scandal, would have every bit as much motive to keep Tamir from contributing to the case against Khadiga. She would never admit this to Tetisheri, though, and Tetisheri would never ask.

"Eurythmy is beauty and fitness in the adjustments of the members. This is found when the members of a work are of a height suited to their breadth, of a breadth suited to their length, and, in a word, when they all correspond symmetrically."

Aristander had traced Dion's home to the Nome of the Bat. Dion was not there and his family hadn't seen him in months. Dion's father had instantly recognized the amulet that had been found with the second body. Like Grafeas, Dion had learned something he shouldn't have, in his case from his master, Dixiphanes.

"Symmetry is a proper agreement between the members of the work itself, and relation between the different parts and the whole general scheme, in accordance with a certain part selected as standard."

Apollodorus was away again on the queen's business. Tetisheri didn't know where, or why.

"Thus in the human body there is a kind of symmetrical

harmony between forearm, foot, palm, finger, and other small parts; and so it is with perfect buildings.

"Propriety is that perfection of style which comes when a work is authoritatively constructed on approved principles. It arises from usage when buildings having magnificent interiors are provided with elegant entrance-courts to correspond; for there will be no propriety in the spectacle of an elegant interior approached by a low, mean entrance."

Rhode had settled into her new employment as house cabriador with very little fuss, donning the livery with its newly designed house insignia of a tiny boat beneath a full-bellied sail, wake foaming back from the bow. She had lost no time in becoming boon companion to Phoebe and Nebet, and the three of them ended every day over tea and gossip around the kitchen fire, and were united in their goal of either moving Apollodorus into the house or Tetisheri out. For women who staunchly eschewed the married life themselves, they seemed oddly insistent that Tetisheri not embrace the same fate. The fact that they were all three a little in love with Apollodorus themselves might have had something to do with this determination.

"There will also be natural propriety in using an eastern light for bedrooms and libraries, a western light in winter for baths and winter apartments, and a northern light for picture galleries and other places in which a steady light is needed; for that quarter of the sky grows neither light nor dark with the course of the sun, but remains steady and unshifting all day long."

Half in jest, Tetisheri had renamed Babak and Company the Order of the Owl. "They're wise and stealthy and secretive, and they hunt at night," she had told them when they asked why. Babak and his friends were entranced by the notion, especially when she had had Matan design a brooch for each of them featuring the eagle-owl of Egypt, to be worn only on dress occasions. Much of their work would of necessity be incognito. She only hoped they'd be better at it than she was.

"Economy denotes the proper management of materials and of site, as well as a thrifty balancing of cost and common sense in the construction of works. This will be observed if, in the first place, the architect does not demand things which cannot be found or made ready without great expense."

Nenwef had gone home to his rich and long-suffering wife and for the moment remained there.

"A second stage in Economy is reached when we have to plan the different kinds of dwellings suitable for ordinary householders, for great wealth, or for the high position of the statesman."

Tetisheri had visited Archeion and Eirene to tell them that the queen had found Grafeas' killer and brought them to justice. They were already predisposed to believe the worst of Khadiga and had accepted Tetisheri's explanation without protest. His remains had been returned to them and had been entombed with all the traditional funerary rites.

"A house in town obviously calls for one form of construction; that into which stream the products of country estates requires another; this will not be the same in the case of money-lenders and still different for the opulent and luxurious; for the powers under whose deliberations the commonwealth is guided dwellings are to be provided according to their special needs: and, in a word, the proper form of economy must be observed in building houses for each and every class."

When Vitruvius finished speaking there was enthusiastic applause, after which he took questions for another hour.

"An interesting thesis," Cleopatra said. "I like the notion of a unifying theory of everything, and that how and where we build should reflect that."

"He's an interesting man."

"And discreet."

Tetisheri answered the hint of a question she had heard in the remark. "I have heard nothing to indicate that he has spoken of that day with anyone." She smiled a little. "He's probably saving it for his memoirs."

Cleopatra snorted.

They watched as students and scholars alike clustered around the lectern. Sosigenes was there, and Yasmin, and Ampelius. Dixiphanes was nowhere to be found, but then Dixiphanes was currently keeping a very low profile. The scene was framed in marble columns and an entablature free of decoration so as not to distract from the action on the proscenium. Above, the sky was a deep, sensuous black, set with stars like chips of mica. A glow in the east presaged the rising of the moon, Nut in all her glory to rise to her station, to watch over the red land and the black.

When the theater had emptied there remained only Vitruvius and the two of them, still seated at the center of the top tier. And the guards spaced at intervals behind the top tier of seats. Those same guards that had been present outside Otho's house on that fateful day. Cleopatra VII Philopater left very little to chance.

"I know why you did it, Pati. Otho is useful to you."

"He is of even more use to Alexandria and to Egypt, Sheri."

"Yes. But if he didn't outright conspire with Khadiga to steal that pozzolan, he knew."

"Oh, yes. I think that is incontestable."

A company of shurta had been dispatched to Syene to find Minius and crew and place them under arrest. After they had set Nenwef ashore at the smallest, dirtiest village they could find, they had gone to ground somewhere upriver. Tetisheri wondered if they would ever be found to give evidence, and if so, if their testimony would ever be allowed to come to light. The risk of exposure to Otho would be great. A case could even be made that Raia must have known enough of her mother's activities that she should have come forward, and the queen had made it abundantly clear that Raia was not to be punished for the sins of her mother.

In that uncanny and uncomfortable way Cleopatra had of reading Tetisheri's thoughts she said, "But there are many more just like Otho who, however corrupt, are necessary to my plans. When that work is complete, things may change."

The work would never be complete, because Cleopatra would never be done building. There was something about the sands of Egypt that made its rulers want to pile blocks of granite into massive memorials. It was one kind of immortality.

"It is interesting to note," Cleopatra said, "that had Khadiga not sent Tamir to kidnap you, she would still be thieving my pozzolan today."

"That thought had occurred to me as well," Tetisheri said dryly. "Just another example of the lengths I am willing to go to serve my queen."

Cleopatra chuckled.

"Her reaction was inevitable, though, after she saw me at Dixiphanes' workshop. He called me by name. What with Nenwef's warning the day before, she would have panicked." She paused. "Did she confess?"

"To the thefts and the substitutions, in full. I am happy to say without the necessity of putting her to the test." The queen made a face. "So loud and so very messy. I hate it when they make it necessary."

"Did she confess to the murders?"

"No. No, she continues to insist that she has no knowledge of them."

"And Tamir has yet to be found."

"Yes. Unfortunately." But Cleopatra sounded very tranquil in this assessment.

"And then?" Tetisheri had not missed the conjugation that revealed that Khadiga was still living.

"She is a capable woman. It may be that I have a use for her." Cleopatra's smile was cold. "And it may not. We shall see."

"She's a murderer, Pati. A multiple murderer."

"I am aware of that, Sheri, but she may yet have something of value to contribute to Egypt." Cleopatra's voice dropped, as if she were speaking to herself. "We don't have so many citizens with abilities like hers that I can wantonly waste one."

After three hundred years of debauchery, corruption, and dynastic warfare, Egypt had finally produced a practical Ptolemy. Tetisheri could not wish it otherwise, but the memory of the body on the beach, its feet encased in that implacable block of cement, would be a long time leaving her.

Vitruvius packed away his drawings and papers, sketched a bow in their general direction without looking directly at them, and departed. He was wise enough to know that if the queen had attended the meeting incognito that incognito she wished to remain. An intelligent man, Vitruvius.

They listened to his firm footsteps echoing away.

"You haven't mentioned Nenwef," Cleopatra said.

"Ah. Nenwef. Yes. When questioned by Aristander he denied it, but he has to have had some suspicion of how Grafeas died. How else would he have known to go straight to Khadiga with the news that I was asking questions?"

"Do you think he was blackmailing Khadiga?"

Tetisheri snorted. "If he had tried, Khadiga would have disposed of him the same way she did Muhandis and Grafeas and very probably Tamir and Dion and who knows how many others."

"And you."

"And me. I may never be able to eat fish again."

"Indeed."

"Still," Tetisheri said slowly, thinking it over. "It's clear she paid him for information. I wonder how valuable any of it was." She drew in a long breath and let it out slowly. "You haven't had him arrested."

"No. Not yet." Cleopatra glanced at her. "He could be useful to us. If he returns to Philo's court."

She wanted to protest but she'd had the same idea herself. "He has no true loyalty to Philo, so far as I can tell. He's always been for sale to the highest bidder. Although I don't know that he would make a very good spy."

"He would if the price was right."

"Philo could top it."

"He could, if he knew about it."

"Nenwef could make sure he did. Don't trust him, Pati."

"Who said anything about trusting him?"

Tetisheri was silent for a moment. "I notice that you have said nothing about Dixiphanes."

"No." Her friend's voice was cool. "No, I have not."

"Dion learned something of this business in Dixiphanes' yard and was murdered for it."

Cleopatra chose to answer obliquely. "I called Dixiphanes into my presence soon after the events of that day. As our Royal Architect I felt he should be informed of the circumstances. He professed himself shocked to hear of Khadiga's activities, and of course he was grieved at the loss of two such promising young men, one his own apprentice. I put it to him: Since a person under his direct supervision had perpetrated these heinous crimes, the Royal Architect should take personal responsibility for compensating their families for the loss to them of the value of their life's work."

"He agreed, of course."

"He did. I also made it clear to him that since the throne was in no way at fault that I felt that this remuneration should come from his personal funds."

"He agreed to that, too."

"Indeed, he did."

Tetisheri knew that Cleopatra wanted her to focus on the enormous sums Dixiphanes would be forced to disburse to Grafeas and Dion's families. "So he continues free."

"Yes."

"And with his reputation unblemished."

"Only to the public, Tetisheri. You and I know him for what he truly is."

The moon came out from behind a cloud and the amphitheater seemed to glow like an enormous candle in the darkness. "Sosigenes tells me that several of the books stolen from my Library have been found. The two editions of *The Iliad* and *The Odyssey* among them."

"Yes. Yasmin says they were misfiled in the Room of Thales."

The Room of Thales was where the works of natural philosophy were collected, named for Thales of Miletus. "How very clever of someone."

"Yes, I thought so, too. But at least they are back." She couldn't stop the smile from spreading across her face. "Not the Astyanassa or the Elephantis, though."

Cleopatra chuckled. "Rather too much to expect. I have instructed Sosigenes to conduct a physical inventory to match all existing titles with our records. Little though I doubt the results will please either of us."

"No." They heard the sound of many quick footsteps and chattering voices. "That shelf of books at Otho's. Has anyone looked at them?"

"Sosigenes reports they are a collection of epics, poems, and plays by modern writers, as well as a few volumes of erotica. No works that predate my father's reign."

Young voices, eager, excited, amused, approached on the promenade outside the theater and faded away again. The next generation of scholars. The people for whom the Great Library had been created by the ancestor of the woman sitting next to her.

"You know I love you, Pati."

"I know."

"But sometimes it's hard not to hate you."

"I know that, too." Cleopatra was silent for a moment. "Does it help to know that sometimes I hate myself?"

Tetisheri, ridiculously, felt her eyes fill. "No."

Cleopatra laughed a little. "Well, then." She reached out to take Tetisheri's hand in a warm, firm grasp. "There's hope for us yet."

# NOTES AND ACKNOWLEDGMENTS

My profound thanks to Carl Marrs, to whom this book is rightfully dedicated. When he told me about pozzolan, the notion of Rhakotis sandals immediately presented itself as a means of murder in Cleopatra's Alexandria. Because that's just how I roll.

My thanks to Barbara Peters, She of the Eagle Eye (not to be confused with the Eye of Isis, although she would have made a fine one), who discovered, among other things, that I had been misspelling Syene since the first book. Syrene is a place, but it's in Libya. Oy.

Google "book thefts." The day I did there were 6,710,000 results. Not a stretch.

My thanks as always to reference librarian Michael Cattogio, to whose original classical timeline I am continually adding more names, dates, events, and milestones. I moved the timeline of the books to the Julian calendar in sheer self-defense, although I admit that it makes me feel better knowing that the change is historically accurate to the time. Can you imagine how confused everyone was, and how long it took for the change to percolate out into the hinterlands?

Susan Walker and Peter Higgs' *Cleopatra of Egypt from History to Myth* and Stacy Schiff's *Cleopatra* are the two books that have most informed this series, but I have two full shelves of more reference works to guide my way as well. And let's not forget Wikipedia when, purely for craft's sake, I need the names of two battles waged by Alexander the Great beginning with the same letter but occurring as far apart as geographically possible.

The Rhakotis sandals were of course inspired by the cement overshoes of legendary Chicago infamy. Maybe Jimmy Hoffa's wearing a pair of cement overshoes, maybe he isn't. Maybe Muhandis and Tamir are both wearing a pair of Rhakotis sandals, maybe not. Mysteries yet to be solved, but not in this novel.

Vitruvius was a real person. I have a copy of his book on my iPad, which includes a chapter on pozzolan. He was in Egypt with Caesar's forces as an engineer, after which he became an architect of historic renown (see da Vinci's *Vitruvian Man*). It is inconceivable to me that he didn't haunt the Great Library as did every other seeker after knowledge who ever came to Alexandria. I have no idea if he met Cleopatra but I like to think he did so I wrote it that way, and during my research I have seen suggestions that Cleopatra might have attended lectures at the Great Library. Certainly Tetisheri would have made ruthless use of his special knowledge in her investigation.

Cleopatra was called many names by contemporary, quote, historians, end quote, during her lifetime. Yes, Builder and Whore were among them. She did orchestrate the rebuilding of Alexandria following the war. She didn't always pay for the books she appropriated for the Great Library, but then neither did the other Ptolemies. Yes, the royal family fronted room and board for scholars who came to Alexandria. Whatever else they were, the Ptolemies cherished knowledge and were determined to collect as much of it as possible under one roof of their own building.

There are too many men named Ptolemy in Cleopatra's life, including her father, her two brothers, and her son. Auletes was actually called Auletes and Caesarion Caesarion, but I'm calling Ptolemy XIII Theo (from Ptolemy XIII Theos Philopator) and Ptolemy XIV Philo (from Ptolemy XIV Philopator) so we can all keep them straight.

And since we are still speaking of Ptolemies, the resemblance between Ptolemy I and Alexander the Great on Otho's frieze is just my little joke, fueled by speculation among some historians that Ptolemy was the illegitimate son of Philip of Macedon and therefore Alexander's half-brother.

Julius Caesar took his time getting home from Egypt, eliminating multiple enemies along the way, but the most dangerous ones were waiting for him in Rome. It's easy to imagine loose talk around the dinner tables of the high and mighty repeated by servants and slaves around the Forum, where Nebenteru and Simon could hear them and carry them home with the rest of the cargo.